The

Lives

of

Desperate

Girls

MacKenzie Common

PENGUIN TEEN

an imprint of Penguin Random House Canada Young Readers, a Penguin Random House Company

Published in hardcover by Penguin Teen, 2017

Published in this edition, 2018

1 2 3 4 5 6 7 8 9 10

Publisher's note: This book is a work of fiction. Names, characters, places and incidents either are the product of the author's imagination or are used fictitiously, and any resemblance to actual persons living or dead, events, or locales is entirely coincidental.

Manufactured in Canada

Library and Archives Canada Cataloguing in Publication

Common, MacKenzie, author
    The lives of desperate girls / MacKenzie Common.
Previously published: 2017.
ISBN 978-0-14-319873-4 (softcover)
    I. Title.
PS8605.O5456L58 2018   jC813'.6   C2018-900402-9

Library of Congress Control Number: 2016956759

www.penguinrandomhouse.ca

Penguin
Random House
PENGUIN TEEN CANADA

To my family, who taught me to keep an
open mind and an open heart.

And to Marlene Bird.
I have never met you but I have never forgotten your story.

Chapter One

February 22, 2006

I look back on February 22, 2006, as the day they found Helen, but that isn't really true. You can't find something if you were never looking for it. How could they care about Helen when a girl like Chloe, so pretty and white, had disappeared only three weeks earlier? The truth was that they didn't *find* Helen on that snowy morning. They stumbled over her.

I woke up early that day, eyes wide and staring at my bedroom ceiling. I had been dreaming of my best friend again. During the day I could distract myself, but at night, all I thought about was Chloe.

The gray light that washed over my walls meant morning was breaking on the snow banks. Snow may prevent a winter night from ever really being dark, but it can blind you on a February morning. I lay there listening to my breath rasp against the edge of the duvet. I couldn't sleep anymore, but I also couldn't think of a single reason to get out of bed. The early morning kept the realities of Thunder Creek from unfurling across my consciousness. I wanted to savor that sleepy lack of awareness before I limped through another day, flinching every time someone said Chloe's name.

At that moment, I had no idea that a trapper named Guy Robideau and his eleven-year-old son Jamie were walking down a disused snowmobile trail on the outskirts of Thunder Creek to check their traplines. It had been an early morning, but they hoped to fill the empty space in the truck bed before the school bell rang. The pair were bundled up, the hoods of their winter jackets forcing them to pivot their torsos with every glance. That limited range of sight meant they didn't see the snow-laden corpse until Guy stepped on her ankle.

It must have looked just like any other snowdrift. Something to barrel over with the rubber-tipped, fleece-lined boots that were ugly but necessary in a Northern Ontario winter. However, when Guy put his foot down, he would have noticed that he had stepped on something more substantial than fresh powder. The snowfall the night before had covered Helen, enough to conceal her but not to bury her completely. From the moment Guy looked down, he would have understood exactly what lay beneath his feet.

I hope the trapper sent his son back for the cell phone before he brushed the snow off the corpse's face. I'd like to believe that the son never saw how grotesque Helen looked; the sight of her bare legs so wrong for a winter morning twenty degrees below freezing. The white snow obscured some of the violence wrought on Helen, but it didn't cover up her brown skin. That shouldn't matter, but it did.

I got up around the time a police car drove out to inspect Helen's body. I showered and wrapped myself in a towel just as they draped a cover over her naked form and carted her out of the woods. Her body would have swayed on the stretcher across the uneven trail packed down by police boots. I hope they wrapped her tightly, that they made a symbolic stand against the Canadian cold taking up residence beneath her skin. Keeping her warm would have shown that they didn't see her as just another dead girl bound for a frozen grave and an ice-encrusted headstone.

The investigators pored over her skin as I rubbed makeup on mine in the mirror over my desk. They photographed every bruise and cut as I applied layer after layer of foundation to obscure the spots on my face. Finally, they zipped a body bag up over her just as I closed a sweatshirt over my chest. When I was done, I stared at myself in the reflection. I was looking for some scar, some obvious sign that I was suffering on the inside.

All I saw were the same gray-blue eyes that always met mine in the mirror. My grandmother was Dutch, and I knew that I looked like her—tall and pale, my body sturdy, as if destined for a life of farming. You might think I was lucky because so many girls wanted to be tall blondes. But they also wanted to be attractive, and I was undeniably plain. My face was bland and forgettable, the features average and everything so pale it was as if my colors had run in the wash. I was a glass of milk, a lump of potatoes, vanilla ice cream when you had thirty other flavors to try.

The only thing that made me look different was my thick layer of freckles. I was coated in a snowstorm of specks when most people never had more than a flurry. I hated the way the freckles looked like some sort of creeping skin disease, an infection that would eventually consume everything.

I looked down and realized that I was clutching my hair-brush so hard that my knuckles had gone white. I shook my head and grabbed my jacket and school bag. I checked one last time to make sure the mitten was still under my pillow; I wanted to keep it safe. Then I shut my bedroom door, trying to resist the urge to lie back down on the mattress. Now that I was out of bed, I just had to get through the rest of the day. Then, finally, I could go back to sleep.

Chapter Two

My mom had already left for work when I came downstairs. She worked as a waitress at an all-night diner. It was a hard way to earn a living, but she had been there for ages and she liked the people. Still, I knew she wanted better than waitressing for me. I'd felt the weight of her expectations settle on me when I started high school. It was as if we were in a relay race and she was barreling up behind me, waiting for me to take the baton and go farther than she could. Unfortunately, I wasn't the kind of exceptional kid who beat the odds. If you asked me what I liked doing, I could tell you a lot of things. But if you asked me what I was *good* at doing, what I was better at than even the tiny proportion of the world that was in my high school, I would be at a loss.

Chloe wasn't like that. She was creative and great at singing and acting. Her grades were average, but teachers always told her that she was very intelligent and just needed to apply herself. That assurance was enough for her, knowing that someday she would pull back the curtain and reveal the brain she'd hidden behind the apathy of a teenage girl. Chloe always understood that high school would end, and when it did, being smart would no longer be grounds for judgment.

I was six years old the first time I met Chloe Shaughnessy, just after her family moved to Thunder Creek from Toronto. Her father had retired from his Bay Street finance job, intending to spend more time with his family and write. I don't think he ever actually succeeded at either.

Chloe had started school a week late. Our new shoes were already scuffed by the time the teacher ushered her into our classroom. Chloe was delicate-looking, with porcelain skin and shiny sable braids. However, she was doing her best impression of a tough girl, flouncing across the room with her hands on her hips. But I remember how she gnawed on her lower lip. I always liked that vulnerability in Chloe. She tried to hide it but it shone through the cracks, winking briefly in unguarded moments.

At recess, I walked right up to Chloe as she sat on a swing. She was ignoring everyone, pretending not to care that she was playing alone.

"Hi, I'm Jenny Parker. I like your jacket," I said. Her windbreaker was teal, with pink bunnies populating its nylon expanse.

Chloe narrowed her eyes and slowly examined me up and down. She had to crane her head because I was already considerably taller than her. I could only imagine what she saw; ratty blond pigtails, freckles everywhere, the ragged edges of my thrift-store jeans. Her eyes finally stopped on my fingers, coated in the glitter nail polish that I had begged my mother for in the drug store.

I felt awkward standing there allowing myself to be judged. Chloe sat on the swing like a princess, her feet a few inches off the ground. What was I thinking, trying to be friends with her? She was a pretty little girl from the city and I couldn't be anything farther from that.

Then, suddenly, Chloe smiled and her whole face changed. Her green eyes shone, and I felt strangely happy that I had made her smile.

"I'm Chloe, and I like your nail polish!" she said. "My mom won't let me wear it." Her exasperated tone indicated that this was a grave injustice over which countless whining campaigns had been waged.

"I bet she will soon," I said, sitting on the neighboring swing.

And we've been best friends ever since. Or at least we were until three weeks ago, when Chloe went missing and I was the last person to have seen her.

I climbed into my secondhand Chevy Malibu and started the engine. I had bought it in September, and it still amazed me how working with my mom at the diner all summer could have produced something as liberating as a car. Over time, I had grown less enamored with the responsibility of driving, but passing my old school bus still gave me a jolt of smug superiority.

I cautiously pulled out of my housing complex onto the main road. A gray sky was draped over the garish fast-food signs that dotted the street. I could tell by the clouds that more snow was on the way. The dirty sign announcing that I lived in "Birch-Bark Village" was already half obscured by it. I had always hated the dinginess of that sign, but the one welcoming people to our town was even worse. I cringed every time I passed it and read "Thunder Creek: Come for a Visit, Stay for a Lifetime." They may have meant it as a promise, but to me, it sounded more like a threat.

I watched a lot of TV shows set in exotic places like California and New York. I saw girls standing in ocean-facing kitchens with perfectly tousled "bed hair." I saw other girls in loft apartments drinking coffee and talking about the latest gallery opening. Television taught me that there were only a few places on earth that mattered, and they were nowhere near my hometown.

I understood why there was nothing like Thunder Creek on TV. There was no fantasy in an impoverished town in Northern Ontario. Admittedly, the wilderness around Thunder Creek was beautiful (especially if you were from down south), but the city was nothing special. The view from my kitchen was of a scrubby backyard, a peeling fence and the top of a garbage can just visible above the snowdrifts. Beyond our fence was another house, which was so close that as a kid I had the hyper-aware feeling that I was playing on a stage. I spent a lot of time back there trying to analyze whether how I played seemed "normal" to them, the invisible eyes. Not that people bothered to watch each other in my neighborhood. Everyone had their own problems to deal with, and the infidelity and romance that happened around here made you want to look away, not look closer. It all revealed too much about the fallible, low side of human nature.

The whole city was built to be functional, except for a pocket of upper-class housing along the lake and a neighborhood of professional families perched on top of Blueberry Hill. Those beautiful houses were exceptions in Thunder Creek, where most buildings were short and squat, hunkered down against the barrage of winter winds. Chloe lived up there in a huge house with a hot tub.

The people of Thunder Creek looked equally utilitarian. Their wardrobes adhered to the drab uniforms of the working poor. People my age wore cheap jeans and hoodies to school, clothes that began to fray and stretch on the short journey from hanger to register. The girls pulled their bushy hair back into ponytails and didn't bother with lip gloss unless there was a school dance. Kids would buy a new ski jacket and wear it every day for the next three years. I always recognized my friends first by their jackets, before their faces even registered. A friend's coat was an indelible part of them, like their eye color or smile.

But Chloe was different, and not just because she had money, or because her mom took her shopping in Toronto. It was more that Chloe refused to be normal. She had such an aversion to blending in that if everyone in school started wearing her usual leopard-print jackets and red lipstick, Chloe probably would have bought a gray hoodie.

My best friend had an amazing wardrobe of sixties dresses, denim cut-offs and crop tops. She spent her free time combing Internet sites and the local Value Village for inspiration. It hurt me to think of her carefully curated collection hanging forlorn in her closet. I imagined that somehow the colors would seem muted, the patterns metamorphosed into incoherent splotches. They couldn't have looked so special without Chloe inhabiting them. I felt the same way about the mitten, but it still seemed to have a bit of her magic left. I had knitted Chloe a set of mittens a few years ago when I was going through a short-lived knitting phase. I had found one after her disappearance, but I was still looking for the other. Finding that second mitten mattered a lot, probably more than I could explain.

I pulled up to my school and took a deep breath, inhaling the stale but warm air blasting from the car heater. I told myself that at the end of the next breath, I would get out of the car, but I couldn't make myself move. My school was built in the sixties to push the baby boomers through to jobs in forestry and mining, to lives lived less than thirty blocks from this building.

My mother had gone here, and it was likely that my children would go here someday as well. The thought of that continuity was more depressing than comforting.

Finally, after I couldn't wait any longer, I got out and trudged through the brown slush in the parking lot. My backpack hung from my rounded shoulders like a deflated balloon.

I walked down the warm hallway, ignoring all of the people standing at their lockers and sneaking looks at me over their friends' shoulders. I could hear their whispers run down the hall like faucets switching on.

"Isn't that—"

"Last person who saw her."

"Why isn't she—"

"She must know . . . "

It was that final comment that had reverberated in the last three weeks, echoed by parents, the school, the police. Everyone was gentle at first, but within days they became frustrated and accusing: "You must know something . . . you were her best friend . . . surely . . . *something*."

"Hey, Jenny," Taylor Sullivan said, looking uncertain as she walked up to me. I could feel Taylor's nervousness, as if she suspected that I would contaminate her with loss.

Taylor wasn't my friend. In the last year all she had ever brought was bad news delivered with a sticky smile. Taylor was the person at your birthday party who gave you bath gel as a gift, a practical but impersonal present. A shower set implied that the giver didn't know anything about you but at least assumed you washed. We had been friends when we were kids, but by middle school we had drifted as far apart as was possible in the close quarters of Thunder Creek. Taylor and I had rarely talked before Chloe disappeared, and we certainly hadn't talked after.

9

"Hey, Taylor," I said, knowing that I should try harder to be social. I smiled, but it felt strange, as if I was mechanically pulling the corners of my mouth up to unveil teeth.

"Did you hear? They found a body in the woods this morning," Taylor said, flicking her honey-colored hair back with satisfaction. She loved to be the person who delivered the headlines.

My blood went cold. I actually felt my knees shake as I stared into Taylor's wide blue eyes, which were locked onto my face to gauge my reaction. *Was it finally over?*

"Was it—" I started, almost choking.

"Oh!" Taylor said with a jolt of realization that made me hate her intensely. How could it not have occurred to her what I would think? Was she being thoughtless or was everyone *that* sure that I knew where Chloe was?

"No! Jenny, it wasn't her," Taylor said. "My brother's a cop, and he came in this morning so I asked him who it was. It was actually this other girl who went here."

"Who?" I asked, mentally running through the faces of all the girls who shared this building with me. Which one was gone?

"Some girl named Helen," Taylor said with a shrug, her eyes flicking over my shoulder. She was probably aware of how many people were staring at me. People seemed to assume that they could divine Chloe's whereabouts from my appearance.

"I don't know her," I said.

"Well, you know, she lived on the reserve," Taylor said, as if that explained everything. In a way, it did. I didn't have any friends on the Native reserve. It was a patch of houses in the woods, about twelve miles out of town, and there was no reason to go there, unless you wanted cheap cigarettes. It was where all of the parents in my neighborhood got theirs, my mom included. They sat on top of our microwave in a large, translucent bag that would last her three weeks so long as she wasn't working doubles.

"How did she die?" I asked.

"All my brother would say was that someone killed her . . . someone really twisted," Taylor said.

I felt a chill steal over my spine. Things like that didn't usually happen in Thunder Creek, and it seemed unlikely that this would be the year of coincidences. We didn't have a lot of murders, and when they did occur they were much more personal. People were killed in bar fights, in domestic disputes and on hunting trips where the perpetrators could claim that it was an accident. Admittedly, the hunting defense was a stretch when the friend was three feet away and wearing a bright orange vest. Thunder Creek had an extremely low rate of murder but an extremely high rate of hunting accidents.

"First Chloe? Then this? I mean . . . ," Taylor said, encouraged by my sudden interest. "Do you think maybe this guy also got Chloe and—"

"I have to go to class," I interrupted, my heart contracting at the casual way Taylor mentioned Chloe's name.

I dodged past her and walked quickly down the hall. Taylor had always been more interested in a story than the people involved. In the excitement of someone reaching out to me, I had almost forgotten how badly she'd treated Chloe. I felt disloyal just thinking about it.

"What? Wait, Jenny? No . . . ," Taylor called out, but I was already gone.

The school suddenly felt overheated, as if the building was closing in on me. Pressure built in my head and I took shallow breaths, forcing the air through the crumpled cage of my ribs.

I walked down the hall as fast as I could without breaking into a run, my ski jacket making a scratching noise as I swung my arms. I tried to focus on the door instead of the sick feeling washing over me. When had this become my life?

I burst out of a back door by the cafeteria, stumbling as I crunched down into the shin-high snow. Dropping my ski jacket on the ground, I let the cold air begin to dissipate the heat raging under my skin. I stared up at the sky and tried to calm my racing heart.

The bell rang. Class had started, but I had no intention of going back inside. I'd never realized how intolerable school could be until Chloe was gone. We had always complained about school, about the people we knew, the town we lived in, but being alone made everything seem so much worse.

That Helen girl. I wondered if her parents knew yet. I hoped so, because it made me queasy to think I might have heard about her death before they did. I didn't need any more secrets.

Suddenly, the door swung open and a guy hopped out into the snow. He wasn't wearing outdoor clothing, just a black sweater, jeans and Converse. I glanced at his face, meeting dark eyes half-obscured by thick eyebrows and a head of rumpled light brown hair.

It was Tom Grey. I averted my eyes because I didn't really know him. He was only a grade above me but I had never said a word to him. Tom had moved here from Vancouver when I was in seventh grade. Our class had been a grade seven/eight split, an arrangement that resulted in students running wild and the teacher taking early retirement.

I could remember the first day he'd walked in and flopped down at a desk in the back row. Tom hadn't bothered to scope out the other people and figure out where he belonged. The sulk on his face made it pretty clear that he didn't want to fit in here. He had spent the whole year in the back, slouched down in an uncomfortable position. It was always a shock when he stood up and you remembered that he was a head taller than everyone else.

We heard that he'd been sent to live with his dad in Thunder Creek after he started getting into trouble in Vancouver. Everyone had their own theories, but most people assumed it had been drugs that landed him here. It didn't escape me that living in my hometown had been his punishment.

I barely saw Tom in high school. He skipped most classes and was so unresponsive that the teachers had to conceal their disappointment when he did show up. He hung out with the dirtbags, kids who stood in the parking lot smoking and heckling the freshmen who scurried by. Still, compared to a bland person like me, Tom had a certain mystique . . . even if he did have an unmistakable "lone school shooter" vibe.

"Hey," Tom said. I snuck a glance at him. He was lighting a cigarette, his hands already turning pink from the cold.

"Hey," I said.

"You're Jenny, right?" Tom asked. His voice was nice, a warm tenor that was smoother than I would have expected from a smoker.

"Yeah," I said, looking back up at him. I was leaning against the wall, my back pressed against the frozen bricks. He leaned next to me, facing the forest as he exhaled a ribbon of smoke.

"Why are you here?" he asked bluntly. I tensed up and turned to leave, but I felt his hand gently grab my shoulder.

"No, wait. I just meant this is a random place to hang out," he said in a rush. It was surreal to hear him apologize, to say anything nice. He was more awkward than I would have expected.

"I don't know," I said, turning my head to look at him in profile. Tom had high cheekbones and his cigarette rested on full lips. He had an angular face with the bright, alert eyes of a crow. I had never noticed how attractive he was, never even made eye contact with him before. I could almost hear Chloe whispering in my ear: "Tom Grey! He's a hottie. Total weirdo but, you know, that can change." I felt an ache in my heart as I tried to remember if I had ever actually heard her say that. It was more likely that I knew Chloe so well that I could apply her memory to any situation and generate a result. Forget about checking in with Jesus; I seemed to unconsciously ask, "What would Chloe do?"

"I guess . . . I just got sick of being around so many people," I said finally. He nodded and we stood there, idly watching a middle-aged man jog down the bike path in winter gear, his labored breathing creating white puffs in the air.

"What about you?" I asked.

"Ah, no real reason," Tom said, smiling slightly and ducking his head. He looked up at me through his shaggy hair and I felt myself involuntarily smile back. It was like he was sharing a secret with me even though he hadn't said much of anything. "I have drama and it's the week everyone has to perform a monologue they wrote. It's pretty lame. The low point was yesterday when Marie Bouchette started dancing around the stage with a sunflower."

"Ouch," I said sympathetically.

Marie was overweight and had bushy eyebrows, but she was sure that someday she would be a star, and that belief left her puffed up with confidence in her own evolution. Her self-esteem was admirable, but I secretly hated her for believing her destiny was somehow more special than mine. As if she would look back on these years someday as the difficult times, whereas I was supposed to treasure my mediocre youth. Chloe had openly mocked her, but I knew it was because they shared a dream. Chloe was always threatened by the idea that someone near her might hijack her success story. It must have comforted her to have a best friend like me, someone with such low expectations for the future.

"Yeah, I couldn't face it today," Tom said. "So, what's the plan now?"

"I dunno," I said. "I'm not going back to class. I guess I'll just kill time until I can go home," I finished lamely, unable to think of a single thing I could do.

"Want to kill time together?" Tom asked, smiling broadly at me. I bit my lip, momentarily thrown off by this random turn of events.

"Yeah, okay," I said, grabbing my jacket and folding it over my arm. We set off toward the parking lot, our feet sinking into the hard-edged crust of snow.

I had been trying to find a way to fill the days since Chloe disappeared. The last three weeks had inched along, each day a little harder to get through than the next. Maybe Tom Grey could help.

Chapter Three

I t would have been cool to climb into Tom's old truck and drive right out of Thunder Creek. We could have headed to Toronto, or Ottawa, or at least to Sudbury, which had the big movie theater and a Starbucks. But we didn't. We drove up Carswell Hill on the edge of town, to the old monastery.

I understood why they would put a monastery there. There was nothing in Thunder Creek to distract you from praying. But the monastery had been closed years ago and sold to the technical college in town. The building was empty now, used only for storage.

Tom parked the truck and we sat there with the heat of the cab draped around our shoulders. The warm air contrasted sharply with the chill that pressed against the windows, begging to be let in. I watched him unroll his window and felt the cold air strike my face, a late winter sting on my skin.

Tom reached into the glove compartment, his arm brushing my knee as he tried to stop old CDs and papers from falling out. I could see a scar on the top of his scalp, a shiny patch of pink skin in chestnut hair.

He pulled out an Altoids mint case and opened it up to reveal pot, already ground. I looked away, shy in front of this guy I barely knew and his own personal stash. I had smoked pot a few times before, but Chloe had always been there. She was the constant variable, even if she was just part of the group at a party filling the air with the sickly sweet but sour smell of weed.

People in Thunder Creek smoked a lot of pot. It wasn't uncommon for parents to get high with their teenage children, curled up in the safety of their own living rooms. I had even been to parties where mothers sat by campfires, passing joints to their teenage children's friends. They were usually mothers who'd had children early and were now determined to live their forties like they wished they had lived their twenties. My own mother had been young too, but she wasn't like the party moms with their Walmart tube tops and Donald Duck tattoos. My mom rarely drank, and her idea of a great night was a Danielle Steel novel and a bowl of popcorn.

Weed was the perfect drug for Thunder Creek. It restricted your desires to things that even Northern Ontario could provide: snacks, funny movies, good conversation. Pot forced you to forget the world beyond what you could see in order to appreciate what you had. Sometimes it was difficult to grow up in such an isolated city, surrounded by nothing but hundreds of miles of forest. Pot helped you forget about your secret list of hopeless dreams.

I wasn't even sure if I liked getting high. Chloe did, if only because she thought we needed to do it to get high school right. It was as if Chloe had a mental to-do list, gleaned from teen movies, senior stories and her own beliefs about what she wanted to remember in the future. But now she was gone and I didn't know what I wanted to remember from high school . . . maybe none of it.

Tom got a pipe and a lighter from the back pocket of the car seat and packed the bowl. I watched him light up, the green clumps flashing red before curling into blackened rinds.

He swallowed the smoke, involuntarily tipping his chin into his chest, before finally, with one wheezy cough, exhaling out the open window.

"Here," Tom said, passing the pipe to me. "You smoke, right?"

"A bit," I said, lighting up and inhaling. I felt warmth curl in my chest. The smoke made me aware of my lungs and how the space inside my rib cage could stretch. I didn't hold it as long as Tom, but I could already feel tiny bubbles of space appear in my mind. "How did you know I smoked?" I asked.

"I saw you at a party last Halloween. You and Chloe," Tom said, staring out the window as he lit up again.

"Oh," I said. "I don't remember seeing you there."

Tom smiled at me, his lips sealed shut to keep the smoke back. I felt something inside of me squirm as we made eye contact. I couldn't tell if it was the pot or something more personal.

"Well, you guys were always so together. Not like . . . *together*," he said, rushing to explain. "It just felt like you didn't have time for other people." I took the pipe from him and lit up again, trying to distract myself from how much I hated my life right now.

"I don't want to talk about her," I said finally. "I'm sorry, it's not anything you said. I just . . . can't."

"Let's just chill then," Tom said, his voice slow and stoned. "No talking required." It occurred to me that Tom's bad reputation might be caused by social awkwardness rather than any real urge to rebel. One-on-one, he seemed more comfortable, and I wondered if, like me, he felt consumed by the chaotic crowds at school.

We sat there and stared out at the view, at Thunder Creek lying at our feet. I felt bundled up in the high, as if it was sitting on top of my ski jacket, making me feel untouchable. I breathed slowly, wondering if it would get better from now on, or if it could only get worse.

We left when dusk wafted across the valley. It was almost five o'clock—it surprised me when I realized that I had spent the whole day with Tom.

As he drove me to my car, I began to feel the day trickle back into my consciousness. Shamefully, it was the first time I remembered the news about the dead body and what it might mean.

"Did you . . . did you hear about the girl the cops found?" I asked hesitantly, staring out at the gray-blue dusk.

"No . . . what was she doing?" Tom asked, frowning at the road. He was probably imagining the gossipy sex stories teenagers traded like currency. The stories always involved household products used for twisted purposes or people catching others going at it. I didn't tell those stories anymore.

"She was dead. They found her this morning in the woods," I said. Tom whistled but didn't look particularly concerned. Likely, he was still stoned. He had kept smoking long after I had stopped. I hoped he was okay to drive, but I didn't know how to raise the issue without looking supremely uncool.

"Huh. Who was she?"

"I didn't know her. She was from the reserve. Her name was Helen," I said, my sentences awkwardly parsed: I was talking about Helen but my thoughts were consumed by the realization that yet another girl from Thunder Creek wasn't coming home tonight.

"Oh. I've never heard of her," Tom said with a shrug.

I looked out my side window, watching the drab houses and gray snow banks slide by. We passed the Sugar Bowl, a sledding spot, which was teeming with kids in a kaleidoscope of snowsuits.

"I think that's what's even worse. That I didn't know her, that she died today and I have no reason to care," I said.

"I dunno, Jenny. I grew up in Vancouver. A lot of people I didn't know died there," he said. "Like, it's sad, but what can you do?"

I nodded. I'd never been to Vancouver; all I really knew about it was gang shootings, heroin addicts and that serial killer pig farmer. A girl in the woods probably didn't pack the same punch for Tom.

"I guess you're right," I said and shut my eyes.

Tom noticed that I looked upset and patted my shoulder. His hand felt heavy on my arm. I realized he had just made the connection between Chloe and Helen.

"Sorry," Tom said finally.

"Don't worry about it. You didn't know either of them," I said.

I wondered if Helen had a best friend. A girl who had grown up with her and who saw Helen's bedroom as just as much hers as Helen's. Someone who always checked both horoscopes in a magazine even when she was alone. I did that. I was still finding Chloe's old socks and mascara tubes in my room. Even now, I couldn't help checking Gemini before I checked my sign, Aries. I wasn't willing to turn down any insight to Chloe, even if it came from a five-dollar magazine written by someone in New York City. I wondered if Helen had a Jenny, someone who was currently having the worst day of her life.

Thunder Creek was becoming a dangerous place to be a teenage girl.

Tom pulled up next to my car and I sat there for a second. I wasn't sure if we would do this again or if it had been a one-time thing fueled by pity. I didn't know what Tom thought because I barely knew anything about him.

He turned off the truck and we both climbed out. My eyes scanned the sky until they stopped abruptly at the dark line of evergreens that bordered the football field. The parking lot was mostly empty. There were no games or concerts at the school that necessitated people staying late. At this time of year, any displays of school spirit would be across town at the hockey arena. The parking lot resembled a frozen wasteland, with gusts of grainy snow skittering across the surface and clinging to the sand-crusted wheels of cars.

Tom's eyes met mine over the hood of the truck. They seemed darker against the faded landscape and I felt myself swallow, unsure of what would happen next.

"So, I'll see you soon," Tom said. It didn't feel like a question, more of a confirmation of what he already knew.

"Yeah," I said. "And uh . . . thanks. For today. I needed it," I said. I didn't know what part exactly I needed: the break from school, the drugs or Tom's company. Maybe all of it.

"I know," Tom said simply. "It was chill." And then, suddenly, he was jogging around the truck and, before I knew it, he had hugged me. He stuck his arms under my undone jacket and I could feel them press against my back. Tom hugged me so tight that my heels left the ground. Then, quick as he could, he kissed my forehead and let me go.

"See you soon!" he said and hopped back in his truck. I waved and then turned around, focusing on finding my keys in my pocket so he didn't see how punch drunk I looked. It probably meant nothing. It was just a hug. But it seemed so . . . important.

I shivered as I climbed into my car. It would take forever for the heaters to work, and I'd likely be home before the car was bearable.

I wished that I could go over to Chloe's house and tell her what had happened. But would Tom have ever hung out with me if she hadn't disappeared? It wasn't likely. For a second, the weak side of me was glad that she was gone. But that wasn't right. I couldn't just erase my best friend.

I parked in the communal parking lot in front of the government-subsidized town house where I'd spent my entire life. I was surprised to see that my mom was home. I felt a wave of nerves wash over me as I wondered why. What if she'd been laid off? It had happened once before, when I was really young and the restaurant she worked at had closed. That was when I realized how close to the edge of poverty we really lived. A couple of missed paychecks had sent us to the food bank, our cheeks burning with shame. When my mother got a job at the place she currently worked, we had celebrated by eating a meal that wasn't composed of non-perishables.

I walked up the steps, gripping the handrail tightly just in case I slipped on the ice. I could see my mother standing in the kitchen, her shoulders and upper back rounded as she stirred a pot on the stove. Sometimes I hated seeing people when they thought they were alone. It denied them the chance to stand up straight and unfold an expression across their face. Right now, with no one watching, my mother looked utterly ordinary in her oversized sweater and jeans from the early nineties. Her face was slack and she looked so normal that it made my heart hurt.

I opened the door and kicked off my boots, my socks getting coated in the round clumps of snow that had formed in the treads.

"Hi sweetheart," my mom said as she walked out of the kitchen. She was holding a wooden spoon stained with tomato sauce.

"Hey." I tossed my jacket over the end of the bannister. My mom frowned. Ordinarily, she would have told me to hang it up, but since Chloe's disappearance she had been extra-lenient. Tragedies made people give you a lot of free passes.

"How was your day?" she asked.

I stared at her. I looked a lot like my mom, despite the fact that I was six inches taller than her and freckled. We both had blue eyes and blond hair, although hers had been stripped of its youth and was shot through with gray. When I was a kid I used to read princess novels and wish my mother was beautiful or that my real parents were rich and glamorous. I felt bad now that I could ever have hated her for not being pretty, not when she was so busy trying to be capable.

"Uh . . . okay," I said, hoping that she couldn't tell I'd been smoking pot. There were limits on how much leeway I could expect. "A girl at my school died. Well, not at the school—"

"I know!" my mom burst out, pulling me into a hug.

"When I heard they found a body, I just couldn't help thinking . . . Well, you know . . . *Chloe*," she said into my shoulder. I stiffened.

"Well, it wasn't," I said loudly. "It wasn't her, but that girl, she's still dead!" My voice rang out, loud enough that our neighbors probably heard it through the wall. I knew I was acting erratically but I couldn't stop.

My mom pulled away to look at me, her head tilted in confusion. We usually got along well, but lately I couldn't seem to stand the things people said to me. Everything just made me mad.

"I know, sweetie, I know. And it's scary that the killer's still out there. He might even have had something to do with Chloe. But I just meant—"

"She was somebody's Chloe," I said flatly. Then I turned around and went upstairs. I hated myself for hurting my mother's feelings, but that only made me want to be alone even more. Clearly, I couldn't be trusted to be around normal people.

I flopped on my bed, the only light coming from the amber glow of the streetlamp in the parking lot. It had started snowing again, and I watched the faint whispers of winter spiral downward past my window. The mitten was under my pillow and I found myself hugging it tightly against my chest like a teddy bear. It didn't make me feel any better but I would have felt worse without it. I thought by now I would have found the other mitten. I looked for it wherever I went. It felt like a clue to what had happened to Chloe, to where I had lost my best friend. I lay in my dark room, listening to my mom move around downstairs, imagining her settling in for an evening alone, her only daughter sealed away upstairs like a dirty secret. My mom was worried about me and there was nothing I felt I could do to wipe away her concern.

I watched the snow fall past my dark room and I felt incredibly alone.

Chapter Four

February 23, 2006

The next day, I daydreamed through my morning classes, staring out the window and failing to process anything the teachers said. It was frustrating to feel like I had to kill time at school every day, not getting anything out of class but not being allowed to leave. It reminded me of working at the diner in the summer, and how, even if there were no customers, you still had to look busy and couldn't just put your feet up and read a magazine.

I hurried out of the classroom when the lunch bell rang, anxious to leave before anyone tried to talk to me, avoiding the cafeteria, a place I hadn't visited in weeks. It was the epicenter of gossip and I couldn't face the rows of watching faces, an audience waiting for me to do something interesting. I hadn't eaten there even before Chloe went missing. We just drove to McDonald's or Subway.

I passed by the glass doors and came face-to-face with Liam McAllister. His hand hovered on the door handle but he didn't open it. He just stared at me through the glass. Liam had a little gap between his front teeth, which, as his only visible flaw, enhanced his attractiveness. He had dark hair and the kind of olive skin that made people ask about his ethnicity, because it seemed too exotic for Thunder Creek. Liam was handsome, but he left a bitter taste in my mouth now that I knew the truth.

Liam always looked amused, as if he was so cool that he thought everything you did was pathetic and funny. His expression used to make me feel awkward. Now it just made me angry.

Liam was Chloe's ex-boyfriend. The first boy she ever loved, the first boy who broke her heart and well . . . a lot of firsts. I hated running into him at school. It made me feel nauseous, a flood of nerves and anger overwhelming me.

Liam raised his hand, a mocking wave. He was so confident that I wasn't a threat to him; he had total control over the situation. I didn't wave back. I just glared at him, then turned away and walked down the hall.

Liam might have been the first boy that Chloe ever loved, but he was also the first boy I'd ever hated.

⌒

I drove to the Mike's Mart a few blocks away. I came here a lot. There was a Subway inside the convenience store, which made it easy to buy lunch and stock up on Red Bull and candy at the same time. This time, however, after eating my sub, I did something I had done only once before in my life: I bought a copy of the local paper—the *Thunder Creek Tidbit*. I walked out of the convenience store clutching the daily and slid into my car. Even though class was starting in five minutes, I didn't turn the key. Instead, I took a deep breath and unfolded the newspaper, resting it against the steering wheel.

The last time I bought the paper I was twelve years old. I had been in the middle-school choir and at a performance I noticed the *Tidbit* cameraman snapping photos. I did my best to look picture-worthy, making eye contact with the camera and opening my mouth really wide to show I was singing. The next morning

I'd walked to the store and bought the paper, thrilled with the prospect of seeing myself in print. I knew that if it was a good photo I might even put it in a picture frame. First though, I'd casually slide it across the table to my mother, say "there's a good shot of me in there today" and let her freak out. She'd probably buy five more copies and take them to work to show her friends.

I remember desperately flipping through that paper on the way home from the store until I found the article about the choir. There was the picture, right under the headline "Spring Choir Recital Hits All the Right Notes." Except it was of the group of altos standing next to me. Despite all of my scheming, the only visible bit of me was my elbow, veering into the side of the photo by Bethany Morris. I noticed that none of the people in the photo were looking at the camera or opening their mouths very wide. I must have looked deranged and desperate and that was why I had been cropped out. I threw the paper away and never told anyone that I'd been lame enough to care about it. I also quit choir the next year, but that was more to do with a lack of talent than the newspaper disappointment.

Now though, I wasn't searching the pages for me. I just wanted to know what they had said about Helen.

I turned to the first page, expecting to see a giant photo of Helen just like there had been after Chloe was gone a week and the seriousness had sunk in. But the first page was a big story about the government cutting health care. Instead of a smiling, beautiful shot of a teenage girl, there was a collage of tired-looking nurses and the defeated elderly in hospital beds. I exhaled and turned the page. And then again. One more time.

I found her on page seven. The article ran down the side of the page next to the crease, so that you inevitably gouged into it if you tried to rip the page in half. The photo was tiny, about the size of a business card. Chloe's picture had been a full page and made you care instantly that someone so pretty was gone. The newspaper had contacted her parents, who had sent them a professional shot, with Chloe's red-brown hair elegantly draped over one shoulder.

I squinted at the photo. It was clearly a yearbook picture. I recognized the emerald green sheet they had hung behind us last year, the arms folded over a school desk, the awkward smile that hinted at the fact that there were thirty people lined up behind her, waiting for her to finish.

Helen wasn't very attractive. She had good skin, a warm caramel color, and long eyelashes rimming dark eyes. But her hair was a frizzy, bushy mass that looked like it needed a bucket of conditioner and a good cut. She was also overweight. Not obese, but pudgy enough that her arms swelled out of her T-shirt in fleshy circles and the features of her face were obscured by its roundness. Her smile was closed-mouthed, the edges pulled up just slightly, which made her look nauseous. I felt a bit disappointed. I had imagined her as a Native version of Chloe, with shiny dark hair and the high cheekbones people always talked about when they talked about Natives. I didn't know why it mattered whether she was pretty, how that affected what had happened to her, but it did.

I scrutinized her face. Had I seen her before? The school was big, but not *that* big. I would have thought I'd be able to recognize most of the faces. But I wasn't sure about Helen. Maybe I had never noticed her, just another girl whose weight and cheap (almost matronly) clothing had made her seem more middle-aged than sixteen.

The article said Helen had been found in the woods. That foul play was suspected. That the police were investigating. It said

Guy Robideau and his son Jamie found her and that she hadn't been out there very long. It didn't say much, but somehow what it didn't say made the story all the more tragic. The white spaces in the article lodged in my brain, sinking in their hooks. Did she freeze to death? Or had she been stabbed and bled out in the woods? Was she already dead when she went into the snow?

The newspaper told the facts like they were synopsizing last night's *Law and Order* episode, but it didn't tell me what I wanted to know. In fact, the article just left me with more questions. Why wasn't Helen's story on the front page? Thunder Creek didn't have enough murders to be nonchalant about homicide, especially when it happened so soon after a girl disappeared. Why wasn't this the biggest news in town?

The last paragraph in the article made me moan. It simply said: "It is unclear whether this homicide is connected to the disappearance of Chloe Shaughnessy earlier this month, a tragic event that the police have made their highest priority. At present, the discovery of the homicide has produced no new evidence on Chloe Shaughnessy."

I pulled my seatbelt on and started the car. Then I folded the paper and zipped it into my backpack. I squinted out at the blinding white snow banks that lined the street leading up to the high school. They bled into the road, which hadn't been ploughed recently, so the street was just as bright. But the road was dangerous. Not because of what was on the surface but because of what the snow could obscure. Long streaks of thick ice and unexpected street curbs could catch you unaware. In one sickening second, your car could be wrecked or you could be stuck in the snow. The annoying thing was, you knew the roads were dangerous, but there was nothing you could do about it. Except wait for summer.

Chapter Five

After school, instead of heading home to a night of reality television and questionable food choices like a normal teenager, I had to go to the police station. I had already been interviewed a number of times in the last three weeks but apparently they would be trying again today.

The first time I'd met Officers Trudeau and Bragg was two days after Chloe went missing. They'd been more sympathetic back then, sure that I would tell them everything because I was so worried about my friend. They'd come to my house that time. Now they just made me come to the station. They were sick of talking to me and getting the same answers. The feeling was mutual.

I parked by the front doors, staring up at the bland cinder-block building with a large Canadian flag hanging limply out front. Walking up the stairs, I already felt exhausted by the fact that I could be here for ages, answering the same questions over and over. They wanted something from me, something I wasn't prepared to give them. Their only recourse was hoping that I'd finally crack under the threat of never-ending interviews.

The police station smelled like burnt coffee and the warm ink of freshly printed papers. I asked the receptionist where I should go and she pointed toward the same meeting room I'd been in last time. The door was shut so I sat outside, wishing I'd thought to bring a magazine with me. The station only had old copies of *Reader's Digest* and *Canadian Parenting*. Rather than pick one of those up, I sat there trying to remember what I'd told the police before so I didn't deviate from my story.

The door opened and Officer Trudeau stepped out, talking to a person behind her. She moved out of the way and Liam McAllister walked into the hall.

Inwardly, I groaned. It was awful luck, running into him twice in one day. He must have come over here while I was still in school, maybe on a fourth-period spare.

"Jenny, we'll be right in. We're just going to grab coffee. Do you want anything?" Officer Bragg asked. I shook my head.

Liam waited until the officers had moved off and then shot me a vicious look, clearly angry to be here again. I was the one who'd told them he'd seen Chloe the night she disappeared. It pissed me off that Liam thought he was some sort of victim, being investigated by the cops; I knew he deserved far worse.

"Another wasted hour, thanks to you," he hissed, standing uncomfortably close. I could smell the spearmint gum on his breath and the musky scent of his deodorant. It made my skin crawl.

"Just tell them what you did then," I whispered back. It was unsettling, being alone with him even for a moment. I pushed past him toward the meeting room.

"You're a freak, you know that? I can't believe Chloe ever hung out with you," he murmured.

"I think the same thing about you," I said, closing the meeting room door in his face. I pressed my back against the door, trying to slow my pounding heart.

The doorknob turned once, but I stayed pressed against the door. Then I heard his footsteps move down the hall, leaving the station. I counted to twenty and then sat down at the table.

Officers Trudeau and Bragg walked in a couple of minutes later. They were both holding takeout coffees from the place next to the station. I wondered if they'd taken their time on purpose, in an effort to make me sweat. Anything was possible.

"How are you today, Jenny?" Trudeau asked. She looked young to be a cop, though it might have been because she was on the shorter side. She also looked strong, like a gymnast. Her dark hair was scraped back into a bun and her eyes were a stormy green-gray. She seemed both smarter and meaner than her partner, Bragg, who was a middle-aged man with a thick black moustache that had likely remained untouched since the seventies.

"Okay, I guess," I said flatly. I folded my arms and stared at them. Trudeau shot a look at Bragg, who laughed.

"Well, let's just jump into it. I'm wondering if you've remembered anything new since the last time we talked. Anything you think we should know?" Bragg asked.

"Nope," I said, shaking my head.

"That's surprising, since you've given us so little to work with. Okay, so let's go over that last day. It was a Thursday, so why was Chloe staying at your house?"

"Her ex-boyfriend Liam had invited her out to pizza. She thought it was a date and she thought it'd be fun to get ready at my house and then sleep over afterward," I said. I felt as if I was talking about something that had happened in another lifetime, not three weeks ago. Things had been so different then, even if they hadn't been ideal.

"But she didn't stay over?" Bragg asked.

"No. It turned out not to be a date. Liam was just being a friend. Chloe was so disappointed that she wanted to go home," I said, the well-rehearsed lie still feeling funny in my mouth.

"That's it? She was just disappointed?" Trudeau asked skeptically. I shrugged.

"Yeah. Maybe embarrassed too, because she'd thought it was a date," I said. I wished I could tell them the truth, but the lies I'd told in the first interview had trapped me, and I was scared to change my story now.

"Did she seem upset about anything else?" Bragg asked, clearly unable to believe that anyone, even a teenage girl, could get that flustered about being put in the friend-zone.

"Not that I know of," I said.

"Did you notice any recent changes in her? Was she acting differently? Or hanging out with new people?" Trudeau asked, glaring at me. She knew I was lying about everything, and the fact that she had to keep up this charade really pissed her off. I was pretty sure she would have hit me with a telephone book if she thought she could get away with it.

"Nope," I said, my face stony.

"So, your story is that Chloe was totally fine, just a bit disappointed, and you don't know what might have happened to her?" Trudeau asked.

I nodded.

"Well, we'll have to have you back in here again soon, Jenny, just in case you remember anything else," she said sourly, moving to stand up. It was a shorter interview than usual, but maybe I'd just caught her on a bad day. Trudeau would likely be back to the marathon interview sessions after a nap and a good long scream into her rage pillow.

"Hey, are you guys investigating that murder? Of that girl Helen?" I asked suddenly. Trudeau shook her head.

"No, we're focusing on Chloe," she said, leaning by the door.

"But I'm sure there's a lot of people working on that, right?

33

I mean, I bet you guys already have some leads, like on who did it?" I asked. Trudeau smirked.

"Why, are you confessing, Jenny? Did you do it?" she asked. I rolled my eyes.

"No. I was just wondering, that's all," I said.

"Don't worry, an officer's going to look into it. Besides, why are you so worried about that victim? I would have thought you'd be wanting us to devote all our time to finding Chloe," Trudeau said, arching an eyebrow. She was examining me like I was a lab specimen.

"I can worry about them both," I said. "I'm good at worrying."

Chapter Six

September 16, 2005

I t was only the third weekend of September and already the first big house party of the year was upon us. Classes had started and I was deeply regretting the end of summer. It wasn't just because eleventh grade seemed a lot more serious and academic than the year before. It wasn't even because I was worried about time passing and the end of high school getting nearer and nearer. The real reason was that over the summer I had grown really close to Chloe again because she had broken up with Liam.

When Chloe had begun dating Liam the summer before tenth grade, I had sensed a distance in our friendship. He was her first serious boyfriend, and this disconnection had only widened when Chloe and Liam started having sex. I felt like Chloe was surging over some major milestones and I was being left behind. Sex and love had somehow made Chloe much more worldly and adult than me. I had secretly fretted about my deficits, running through lists of potential boys in my head, ones who I could tolerate and who might actually consider dating me. The list wasn't very long.

But over our summer of singlehood, Chloe and I had reconnected. We spent our time tanning on the beach at Fisher Lake and drinking strawberry Bacardi Breezers in Chloe's backyard. The distance of the year before was erased by August. And yet, I couldn't help worrying that a new school year would upset the balance, and that Chloe would find new boys to date and friends who were as experienced.

Still, there was something exhilarating about a house party, especially the first one of the school year. Everyone would whisper fervently about it in class, hashing out plans of where they would sleep, who had booze and where they would meet beforehand, because it simply wasn't possible to show up alone. The air felt electrified on Friday afternoon as everyone hurried home to get ready.

By the time Chloe and I arrived, the house was packed and we were buzzed. We had shared a water bottle filled with iced tea and her father's whiskey on the walk over. The two of us shuffled into the heaving house, the stairway lined with piles of Converse and ballerina flats with the toes worn down. The noise was incredible, a mixture of pounding bass and screamed conversations that packed my ears with sound. I could feel the stereo sound waves reverberate across my eyeballs, and I knew that the only way to endure such a huge party was to drink more, to apply a muffling layer of alcohol between me and everything else.

I spent the next few hours in the dining room, having insipid conversations with girls who were only interesting when you were smashed. I let guys tell me dumb stories about how they and their "buddies" drank obscene amounts of alcohol and did stupid stunts on their four-wheelers. I played a terrible game of beer pong, cracking under the pressure of my partner's expectations. The crowd moaned with every air ball as if they were spectators at Wimbledon.

The party swirled around me as the alcohol simmered in my stomach. I could feel it bringing color to my cheeks and matting my hairline with sweat. I was so drunk that a delay appeared between the utterance of words and my comprehension. In that hazy, churning world, I finally realized that I hadn't seen Chloe in hours.

When we arrived, we had filled tall plastic cups with vodka and Sprite before going our separate ways. We had spent so much time together recently that both of us must have felt secretly relieved to hang out with other people. Later, I'd spotted Chloe on the back porch smoking pot with some older boys. I considered joining them, but I wanted to prove to Chloe that I wasn't the kind of clingy friend who would be abandoned when the main character falls in love again.

But that had been hours ago. And regardless of what happened at the party, Chloe was sleeping at my house tonight. My mom was working the night shift, and as long as we were back before 5 a.m. she would never know we'd been gone. It was 3 a.m. now, which meant I had to find Chloe soon.

I pushed myself off the couch and chugged my drink before trudging off on my mission. After a look around the main floor, I staggered down to the basement, bracing my hands against the wall and teetering precariously on the slick pile of the carpet. I could smell pot smoke seeping up the stairs. I rounded the corner, assuming that the first thing I would see was Chloe passing a pipe. I would tell her it was time to go and she would make me feel lame in front of everyone by telling me to calm down. Then we would leave, Chloe acting as if I was arbitrarily dragging her away even though she knew we had a deadline.

I turned the corner and saw five guys and girls passing around a glass bong swirled with shades of blue. My heart sank when I realized that Chloe wasn't among them.

I turned back to the stairs and began to pull myself up with the bannister. I could feel the rail strain, but I knew that I wouldn't be able to climb unassisted.

If Chloe wasn't there, and Chloe wasn't on the ground floor, that only left upstairs. For some reason, the idea sent a chill down my spine. I dismissed it as the kind of drunk paranoia that convinced you there was a rapist lurking behind every car on the walk home. I was sure I would find Chloe in a brightly lit room, leaning back in a computer chair and shouting over everyone. Either that, or she was even more hammered than I was and had found a quiet room to grab a nap. If that were the case, she'd be okay once she was outside in the fresh air.

The living room on the ground floor hung in a surreal stillness. It was the fancy living room, with plush carpet and couches all in muted beiges. We had been warned away from this room because the pale colors would show every spill and swipe of a Doritos-dusted hand.

I took a deep breath and began to toddle up the stairs. Once again I found myself clutching the bannister like a lifeline. I was halfway up when Taylor Sullivan started walking down. It was obvious that she had been in the bathroom fixing her makeup. Nobody's lipstick was that pink at 3 a.m. without a recent retouch.

"Hey," she said, her eyes flicking over me. I self-consciously smoothed my hair down and smiled. Taylor always made me feel uncomfortable.

"Hi, Taylor. Having fun?" I asked. I had seen her earlier, shamelessly flirting with Drew Saunders by the air-hockey table.

"Yeah, but, uh . . . ," Taylor began, leaning toward me with the devilish smile she always wore when she knew something about someone. She was the kind of girl who thrived on secrets, whose self-esteem swelled as everyone around her succumbed to moments of weakness. "Jenny, have you seen Chloe recently?"

"No. I'm actually looking for her. Why?" I said. Taylor tried to look concerned but her furrowed brow was no match for the smile spreading across her face.

"Don't tell her I told you this, but she's been a total whore tonight."

"Like, a bitch?" I asked, still clutching the bannister for balance and wishing this conversation had happened three shots earlier. *Whore* could entail all manner of female misconduct, from hitting on a taken boy to making pointed comments in a game of "Never Have I Ever."

"No, like . . . a slut. She slept with Devon *and* Mike tonight! It's pretty pathetic," Taylor announced. She looked like a little kid telling on her older sibling.

"Which Mike?" I asked dumbly. Even in that moment, I knew it didn't matter.

"Mike Doucette," Taylor said. I nodded slowly.

Mike and Devon were a grade above us and on the hockey team, the kind of guys who dressed up as women for the hockey pep rally every year. As if the sight of their muscular legs and broad shoulders filling out a thrift-store dress was so decidedly hilarious that it needed to be repeated annually. Mike and Devon weren't Chloe's type. She had never wanted the kind of guy who saw hockey as their only viable career plan. Her ex, Liam, was also a year older and on the team, but his success in sports was matched with the kind of easy intelligence that saw him aiming for medical school in the future, not the NHL. Chloe had complained that Liam was always worrying about what other people expected of him, but I couldn't imagine her doing a 180 and going for Mike or Devon.

"What? Both of them?" I said, shaking my head. "There's no way she'd have a threesome."

"No, Mike was like an hour ago. Devon's in there now," Taylor said, glowing with the knowledge that a girl had debased herself at the party.

Before she could say anything else, I hurried up the stairs, taking them two at a time. Chloe had clearly lost her mind. I needed to stop her from making any more detrimental decisions.

Of all the doors leading off of the landing, only one was closed. I knew that Chloe was in there, knew it with the startling prescience that can only happen when you brush up against something truly bad in life.

Just as I touched the doorknob it turned beneath my fingers. I stepped back as Devon slipped out of the room. He closed the door so quietly it was as if he were laying it down to rest. His eyes met mine, and I could tell by the flush that appeared on his cheeks that he hadn't wanted an audience. It occurred to me that I had gone to school with him for my entire life. We had never said a word to each other, and yet I knew all about his life and he probably knew a fair bit about mine. Small cities may call that sensation a feeling of "community," but Thunder Creek really just fostered an artificial intimacy with strangers.

"Hey," I said. "Is Chloe in there?"

"Uh, yeah," Devon said. He wasn't looking at me; his eyes were fixed on the hallway behind me, like he was watching for a bus.

"Is she okay?" I asked. I noticed that Devon was wearing a T-shirt and jeans, but he was holding his belt in his hand, as if he had dressed in a hurry.

"She's fine," he muttered, pushing past me and walking down the hall. "Just a bit drunk."

I wanted to stop him. I wanted to grab his shirt in my fists and shake the answers out of him. I wanted to force him to look at me and to explain what was going on. But I knew he wouldn't.

The only thing I could do was to see Chloe for myself. I took a deep breath and pushed the door open. The sliver of light from the hallway caught the pale flesh of Chloe's legs, tangled in a faded sheet. I had seen her bare legs all summer, but they somehow seemed more exposed in the uncomfortable intimacy of the bedroom. Her jeans lay crumpled at the foot of the bed, and I noticed that her underwear, an old pair of rainbow briefs, were on backward—the word *Superstar* wrapping around her pelvis instead of across her butt. Chloe was wearing her bra and her top, but the shirt was hiked up to her collarbone. She was a still form sprawled across the bed, and for a brief moment I thought she was dead.

I felt a wave of nausea pass over me and I gripped the doorframe, wishing desperately that I could close the door and leave this for someone else. I saw myself walking down to the party and drinking enough to black out. Chloe could put herself together and I could pretend that I had never found her. It was an appealing thought, but I knew I could never do that to her. Not to Chloe. She was my best friend, and in that moment I was the only one who could help her.

I pulled her jeans up her legs, shocked by how hard it was to maneuver limp limbs into clothing. My eyes lingered on the backward underwear. They were so old that the elastic waistband had separated from the cotton, framing the skin beneath. I remembered how, when Chloe decided she was ready to lose her virginity, she had bought brand-new underwear. It was a matching bra-and-panties set, blue and white with frilly lace. It wasn't overtly sexy and bore no resemblance to the terrifyingly mature G-strings and mesh panels of Victoria's Secret lingerie. But there was something undeniably adult about a matching set. It hinted that a person might linger in their underwear, that the eyes of others might fall on such an outfit, maybe even remove it.

But this underwear? It wasn't the kind of thing one wore if they thought someone else would see it. Underwear like this was only pulled out when a girl was on her period or had gone too long without doing the laundry. This underwear was the final stop before a lazy girl had to wear bikini bottoms under her jeans. I couldn't imagine Chloe ever choosing to show them to a boy. No, not someone as carefully constructed as she was.

I managed to shake Chloe awake, rousing her out of bed as she slurred incomprehensible questions. I was terrified that even if I had understood what she was asking, I wouldn't have been able to answer.

I looped her arm over my shoulder and begged her to help me get us down the stairs. I promised her that I was taking her home and that we had to leave as soon as possible because this wasn't a good place. In a way, I still believed that if we slipped away from the party without being seen then the events of the night wouldn't become a concrete reality. Chloe seemed to understand what I was asking, because although she leaned heavily on me, she stiffened her back and surged down the stairs. Her drunken focus made me feel strangely proud of my best friend.

Outside, I kept my arm wrapped around Chloe, gently guiding her forward. She was so drunk that she wasn't exactly walking but rather fixing her eyes on the horizon and staggering toward it. Neither of us said a word.

As I walked home with Chloe that night, I felt the autumn winds conjure goose bumps on my skin. I could hear the dry rasp of fallen leaves like bones rattling in graves. Summer was over, and I knew that this night would be a major turning point. In that moment, I felt afraid of what autumn would bring.

I woke up early the next morning, the house completely still. I almost wished for noise to distract me from my pounding heart. My head felt leaden and tender, the consequences of a drunken evening and a near sleepless night.

I tipped my head to the left and was surprised to see Chloe sitting upright in bed, staring out the window. The gray light of morning mercilessly illuminated the particles of mascara ground into her skin, the knots in her red-brown hair and the hickeys on her neck. I knew that when I showered, I would discover bruises blooming across my knees and thighs, the inevitable consequence of a night spent slamming my legs into kitchen tables and catching my hips on doorframes. Still, as I stared at Chloe, I knew that my discomfort was insignificant compared to what she must be feeling.

Even looking at Chloe made my heart ache. A hangover can strip you of your affectations, leaving you unvarnished and vulnerable. You feel inarticulately plain, and you just want your friends to accept you even when you can't be charming. But there was something else in Chloe's blank stare and bite-swollen lip. Beneath the quietness of this moment, I could feel her pain bubbling into a furious boil.

"Hey," I whispered, unsure of how to begin the first conversation after the night before.

"Hey," she muttered back, glancing down at me and trying to smile. It was more of a grimace, but I knew she had tried for my sake.

I pulled myself up and leaned my back against the wall next to her. I could feel the bed coast forward a few inches, but we both ignored the precariousness of our perch.

"So . . . last night . . . ," I said, staring straight ahead. The window illuminated the dust motes floating around my cramped bedroom.

"Yeah," Chloe said quietly. "Last night seems pretty bad today."

"What do . . . what do you remember?" I asked. It was cowardly to admit that I hoped she remembered everything, that I wouldn't have to be the one to tell her.

"I remember lying in bed . . . ," Chloe whispered, keeping her gaze forward. It was easier to share uncomfortable secrets without the intimacy of eye contact. "Just super-drunk, and I remember Mike kissing me, and, you know, I kissed back I think, and then I guess it kept going."

"Oh," I whispered.

"And then, I was asleep, and then Devon was there, and then, uh, I guess sex happened," Chloe said, using a passive tense, as if sex was a phenomenon that spontaneously occurred, like lightning storms.

"Did you . . . want to?" I asked, unsure of how to ask the unspoken questions hanging in the stagnant morning air.

"I don't know," Chloe sighed. "To be honest, I was so drunk, I don't even feel like I knew what was going on. It seemed like they knew what they wanted and I was just . . . *there.*" She choked out the last part in a hoarse whisper.

I understood why she refused to say anything clearer. As long as there was ambiguity, as long as the night was a confusing gray smear in her mind instead of a crime, she didn't have to see herself as a victim. A mistake could be forgotten, but anything more seemed to imply that victim status would be an irrevocable part of her identity. That it would contaminate other aspects of her personality and fester into ugly issues in later relationships.

I remembered how uncomfortable Devon looked outside the bedroom, like he didn't want to be there. Did he feel guilty? Or was he just hoping to avoid a confrontation? I had never thought of high-school boys as dangerous before, but I couldn't shake the feeling that I had witnessed something large and terrible.

Chloe had wrapped her arms around herself. The sleeve of my old soccer shirt had ridden up and I could see fingerprint bruises trailing up her biceps. Chloe used to have similar marks when she was with Liam. She always bruised easily, under even the most delicate of touches. But these particular bruises came from a much uglier place.

Seeing my best friend so vulnerable made me unspeakably sad. Chloe was a force of nature, the sort of person who went out and made things happen. Mornings like this weren't supposed to happen to unstoppable girls.

"Are you going to tell someone?" I asked.

"No need. This is going to be all over the school," Chloe said darkly. I watched her shoulders knot and roll as she tried to keep herself from crying.

"No—what they did to you, your side of the story," I suggested. She shook her head.

"I don't even know what my side of the story is. And I'm not going to accuse a couple of popular Creeker boys unless I'm sure," Chloe said. I heard an unfamiliar grimness in her voice, as if she'd aged ten years overnight.

I nodded sadly. Mike and Devon had grown up in Thunder Creek—in fact, they were probably third-generation Creekers—and they were obvious choices for the communal inheritance of the Thunder Creek way of life. They spent their weekends hunting in the bush, playing hockey and drinking beers with their buddies. While they might go down south for university, it was a safe bet they'd move home afterward, marry a local girl, buy a boat and live a nice middle-class Northern life. Chloe wasn't from town; moving here as a child wasn't enough to make you a Creeker. She was intent on escaping Thunder Creek and everyone knew it.

"What should we do?" I whispered.

I felt Chloe shift her weight closer to me. The bed inched farther forward, the curl of our lower backs exposed in the air between the wall and the mattress. Still, I didn't move; feeling Chloe lean against me, the weight of her legs next to mine, made me feel hopeful.

"I guess just carry on," she said quietly.

I nodded and we sat there, staring out the window, dimly aware that we had just taken a great leap forward into adulthood. When you're a kid, you think life is just one big fairytale. Then you become a teenager and everything seems a bit crappy, but you still believe that you'll be the exception, the person whose dreams will come true someday. Maybe becoming an adult meant recognizing that life was something that just happened to you, and all you could do was try to adjust and carry on.

Of course, if I'd known what was going to happen next, I would have tried harder to get Chloe to speak out. I would have convinced her that it wasn't her fault, and that while the truth may have interpretations, there were very few that absolved those boys of all blame. Instead, we saturated ourselves with secrets and passivity, convinced that it was safer not to point fingers. We were wrong.

Chapter Seven

February 24, 2006

That night was the beginning of something, an unhappy few months where the secrets I kept for Chloe grew every day. I had lied to the police and now I couldn't back down; there were too many hidden things that shouldn't come out. Weeks after she had disappeared, I was still keeping Chloe's secrets. They were stopping me from making new friends, from feeling truly connected to anyone, even Tom.

I didn't see Tom at all on Thursday or Friday morning. I felt stupid every time my eyes snagged on a tall guy in the hall. What did I think would happen? He'd wait by my locker and walk me to class, hand-in-hand? That might happen to other girls but it didn't happen to me. I was the girl you hit on at the party when you were too drunk to charm anyone better. The girl at the school dance who patted your back as you threw up and then pretended she couldn't smell your rancid breath during the slow songs.

Until eleventh grade, Chloe had actually been the kind of girl guys walked to class. That is, on the rare occasions that she would let them. When we were in ninth grade, Chloe went on a few dates with Jay Peterson, an eleventh grader who bought us bottles of raspberry SourPuss with his older brother's ID. The first time he offered to walk her to class, Chloe laughed and flipped her hair. "What? You think I'm going to get lost, Jay?" she asked with a sneer and then strode away, looping her arm through mine. I knew that disdain had probably made Jay like Chloe even more—the exclusive trick of pretty girls who can afford to be harsh on boys. Until eleventh grade, Chloe was never short of guys who wanted to date her, although Liam had been her only serious boyfriend. But things changed, and even before Chloe went missing, no boy wanted to hold her hand.

In English class we were studying *Lord of the Flies*. I liked the book better than *Macbeth*, our last unit, but I still found it disturbing. I had thought the boys would act like a group of tropical castaways, making things out of coconut shells and playing on the beach. It wasn't really turning out that way.

"Why did the boys attack Piggy?" Mr. Greene asked, gently tapping the desk of a guy who had his head down on his arms.

"Because they've gone insane. They're acting so random," Andrea Moore offered. That was always her answer, whether it was *Macbeth* or *Catcher in the Rye*. Andrea was the kind of girl who thought everything in life was random, mostly because she never seemed to completely understand what was happening.

"Well, you could argue that," Mr. Greene said. "But did the island make them crazy?" He was still young enough that he came in every day brimming with new ways to inspire us. It was almost heartbreaking to watch his disappointment when he realized that most people had forgotten their books and weren't really reading along anyway.

"I think it did," Joseph Pitreault said at the front of the class. He glanced down at his book, which was open on his desk and stuffed with Post-it notes marking significant passages. Joseph was one of the only kids who always read the book. "They've been out there so long. And Simon is clearly hallucinating with that pig's head. I think the stress is causing them to fall apart and that's why they're behaving so violently." I stared out the window, watching the people below as Joseph continued talking. My attention was so shoddy these days. I couldn't seem to focus anymore.

"Jenny? What do you think?" Mr. Greene asked. I jumped, snapped out of my reverie.

"Uh . . . ," I said, hoping he would move on. But he didn't. "What was the question again?"

Mr. Greene smiled. "Do you think the stress of being on that island drove those boys to violence?" he asked. I looked outside, where the hockey team was heading to a school bus, probably to take them to a tournament down south. I could see Devon in the group, running away from a guy who was trying to push him into a snow bank. Devon was smiling and laughing; you could never imagine him hurting anyone. But suddenly I found that I knew the answer to Mr. Greene's question.

"No. They were already violent deep down. The island just gave them permission," I said, still staring out the window at the boys.

By second period it was snowing heavily. I stared out the window of my math class, the road in front of the school blotted out by falling clumps. My classmates began to glance cagily at the snow, distracted by the prospect of driving home in a blizzard. The journey would involve inching down clogged roads and staring grimly at the taillights ahead.

Snowstorms in late February could be brutal, the winter seeming to rally for one last onslaught. This storm was even more disheartening because it had been a hard winter. We had fixed the idea of spring in our heads already, determined that by sheer force of will, It Would Not Snow Anymore.

At the end of math class, the announcements began: "Due to the heavy snowfall predicted for the rest of the day, school buses have been canceled. Please make other arrangements."

The other students cheered. It was an unwritten rule that teachers didn't take attendance once buses were canceled. The number of students would slowly diminish until only the kids who had to wait for their parents remained.

Usually, I would have been just as happy for the news. But today it didn't do me much good. I had missed a huge chemistry test a few days after Chloe disappeared. I'd been given a few weeks to study and today was the day I had to take it. I knew my disciplinarian teacher wouldn't accept the snow as an excuse. I could almost hear Mr. Boyle's voice now: "Miss Parker, I don't see why you should be excused when I have to be here. You're Canadian, you can handle a bit of snow."

When I left the class for lunch, Tom was suddenly at my side. He touched my elbow to get my attention and I jumped.

"Whoa, sorry," Tom said with a grin. "Didn't mean to sneak up on you."

"No, sorry," I muttered, my heart beginning to pound as the prospect of talking to Tom again sunk in. "I was just . . . thinking."

"Well, are you free now? Want to get out of here?" Tom asked. We started walking down the hallway past kids shrugging on jackets and jamming books into their bags as fast as they could.

"I can't. I have this . . . thing I have to do here, after school," I said.

I was cringing at the idea of telling him I had a science test. It sounded so lame, especially when Tom acted like he never had to be bothered with trivial things like tests and parents. But my grades were hovering around the pass line and missing the test would mean an automatic fail in chemistry.

"Well, come hang out now. I have something to tell you," Tom said, winking at me conspiratorially.

"Okay," I said. To my surprise, he looped his arm through mine and guided me smoothly down the hall. As we walked, I noticed people watching us with interest. Tom and I had never been seen together, and in Thunder Creek, the kids saw everything, or at least they *thought* they did. Walking down the hall like a couple was quite a statement. It was a new experience for me, feeling chosen by a boy. I already liked Tom more than I would have expected. He was warmer than his reputation had led me to believe.

We walked out to his truck and he drove to the parking lot of the hockey arena. The lot was empty, the snow rapidly filling up the crevices that the tires had etched into the ice. Tom parked at the far corner so we could see any cars approaching and then he sparked a joint.

When Tom turned off the truck, silence flooded into the space, punctuated only by the sound of him inhaling deeply. I waited for him to talk. He seemed more focused on getting high, though, so I shared his joint, hoping it would wear off by test time. Finally, with the joint done, Tom stared out the front window, his dark eyes reflecting the bright snow all around us.

"You know how you were talking about that dead girl the other day?" he asked. I nodded. He hesitated, and for one second, in a fit of stoned paranoia, I thought he was going to tell me he murdered her.

"Well, my dad's girlfriend works at the police station. I heard her talking to him about the case last night. Apparently, the last time someone saw that girl, she was just outside Birch-Bark Village. She was at the road, so they're assuming she was trying to hitch a ride back to the reserve," he said. My stomach dropped.

"That's where I live," I whispered. Tom nodded.

"Yeah, I figured you had to live around there. Because you went to my middle school, remember?" he said. My cheeks flushed. Birch-Bark Village was the poorest area on the west end of town, which meant that Tom had assumed I didn't live anywhere nice. That stung, but I tried to focus on the information he'd shared.

"Do they know why she was there?" I asked. He shrugged.

"Nope. I'd guess visiting someone, but that's pretty far to travel if you have to hitch back."

"No buses go out to the reserve?" I asked.

"I don't think so," Tom said, shaking his head. "They're not really part of the city, are they? Maybe school buses."

"So, they think whoever picked her up killed her?" I asked.

"Yeah, I think so," Tom said. "Maybe the guy who killed her lives in your neighborhood."

"Thanks for telling me," I said quietly.

"Be careful," Tom said. I didn't reply. It seemed like such an irrelevant comment. I wasn't doing anything dangerous, and I couldn't help the fact that I was a girl in Thunder Creek. I was just going to have to take my chances.

And then, slowly, he leaned over and kissed me on the lips. Something dropped inside of me and I kissed back harder. I could feel the contours of his full lips against mine. His hand slid down my face, past my neck and inside my jacket to my chest. I ran my hands through his hair as he kissed my neck. Some of the numbness that had crept into me after losing Chloe evaporated as I felt Tom's warm hands under my sweater, just over my heart. Finally, we pulled away and Tom drove me back to school. I wondered if anyone would be able to tell how I had spent my lunch hour, if the unfamiliar smells of pot and boy would sit on my skin like a perfume borrowed from an older, worldlier cousin.

I felt exhilarated as I climbed out of Tom's truck. I couldn't believe that this was actually me kissing a good-looking boy at school. But as I watched him drive out of the parking lot, I didn't forget what he said.

Be careful.

Chapter Eight

I spent most of the afternoon staring out the window, letting the lessons wash over me. The classes were all half full because so many people had gone home. But I still felt like a ghost haunting the classrooms. No one asked how I was or even tried to talk to me anymore. I wondered if people would have treated Chloe the same way if I'd been the one who disappeared. The thought seemed unimaginable, me anywhere but Thunder Creek. Chloe had always been poised at the doorway, while I was always the one begging her to come back inside.

The light was already fading by the time I wrote my test. My mind still felt slow and stuffy after the pot, and I regretted smoking it. I was starting to get the sense that Tom was the kind of heavy stoner who treated pot like a daily occurrence, a far cry from my limited experience. Still, I soldiered on under Mr. Boyle's intense glare, and by the end I knew that I had passed. A pass was enough when so much else was happening in my life.

I walked down the main hallway to the exit. A gust of snow lifted my hair as I stepped outside, sending frozen air down the strands right to my scalp. I walked as quickly as I could to my car, curling stinging hands in my pockets as the snow battered my body. I couldn't wait to be home, curled up in my room with a hot chocolate and my feet under the covers.

The road was empty. Anyone reasonable was already home, and no one was going out again tonight. I decided to take the highway that looped around town, because it was always better maintained than local streets. Northern Ontario tended to treat those who were passing through better than those who stayed.

I was almost to the set of lights where I would turn off the highway and drive west to my neighborhood when I saw the boy. The fluorescent orange of his jacket made him stand out in the kaleidoscope of grays and whites that filled my windshield. He was hunched over, walking into the snow with no hat. And he was clutching a musical instrument case with the name of my high school stamped in big letters on the side.

He was at the perimeter of town, heading down the Trans-Canada Highway. The highway here had wedged itself between two towering rock faces dotted with scraggly evergreens. To make the road they'd had to blow right through the rock, and there was almost no shoulder for pedestrians. One car skidding was all it would have taken for the boy to be in serious trouble.

So I stopped my car. I didn't normally offer rides to strangers, but this was bad weather and he was from my school. And maybe I had started to notice other people more lately, now that I wasn't taking care of Chloe.

I rolled down the passenger-side window and honked my horn. He turned around and I motioned him to come over. The howling winds were so loud that I had to lean across the car and shout to be heard.

"Hey, you go to Thunder Creek High, right? Can I give you a ride?" I asked. The guy hesitated. His black hair was coated with snow and even his eyelashes were fringed with ice.

"Are you heading toward the reserve?" he asked.

"It's no big deal, really. I don't mind dropping you—the weather's shit!" I said, trying not to look like the kind of person who regularly encouraged people to get into her car.

"Okay, thanks," he said, opening the car door and climbing in. He wedged his instrument case between his legs and I rolled up the window.

I didn't recognize him, but he looked pretty young. By eleventh grade you stopped noticing freshmen; it was the natural order of things. He was tall and skinny and had the gangly look of a junior basketball player. I knew he wasn't, though, because there were no Natives on our basketball team. It occurred to me that he must have been desperately cold to accept a ride from a stranger. But I guess if you're stuck in a storm you have to run the risk that the only person offering help may hurt you.

"I'm Jenny," I said as he warmed his hands on the dashboard vent. He couldn't have lasted much longer outside without getting serious frostbite. It was a scary prospect when the reserve was still over six miles away.

"Bobby," he said quietly. I cranked the heat up as far as it could go, even though the hot air blew my hair back and made my eyes feel dry. I could tell he was so chilled that getting warm again would be an ambitious project, with hot showers and soup and an evening spent huddled by the radiator.

"What grade are you in?" I asked, feeling like the awkward mother of a teenager, driving one of her children's friends home.

"Nine," he said.

"Oh. I'm in eleven," I said, even though he hadn't asked.

"What instrument do you play?" I asked.

"Trumpet," he said. I nodded and the conversation promptly stalled.

I stared straight ahead at the road as we inched along. I knew how to find the reserve. It was down a twisty road off the highway, on a patch of land randomly cut out of the woods.

My mom had taken me along a few times when she wanted to pick up cigarettes from the reserve store.

I drove down the road and over the train tracks. A few more miles of icy roads passed before we finally arrived at the reserve. Little beige houses with ramshackle porches rose from the ground along the road while the trees receded behind them. Looking at this little clump of homes in the wilderness, I couldn't help feeling lucky that I lived right in town. At least we had a beach and a movie theater.

Bobby pointed at a little house up the road. I noticed that there was no car in the driveway. We slowly cruised past the store with its billboard advertising "Cheap Smokes." The neon yellow letters seemed jarring against the gray-white landscape of winter. When I pulled up in front of his house, I saw a curtain flick shut. I wondered if Bobby's mother had spent the afternoon nervously peering out at the road, unable to do anything but worry about her son. It was comforting to know that she would feel better because of something I had done. Now she could spend the next hour babying her son instead of praying for him on that unforgiving highway.

I put the car in park and looked at him, the car silent despite the background noise from the heater.

"Thanks," Bobby said.

"No problem."

"Why'd you stop?" he asked. I shrugged and looked out the window at the snowflakes collecting on the windshield, settling for just a second before the wipers violently pushed them aside.

"It's dangerous out there," I said. I could have been talking about the weather, but I wasn't and he knew that.

"It always has been," Bobby said stiffly.

"Did you know her?" I asked, almost certain that he would bristle and tell me that not all Natives knew each other. Bobby opened the door of the car and got out, the cold air washing over my flushed cheeks.

"She was my cousin," he said simply. Then he shut the door and trudged up the driveway, still holding his case.

Chapter Nine

February 27, 2006

On the Monday morning after I gave Bobby a ride, I woke up disappointed to find that my life was still the same. I sat up in bed and decided that today I couldn't be bothered to go to school. I went back to sleep, knowing I could convince my mom to give me a sick note for tomorrow. I woke up again around eleven and decided to make a McDonald's run, the perfect complement to an afternoon of watching daytime TV.

I was just pulling out of the housing complex parking lot when a truck rolled up in front of me. It was Tom Grey, his eyes obscured by black Ray-Bans. I swallowed hard, feeling a sickening flip in my stomach. Was I happy to see him? I wasn't sure. I didn't know him well enough to be totally comfortable with him. Yet somehow his presence seemed to make everything a little more exciting, a little less predictable.

I rolled down my window and he did the same, looking down at me in my tiny car.

"Hey," he said, his mouth pulling up in a smile.

"Hey . . . what's up?" I asked. He shrugged, the movement exaggerated by the black snowboard jacket he was wearing.

"I have something that might be useful. Can we go to your place?" he asked. I nodded hesitantly.

Anxious thoughts flickered across my mind as I parked my car. What did he have? Was it a clue about Helen? Was it drugs? Was this all a clever way for him to suggest we hook up?

I unlocked my front door while he stood behind me. I tried to breathe normally and open the door the same way I always did, regardless of his presence. It worked . . . sort of.

My house was the middle column of a row house divided into three segments. It was like a novel on a tightly packed bookshelf. I didn't know where Tom lived, but I felt ashamed as my eyes drifted past full ashtrays, yellowed linoleum with curled edges and a faded floral couch. Our house wasn't dirty but it was untidy, and there was an undeniably dingy quality to the interior. It was a home full of secondhand things and second-rate lives, both of which we couldn't afford to replace.

I threw my jacket on the easy chair and sat down on the couch. Tom lingered in the doorway for a moment. He was taller than the frame and was slouching almost unconsciously, as if he'd spent his whole life trying to make himself small enough to fit places.

"So, what's up?" I asked as he settled next to me on the couch. Tom unzipped his backpack and pulled out last year's yearbook.

"Helen was last seen in Birch-Bark Village," he said, his large hands resting on the pebbled black cover. "So why was she here? Who was she visiting?" he asked, flipping his inky hair out of his eyes.

"It was probably another kid," Tom continued before I had time to guess. "So, I got the yearbook. I thought we could pick out which people live in your neighborhood."

"That makes sense," I said. I cracked open the book, ignoring the stamp that indicated Tom had stolen it from the school library.

"There's not a lot of teenagers around here," I said, my face growing hot. "It's mainly old people and young families. Most people move into bigger places before their kids are in high school."

I pointed out a couple of freshmen, but the only older kids were Brittany Robichard and Jake Depuis. I couldn't imagine Brittany knowing Helen. She was a star basketball player, and like any girl who was talented and pretty, Brittany seemed to stroll through life with an ease I hadn't picked up in my sixteen years on the planet.

But Jake . . . Jake was in the school band. He played the trumpet, like Helen's cousin Bobby. I only knew this because we used to ride the same bus to school. Every morning Jake would be standing in front of Birch-Bark Village, carrying a school trumpet in a battered and frayed case. Even on the bus, after he had aligned the instrument on the seat next to him, Jake would never let go of the handle, probably afraid to let the case slide off the seat. Someone in his family had no doubt made it clear to him that they didn't have the money to pay for repairs if the trumpet was damaged.

I pointed at the black-and-white picture of Jake smiling hesitantly, his skinny shoulders hunched.

"I think that guy might know Helen's cousin. Maybe that's the connection?" I said. Tom furrowed his brow, examining Jake's picture in the yearbook.

"I guess it's possible. I mean, do you know if she was close to her cousin?"

"I'm not sure," I admitted. "I just met him yesterday. I gave him a ride out to the reserve."

"What's up with that anyways?" Tom asked, his voice growing louder. "I mean, it was the same out in B.C. You always saw Natives hitchhiking, even when they knew people had been killed in the area doing that. You'd think they'd learn."

"How else can they get around if they don't have a car and the buses don't run out there?" I asked, a little shocked that Tom would wonder about something so obvious. Then again, judging by his car and his clothes, Tom had never been short on money.

"Maybe, like, a carpool between them, where they all chip in and buy a car? I mean, there's always a solution if you get creative," Tom said self-righteously.

"Yeah, you're probably right," I said. I didn't actually agree with him. I knew that it was easy to demand that people come up with clever ideas without acknowledging that being poor made you feel unable to change anything in your life. There was an overwhelming sense of powerlessness that was ground into your bones. Still, I wanted desperately to keep liking Tom, since he was the only person who had treated me like a normal human being since Chloe disappeared.

"Anyways, do you think you could talk to this Jake kid? Maybe see if he knows anything useful?" Tom asked, changing the subject abruptly. He must have known that I was being insincere but wanted his win intact.

"I can try. Jake's pretty quiet, but it's worth a shot," I said.

"Good!" Tom said, taking the yearbook from me and dropping it carelessly on the floor. "What should we do now?" he asked, his eyelids heavy and his lips open.

"This," I said hesitantly, leaning forward and kissing him. I wasn't sure if I did it because he was good-looking or because he seemed as out of place in Thunder Creek as my best friend had been. Maybe I just didn't want to be alone. Still, I felt a thrill of electricity when our lips touched, and some of the tension in my head melted away.

We didn't do anything more than kiss. After twenty minutes of making out on the couch, Tom told me he had to go. A strange mixture of relief and disappointment settled over me when he left. It felt good to kiss Tom, but I'd been worried about how far he might think things would go in an empty house in the middle of the day. Still, the house seemed particularly empty with him gone, and I found myself fantasizing about how we could have spent the day if he'd stayed.

Tom had dated girls before. When he was in grade ten, I would see him around school with this artsy punk girl in the eleventh grade. Her name was Vanessa and she was so pretty that she elevated dyed black hair and dark purple lipstick beyond the cliché. Tom and Vanessa would make out in the student parking lot, their hips pressed together. They had that ease with each other's bodies that silently telegraphed the fact that they were having sex. To think that Tom might be unconsciously comparing me to Vanessa was terrifying.

I had never done more than kiss a boy. There had been a handful of moments at dances and parties, moments swollen with the potential of future romance, but they never developed into anything more. I'd never had a boyfriend. It was disappointing in a way; I had always assumed that I would have a high-school sweetheart. He would be someone who I could eventually marry and settle down with in Thunder Creek. It would have been so easy to wrap my future in the promise of love, but it never materialized. People occasionally joked that I was in love with Chloe, which wasn't true. But maybe I had been waiting for a boy as exciting as Chloe, someone who could make my small life feel special.

Obviously, I was still a virgin. It hadn't mattered initially, but as the years of high school trundled along, the ranks of virgins had begun to dwindle. I was petrified that eventually, I would be the only virgin left, and the fact that I hadn't changed would be considered terminally bizarre. When we hit eleventh grade, Chloe began to refer to my virginity as embarrassing, and often told me that I just needed to find a guy to get rid of it. It wasn't an appealing idea, especially after I saw how sex had hurt Chloe.

Many adults thought teenage drug use was perfectly harmless so long as you weren't stupid enough to get caught. You could buy condoms and birth control in Thunder Creek, and plenty of couples had sex in high school. But you couldn't be a whore. If you were a girl, you waited until you were dating someone before you had sex. You stayed with that person for at least six months, and if you broke up, you didn't have sex again until the next relationship was firmly established. Having a boyfriend legitimized a girl reading *Cosmo* and playing confessional party games. As long as you had a boyfriend in the daylight, no one cared what you did at night.

Chloe had slept with a few too many guys in circumstances that were a bit questionable. Suddenly, she was soiled, and lurid stories of her depraved behavior began to circulate at school. The girls were the worst. Chloe had been so colorful and vibrant, so sure that she was better than Thunder Creek. In comparison, the third-generation Creeker girls had always seemed so dour and plain in their boyfriends' oversized hockey sweatshirts. In other circumstances, it might have been comforting to see Chloe taken down a peg. She had always been better than me, her freckled Creeker sidekick. But there was nothing fun about the ugliness that Chloe endured.

They made websites about her. They told jokes. Boys called her house, wanting to know if she'd like to "party." By the end,

I couldn't tell if Chloe's true error had been having sex too casually or simply believing there was something out there better than Thunder Creek, better than the plain dreams of girls like them, girls like me.

It was safer to stay a virgin.

Chapter Ten

At the end of the school day, I went outside and walked down to the place where the school bus stopped. I was waiting for Jake when the bus pulled up. He walked out with his head down. Jake was a rock in the river of elementary-school kids clutching the straps of their cheap nylon backpacks. He trudged toward his place, his trumpet like a briefcase on the arm of a miserable businessman.

"Jake!" I called, my hand clamping down on his shoulder. Even through the canvas of his army jacket I could feel the surprising hardness of bone instead of the expected mix of muscle and fat.

Unfortunately, Jake was one of those people who had a bundle of unattractive features, the kind of ugliness that averaged out the unworldly beauty of supermodels. He was small and thin with an overbite so pronounced that it pulled his features forward and gave him a rat-like appearance. He wasn't helped by a buzz cut that threw his features into sharper relief, as if he were standing under a fluorescent light.

"Yeah?" Jake said, turning around. His eyes widened when he saw that it was me. We had never really spoken before.

"Um, do you have a few minutes? I need to talk to you about something," I said.

Nearby, kids were climbing the dirt-encrusted snow banks that bordered the curb. Their mothers were standing nearby, smoking cigarettes and gossiping.

"Uh, I don't know . . . ," Jake said, glancing past my shoulder as if trying to come up with a reason to say no.

"Please, it's important," I said, taking a deep breath before going out on a limb. "It's about Helen."

Jake's eyes registered pain as he stepped back in shock. Whatever he thought I wanted, it was clear that he hadn't expected this. He stared down at the trumpet case clutched in his hand then slowly pulled his gaze up to meet mine. His eyes were a golden-brown and fringed with long, oddly feminine eyelashes.

"Okay," he whispered, walking toward his house and beckoning me to follow.

———

Nobody was home at Jake's so we sat in the living room. Jake was avoiding my eyes. It was obvious that he was speaking to me out of some sense of duty rather than any genuine desire to do so. That was fine with me. I was looking for information, not a new friend.

"So, Helen was visiting you the day she disappeared?" I asked, figuring that I should cover the basics before I launched into unknown territory. It was strange, morphing from the person who was always being questioned into the interrogator. Jake nodded tightly and fiddled with his watchstrap.

"How did you guys know each other?" I asked.

"My dad. Uh, he was in an accident on a construction site. He broke something in his back and was in the hospital for a long time. Helen volunteered there, in the children's ward. One day we started talking in the cafeteria and we just, you know . . . became friends. We both had a parent die when we were younger so we kind of understood each other. She hung out here sometimes, but I've never been to her house," Jake whispered, the story streaming out of his mouth in a confessional whoosh.

"What was she like?" I found myself asking. I was overcome with the need to understand a life I had only noticed once it was already over.

"Oh God, Helen . . . ," Jake said, a pained smile breaking on his face. "She was quiet but she cared so much about people. Helen would always listen to your problems. She spent all of her time trying to make everyone happy. She didn't really like school but she wasn't dumb. We both loved historical movies, especially about World War II. We were actually watching *Band of Brothers* the day she . . . that day."

"She sounds like a good friend," I said. I realized I had used the present tense. Somehow, it seemed inevitable as Jake told me what made Helen a person and not just a crime scene. It felt like she was still there.

"She was," Jake said quietly. He looked up and I saw tears brimming in his eyes, trapped in the web of his eyelashes. "She was one of my best friends, even though nobody really knew about it."

"What do you mean?" I asked. Jake sighed and wiped his face with the faded cuff of his army jacket.

"Well, we didn't hang out together at school. I mostly hang out with kids from the band, and I invited her a couple of times but she was funny around new people, too shy. And . . . well, my dad's a bit weird about Natives. He's from Oka, in Quebec, and they had Native protests there, so I only invited Helen over on days when he wasn't home."

"Your dad didn't know about Helen?" I asked. Jake shook his head.

"No, he didn't. I mean . . . " He paused, trying to gather the right words. "My dad's not, like, *racist*. He wouldn't have flipped out if he found her here. He just wouldn't have approved of us hanging out."

Jake was looking at me anxiously, afraid that he had given me the impression that his dad was a bigot.

"Yeah, I totally understand," I said. "What did he say when the cops came by to interview you?"

"What?" Jake looked confused. "The cops never talked to me."

I frowned. When Chloe went missing, the police started interviews and searches right away. Granted, the cops wouldn't have known Jake was her friend, but surely they would have wondered why Helen was last seen by Birch-Bark Village, clear across town from the reserve, the hospital and our school? Tom had noticed that immediately. Either he was an investigatory prodigy or the cops weren't even bothering to ask the most basic questions. I flashed back to something Officer Trudeau had said: we have an officer who's going to look into this. Had that officer even started yet?

"So, no one but me really knows you were friends?" I asked. Jake bit his lip and nodded. "And she was just going home afterward?"

"I don't know," Jake said hesitantly. "She mentioned meeting someone. Helen talked sometimes about this one guy; he sounded sketchy. I think he worked at a bar."

"Did you ever meet him?" I asked. Jake shook his head.

"No. I just figured I had my friends and she had hers. She only mentioned him a couple of times, but I didn't think he sounded like a good guy. He was older than her and she seemed really into him, like in love."

"Okay, thanks," I said, dazed that Jake hadn't considered any of this information valuable enough to be shared with the police. It was obvious that he was keeping quiet so his father wouldn't find out he'd been sneaking around with Helen. I wondered if things would have been different if he'd contacted the cops. Still, it was hard to be angry with someone who had just lost a good friend in a brutal murder. Besides, I knew what it was like to keep secrets about your friends.

"It's hard, isn't it?" I asked suddenly. "To try to act normal after you lose someone?"

"Yeah," he whispered, his tears returning. "I just feel so guilty that I'm still here and she's not. And I can't even tell anyone. I have to pretend like nothing's changed."

"It's almost easier not to," I said. "To just accept that you're different now and you'll never be the same."

"I-I wanted to say I was sorry about Chloe," Jake said hesitantly. "I saw you guys together so much, ever since we were little. What happened to Helen . . . I hope he didn't get Chloe too."

"Thanks," I whispered. "That's nice of you to say."

Jake nodded and I got up from the couch. I didn't have any more questions, and I could tell by the relieved look on Jake's face that he wasn't burdened with any more answers.

I walked down the steps, distracted by the nagging suspicion that I was missing something. Suddenly, the thought dislodged from the murk of my subconscious and floated up to the surface.

"Jake, wait," I said, whirling around. He stood in the doorway, the light from the hall casting a deep shadow across his face. It distorted his features, leaving me with the unshakeable feeling that I was now talking to a stranger.

"Yeah?" he asked. I checked for people nearby, but it was close to dinnertime now and all the children and mothers were tucked away inside.

"You told me Helen was shy around new people. And that she wasn't going directly home." I ticked the points off on my fingers and then looked up at Jake, who nodded. "Everyone assumed she was hitchhiking that night. But she doesn't sound like the kind of person who would ever hitchhike."

"She never mentioned hitching. I don't think she would have done that," Jake said with a frown, trying to understand where I was going with this.

"Then maybe someone picked her up that night," I said slowly. "Maybe Helen knew the killer."

Chapter Eleven

February 28, 2006

The next day, I stopped at the grocery store on my way home from school. I did most of the grocery shopping in the family, my way of reducing my mom's endless list of parental responsibilities. My mother always seemed tired, and I wanted to make her life as easy as possible. Sometimes this entailed doing extra chores around the house, sometimes it meant keeping a bundle of secrets.

"Jenny?" I looked up from my grocery cart and right into the faces of Chloe's parents, Linda and Greg Shaughnessy.

To see them in a place as mundane as the grocery store was surreal. My throat tightened as I noticed how normal they looked. How could tragedy be concentrated so inwardly that grieving parents could have clean hair and scarves that matched their hats?

"Hi, Mr. and Mrs. Shaughnessy," I said. Linda smiled, but the wrinkles around her eyes didn't deepen. Her hands, which rested on the handle of her cart, were shaking.

"Hi, Jenny," she said. "How are you?"

"I'm okay. You know, work and school . . . ," I said awkwardly. My vague answer left out so much that it felt like a lie. But what could I tell her? How, since I had lost Chloe, my life felt flattened and stretched thin? That I was spending more time investigating a teenage girl's murder than doing my homework? The Shaughnessys didn't need any more unpleasant truths.

"It's been so long since I've seen you . . . ," Linda said wistfully. "You should drop by sometime." I nodded, aware that I would never go near Chloe's house. It was too painful.

Greg glanced away, distracted by a child pitching a temper tantrum in the checkout line. I had known Greg for over half my life, but he still felt like a stranger. His presence was usually marked by a closed office door or the back of a steel-haired head watching CNN. He had the air of a person who generally disapproved of any excessive noise or extravagance. Chloe and her father had never been particularly close.

"Well, uh, I hope to see you soon," I said, my heart beginning to splinter as I stared at Linda's face and saw her resemblance to Chloe. It occurred to me that this might be the closest I would ever come to seeing what Chloe would look like as an adult.

As they turned away, I thought of something, the words coming out before I really had time to consider them. "Hey, this is a weird question, but that night, Chloe was complaining about losing one of her mittens. Did you guys ever find a mitten, blue and pink stripes?" I asked, flinching at saying her name in front of her mother. It seemed so callous to ask a woman with a missing daughter about a lost mitten, but I couldn't tell her the truth.

"No, sorry, we didn't," Linda said, a faint frown crinkling her forehead. "But I'll keep an eye out."

"Thanks," I said awkwardly.

"Take care, sweetie," Linda said.

As I walked past her, she reached out and lightly touched my arm. When I glanced back, it was as if her face had cracked open, revealing the raw emotion swirling beneath the surface: confusion, fear, frustration. But there was something else. Her face was shining with hope, like she was waiting for God to vindicate her pleas and put an end to the slow-burning loss of her daughter. Even after Helen's murder, this mother believed her daughter was coming home, that no one could ever hurt a girl like Chloe. The faith in her face made me look away.

That night, I sat on my bed and stared at Helen's picture in the yearbook. I kept switching from it to the pictures of Chloe and me layered on the walls. It was a chronology of our life, the new pictures covering up the years of captured moments that had come before.

I couldn't stop thinking about Chloe's mother and the fact that her life at the moment was completely defined by what wasn't in it. Linda had left her job when Chloe was born because she'd always wanted to be a stay-at-home mom. Now she was just a mother-in-waiting, marking time until she found her daughter.

What remained of a life once it was over? I thought of Chloe's clothes hanging silently in her closet, of the binders and stray gloves that surely remained in Helen's locker. I thought of the pictures in the newspaper, and how quickly that paper aged and degraded, as fast as it took people in town to move on from yesterday's sadness. Finally, I thought about the mitten I had stashed under my pillow. It haunted me to think that once a person was gone, all that remained of their life was a random collection of possessions and a shadow in other people's memories.

It made me feel as if I should live my life in a way that would transcend a closet full of clothing and the private sadness of a mother. More than that, I wanted to right the wrongs that had already happened. I felt a flush of anger as I thought of the people who had hurt Chloe and Helen. I wanted to make them pay, but I felt completely useless.

I looked up at the picture of Chloe and me hugging on her last birthday. She was wearing orange sunglasses and bright pink lipstick. My face was colorless, and I was hunched down like a tissue draped around her shoulders. One of those girls looked like the kind of person who could make her life matter, the kind of girl who could force the whole world to sit up and listen. The other girl would never even be a footnote in a book. She wouldn't be forgotten, because she would never be noticed. The problem was that the wrong girl had disappeared.

I lay in bed for hours that night, tossing and turning as the same thoughts ran through my head like a dog chasing its own tail. Finally, when I couldn't bear to spend another moment thinking about Chloe and Helen, I gave up on sleep and got out of bed.

It was past midnight when I padded downstairs, the house quiet and as still as a photograph. I slipped my snow boots on and shut the door carefully behind me. The night air poked my face with cold needles as I hastily zipped up my snowboard jacket and pulled a hat down over my hair. I was still wearing pajama pants and I could feel my legs grow cold as I walked to my car.

I turned the key in the ignition, gasping at the cold air that blew out of the heater. The steering wheel was frozen, but I knew that my hands would thaw once the heater kicked in.

It was crazy to be out at this hour; I was going to feel terrible in the morning after so little sleep. But my only other option was to stay in my room and obsess over the myriad things that made life unfair. Better to drive.

On nights like these, I always ended up in the same place, parked near Liam McAllister's house. He was the only person I blamed as much as myself. I parked across the street and turned off the engine, just in case anyone was awake to notice me. Pulling my gloves on, I huddled in my rapidly cooling car and examined the McAllisters' home. I found myself searching for Chloe's other mitten, poking out of a snow bank or frozen in the driveway, but that didn't make any sense. She hadn't come here that night.

It was a large brick house that glowed with the comfortable wealth that the McAllister family possessed. They were the kind of family who went on European vacations every few years and had money for the constant hockey equipment purchases required to outfit growing boys. Things had always come easy to Liam, and this house was the epitome of that successful life. I had never liked it when he gave me a ride home; he would peer out his window at my neighborhood like he was on some sort of African safari. So often, I wanted to scream, "Yes! Some houses don't have hot tubs and barbecue pits! Get used to it!" But I never did. Chloe loved him, and I didn't want to ruin our friendship, so I kept quiet, like always.

I balled my gloved hands into puffy fists and tried not to cry. Was Liam in that house, asleep in his bedroom? Were any guilty thoughts poking his conscience? Liam's life remained on track even as mine was completely derailing.

I stared up at the McAllisters' tranquil home and wished that I could burn it to the ground.

Chapter Twelve

October 15, 2005

C hloe and I were sitting on top of the chairlift at the ski hill. It was mid-October, so the hill wasn't open yet and no one was around to stop us from climbing the ladder. Just under the cable was a small platform used by the technicians to fix the lift. Chloe and I had been coming here for years. It was just around the corner from her house, a spacious four-bedroom home with a hot tub in the backyard.

We were sitting on the platform, our feet dangling high above the chairlifts. We had our backs turned to the forest that bordered the ski hill and stretched north without interruption for ages. The whole town was spread out in front of us, curled around the base of the ski hill. At night, surrounded by the inky darkness of the forest and the vast sky, Thunder Creek's cluster of lights seemed to belong to a larger city. You could pretend that the lights kept going beyond the hills. That maybe those lights were nightclubs and modern art museums instead of an endless number of suburban houses and twenty-four-hour convenience stores.

It was a beautiful night, unseasonably warm for October. A breeze slid up the hill, ruffling the long grass and reminding me that while it was warm tonight, I would be in a winter jacket within a month.

We were sharing a water bottle filled with whiskey stolen from Chloe's father's liquor cabinet. He drank a lot, so he didn't really notice how often we skimmed off his bottles. We never took anything from my house. My mom didn't like to drink alone. The only booze in our house was an unopened bottle of Baileys from her work Secret Santa.

The whiskey filled my throat with flannelly warmth even as my mouth puckered. We were drinking because it was the only way we knew how to make *something* happen. Sometimes we would run into people who knew about a party in the woods. Once, we found discarded office chairs on a curb and rode them down the hill. Usually, we just ended up wandering Chloe's neighborhood, the secret drinking electrifying our conversations.

But that night, Chloe seemed distracted. She was drinking quickly, almost with purpose. I caught her glaring at Thunder Creek's lights, which looked like a swarm of fireflies hovering by the lake.

"Look at it, Jenny," she burst out as she took another deep swig.

"Yeah, it's pretty," I said. The Milky Way looked as if someone had smeared stardust across the sky like butter on bread.

"Pretty?" Chloe said with a snort. "It's an ugly town, full of ugly people." She forced the bottle into my hands, but I had barely taken a sip before I felt her fingers clawing it back.

Earlier, we had been in the bathroom at school. I was washing my hands when I heard Chloe gasp from inside the stall. When she came out, she didn't say anything, but she was quiet and distracted. Later, I went back to the bathroom, furtively checking over my shoulder in case Chloe had left her class at the same time.

In the second bathroom stall, someone had written in black Sharpie: "Chloe Shaughnessy is a Slut with AIDS." People had written comments underneath, all agreeing that she was a whore. I sat in that bathroom stall for the rest of my class, methodically covering each comment with white-out, wishing that I could erase it from Chloe's memory as easily. It didn't seem like enough, even then. I wanted to teach them a lesson, force them to leave Chloe alone, but I didn't know how.

"Chloe, are you okay?" I asked. She glanced down at the goose bumps on her knees, poking out from underneath a floral skirt.

"I just wish they'd stop. No matter what I do, they're there," she muttered. I nodded and took another sip of whiskey.

That was the terrible thing about reputations. As soon as a story got started, there was no way to reverse it. Maybe someone gets their stomach pumped after a party. Maybe a boy has an embarrassing erection at the beach. Maybe a girl sleeps with a few too many guys who aren't her boyfriend. In a place like Thunder Creek, there were no pardons. Any black mark on your reputation would count against you long after whatever you'd done to deserve it.

The worst offense was a girl being labeled a slut. Stories would be exaggerated, lurid and seedy details added and narratives exchanged like currency. Everyone would be sickened by the details but would glory in the fact that they were obviously superior to *that* girl. I had heard the same stories about older skanky girls my whole life. There was a girl named Rachel who had graduated high school six years ago, but people still talked about her. They shared her stories when they went off to university, another nameless whore joining endless variations all over the country.

I just never thought Chloe would become ours.

"Don't worry, Chloe. Two more years and you'll be out of here," I said, using the countdown that had comforted her since we were little. Chloe snorted and began to climb down the ladder. She paused on the rails and looked at me, her wild red-brown hair blowing in the breeze.

"Two years might be too much," she said.

I sat up on the platform, drinking the last sips of whiskey while I waited for her to climb down. By the time I started descending, she was far away, walking across the parking lot. All I could see was her shadow, stretched long and thin over the asphalt, disappearing behind her like a fading memory.

Chapter Thirteen

March 1, 2006

Tom was waiting for me at my locker in the morning. He was sitting on the floor with his legs stretched out, impervious to the people awkwardly stepping over him. There was something admirable in his commitment to taking up space when I spent most days trying to be invisible.

"Hey," Tom said, a smile pulling at his lips when he saw me. I felt myself smiling back, my heart pounding a quicker rhythm.

"Hey," I said, trying to ignore the people who were curiously staring at us as they walked by.

Tom stood up and stepped close to me. I could smell pot smoke trapped in his hair and the humid but clean scent of his skin. My stomach squirmed at his closeness, but I knew that he was just trying to speak privately.

"I was wondering, do you want to come over for dinner tonight?" he muttered near my ear. I could feel his breath on my earlobe and a shiver ran up my spine.

"What? Like a . . . ," I asked, panicking that whatever we had been doing was about to culminate in a public show of relationship. I had never dated anyone before, and I didn't know how serious this was to Tom. I couldn't even tell what I wanted, since I was still spending a good part of the day convinced that I was becoming permanently unhinged. I wanted to investigate an unsolved murder with him. And I wanted to kiss him. But I was scared that he would realize how flawed I was if he actually became my boyfriend. Of course, the idea wasn't totally unappealing . . .

Tom must have seen the stricken look on my face, because he stepped back and patted my arm.

"Jesus, chill out, Jenny!" he said with a laugh. "I want you to come for dinner because my dad's having his girlfriend over. The one who works at the police station?" He glanced around and then whispered, "I thought we could wait until she has a few drinks and then see if we can get her talking about the case."

"Ah," I said, heart racing as I thought of seeing anyone from the police station. I would have been happy to never see any of them again. "What was her name again?"

"Leslie. She's an admin assistant," Tom said. I bit my lip. I didn't recognize the name, but I only knew the cops, not the administrative people. Still, I might recognize her face when I saw her. It wasn't an appealing thought.

"Oh yeah, gotcha," I said.

"So, are you in?" Tom asked.

"Uh, yeah okay. What time?" I asked, wondering if this was a good idea. But spending time with Tom was too attractive an offer to pass up.

"Seven o'clock. Our house is 29 Bayview Road," Tom said, turning to walk away. Suddenly, he stopped and turned back.

"Oh, and Jenny? I didn't want my dad to ask questions about why I wanted to invite someone to dinner." He grinned at me. "I'm not exactly Mr. Popular around here. So, you'll have to pretend you're my girlfriend."

"Oh, uh, no problem," I said faintly. I stood by my locker and watched him walk away, a head taller than most of the other students.

I felt off-balance around Tom. I wasn't sure if I liked the feeling, but I did know that the time I spent with him was the longest I went without thinking of Chloe. Maybe that was good enough for now.

After school, I stood in my bedroom, staring at myself in the mirror. What did one wear to a fake date? I had only been on a few real dates in my life, and they had all been to school dances or the movie theater. The best outfit I could come up with was my lavender sweater and black jeans. I felt disappointed by how supremely unspecial I looked in the mirror. But I knew it wasn't about the clothes.

I had always found it hard to describe myself. All of my qualities seemed so tenuous and insubstantial. I was loyal, quiet and thoughtful . . . in other words, boring. I had never been able to see myself clearly before Chloe disappeared. Her personality had always been so bright and big that it threw a long shadow on the people around her. Being Chloe's friend had defined me for so long that I was surprised to see who I was without her.

I retouched my makeup, which always seemed to evaporate by the evening. I had been painting my face with a thick layer of foundation since I was ten years old, and it had become a permanent part of my morning routine. My mother never said a word about my skin. She knew the makeup obsession had started when the kids in my class began to call me "Pongo," after the male dog in the movie *101 Dalmatians*. Even Chloe never mentioned my freckles. They existed in that unspoken space between friends, like the fact that Chloe's family was wealthier than mine. Chloe and I had always been good at leaving uncomfortable truths unsaid.

I turned away from the mirror and shoved a tiny hairbrush and lip gloss into a purse Chloe had given me for my birthday two years ago. If I didn't stop worrying about my appearance and get going then I would be late. Tom lived clear across town, so I had to get on the road. I gave myself one last look. I was never going to be a beauty, but I looked about as good as I could; that would have to be enough.

Bayview Road ran along the edges of Fisher Lake and was one of the nicest areas in town. In Northern Ontario, finding the most expensive neighborhood was easy. All you had to do was look for the lakefront. The next best option were houses perched so high on a hill that they looked out on vast expanses of forest and water. It made sense. If you had the money and you chose to live in Northern Ontario, then you'd better be getting a great view for your troubles.

I drove by large houses made of dark wood and gleaming windows, perched on the shores of the frozen lake. Every home had a pair of jewel-toned SUVs with ski racks mounted on the top. In the summer, I knew I would see speedboats bobbing in the waves, gently bumping docks punctuated with Muskoka chairs.

A lot of these families were rich because of Northern Ontario's resources. These were the folk who owned mining companies and mineral-processing firms. They had started construction businesses or been named executives for the major lumber corporations in the province. These people could afford to treat Thunder Creek like a natural paradise. They spent the summer boating on the lake, trailing water-skiers in their wake. In the winter, there were ski trips to Quebec and evenings curled up in their luxurious homes stoking the fireplace and drinking wine. It was the Great Canadian Dream: a life replete with nature worship and expensive interpretations of rustic living.

Families like mine didn't really benefit from the much-vaunted Northern lifestyle. In fact, like most working-class families, our life was so unadorned that we really could be living anywhere. The view from our front window was of a parking lot. We couldn't afford ski equipment or boats, and even if we had somehow managed to find cheap ones, my mother was almost always working. The only nature I regularly saw was the forested hills that enclosed the city, and the creek behind the high school. Admittedly, I did spend my summers at the local beach, but I would have traded that to live in a less isolated part of Ontario.

Tom's house was a sprawling wooden structure with a deck that wrapped around the home and extended out to an imposing boathouse. On lakefront homes, the most impressive aspects of the house always face the water. Yet, the front of Tom's house still featured wide windows at the top of a peaked entrance. I could see a chandelier glittering warmly through the highest window.

I parked my car and walked up the driveway, feeling my impressions of Tom Grey rearrange themselves. His hatred of Thunder Creek seemed threadbare now that I knew he lived so comfortably.

I rang the doorbell and stood back. When Tom opened the door, I felt a flurry of nerves as I remembered the challenges this night posed. Not only did we have to try to get confidential information from a police employee, I also had to convince everyone that I was Tom's girlfriend. The girlfriend performance would require some serious acting, since I had no real-world experience.

"Hey," Tom said, a slow smile creeping over his face. He was wearing a faded Pink Floyd T-shirt and black jeans.

"Hey," I said, stepping inside the door.

Tom didn't move out of my way, so I found myself facing him, his chin inches from my face. I could feel the warmth radiate from his body, and being so close to unfamiliar skin made my heart beat faster.

I felt Tom's hands rest on my lower back and pull me gently forward, my breath pooling in the back of my throat in anticipation. He was leaning in for a kiss when I heard footsteps approach, shattering the strange and quiet moment. I stepped back abruptly and Tom turned around.

"Uh, Jenny, this is Leslie," Tom said.

"Hi," I said, looking at Leslie. She was a petite brunette in her mid-thirties. I had wondered why Tom's dad, who was clearly wealthy, would be dating someone who worked as an administrative assistant at the police station. Looking at Leslie's full lips and Pilates body, I understood that the missing variable was beauty.

"Pleased to meet you, Jenny," she said.

"Likewise," I said, unnerved by the way her eyes were examining me, as if she was trying to decide whether I was worthy of Tom's company.

"You look familiar. Do I know you from somewhere?" she asked, squinting at me. I swallowed hard. I had thought the same thing about her. I had seen her at the station multiple times, typing away at a computer or bustling down the hallway with an armful of files.

"Uh, I don't think so," I muttered.

"My mistake. So, kids, dinner's probably ready," Leslie said, her hand alighting on her slim hip.

I nodded and followed her down the hall. Tom walked next to me and I could feel his fingers brush against mine. I couldn't tell if it was intentional but it still made me smile.

The dining room of Tom's house was open-concept and shared space with the living room. A wood fire heated the room, the glimmer of firelight reflected in the polished hardwood floors. As I expected, one wall was almost completely made of windows facing the lake, and I couldn't help lingering in front of the bleak view—a vast expanse of black sky and a flat plain of ivory snow stretching out to meet it.

My eyes jumped from the black leather couches to the flat-screen TV, from the mahogany dining table to the soft blankets draped over the arm of the reclining chair. I had never seen a home so luxurious in real life. It was the sort of place I had believed existed only in magazines. I felt my cheeks flush as I remembered Tom visiting my home, with its mismatched furniture and cheap knickknacks. Everything must have looked incredibly dingy to him when he took a house like this for granted.

Tom's father was setting the table. He looked like Tom, tall and lean with thick brown hair. The only difference was that Tom was fairer. His father's skin glowed with a deep tan, as if it were some sort of natural side effect of being wealthy. When he looked up and saw me, he casually tossed the remaining forks onto the table and came over to shake my hand.

"You must be Jenny," he said, his hand warm and soft in mine. "I'm Richard."

"Hi," I said quietly, unsure of how to act. I was quiet at the best of times, but I hated meeting new people.

"Dinner will be about fifteen minutes," Richard said. He smiled conspiratorially, like he was letting me in on a secret.

"I accidentally fell asleep after getting back from the gym tonight, so I'm a bit behind."

"Well, just give us a call," Tom said, leading me away. "I'm just going to show Jenny my room."

"Thank you," I called faintly back to Richard as Tom pulled me down the hallway. I could count on one hand the number of boy's bedrooms I had seen in my life. My pool of experience when it came to boys was so shallow that even the mention of their bedrooms made my palms sweat. I hoped Tom didn't notice.

Tom's room was a complete mess. His floor was covered in piles of laundry that resembled lumpy mountains rising from the carpet. There were dishes everywhere, and cups that he had used as ashtrays. The whole room smelled of cigarette smoke. Books filled his shelves and overflow stacks leaned haphazardly against his desk. His walls were covered in a mishmash of seventies rock posters and exotic scenes that he had torn out of travel magazines.

"I guess I should have cleaned up a little," Tom said sheepishly. "It's usually a bit nicer . . . well, no, that's a lie. It's not."

"What's with all the guidebooks?" I asked, examining his bookshelves. Whole shelves were dominated by old travel books, interrupted only by a few rock star memoirs and books set in far-flung locations. All of the guidebooks looked heavily creased, spiderwebs of cracks traversing their spines.

"Oh, it's kind of dumb," Tom said with a grin, pulling a guidebook to Latin America off the shelf. "When I moved to Thunder Creek, I started buying secondhand travel books at Value Village. A lot of people get rid of them after they go on their trip, so there's a lot there."

"Why?" I asked. "Surely a lot of these are so outdated you can't use them."

"I know," Tom said with a shrug. "But the countries are the same, and I thought it was so cool that these books had traveled to these places. And it just made me excited to think that some-day, I could go to all of these places too."

It surprised me to see Tom so animated about something. His eyes were shining as he replaced the Latin American guide-book and traced his fingers along the spines of books for Indonesia, North Africa and the Caribbean islands. These books represented more than just travel information to Tom; they spoke to him about all the possibilities life had to offer.

"I'm sure you'll see everything," I whispered. "I'm sure it'll be amazing."

Tom leaned down to kiss me. I felt his lips brush against mine for the briefest of seconds, the dry skin on my lower lip gluing ours together, before we heard Richard call for dinner.

As we left the room, I stole one last glance back at Tom's bookshelves. It was the bedroom of a dreamer, someone who believed that his life would be exciting. Chloe's room had been just the same, jam-packed with pictures she'd torn out of fash-ion magazines. I just hoped that, unlike Chloe's, Tom's dreams would actually come true.

Chapter Fourteen

I n the dining room, Richard and Leslie sat at the table, their posture straight-backed and prim as they waited for us to sit down.

"I hope you like cannelloni," Richard said, gesturing toward the table. "It's Tom's favorite."

"I love it," I said, having no idea what cannelloni was. I hoped it wasn't seafood. I hated fish.

Cannelloni turned out to be tubes of pasta with a cheesy spinach filling. It was delicious, and I was relieved that I didn't have to choke down a rancid fish dish in order to make a good impression.

Tom kept refilling Leslie's and Richard's wineglasses. By the fourth glass, Leslie's gestures were becoming looser and more relaxed. Richard had leaned back in his chair and seemed to be struggling to keep up a conversation. I was glad they were drunk; I had felt awkward answering questions about myself throughout dinner. The questions were still coming, but at least I knew they were seeing me through the hazy glow of wine.

"When did you two start dating?" Leslie asked slowly. Her chin was resting on her hand and it swayed slowly back and forth on her floppy wrist.

"A few weeks ago," Tom said, taking my hand.

"Yeah," I said helpfully, hoping the conversation would veer elsewhere.

"Well, that's good. Dating's fun when you're a kid. It becomes more important when you're older, almost like a second job," she said. "Just, you know, don't rush into sex or anything."

I kept my eyes fixed on the table, trying to stop the blush I could feel stealing over my face. I didn't want to talk about sex with an adult I barely knew. In fact, I didn't want to talk about sex with anyone. Why couldn't we just move on to discussing murder, like normal people?

"So, how's work?" Tom asked abruptly. Leslie snorted and took a deep sip of wine.

"You know, the usual," she said, pursing her lips and rolling her eyes.

"I would have thought you'd be extra busy, with that murder," Tom said slowly. I held my breath, afraid that he should have waited until there were more words and wine between them.

"Eh, not really. There are no real leads," Leslie said. "This guy is crafty. He didn't leave any physical evidence behind. He probably picked her up hitchhiking; Natives always do it. Getting her into his car was probably like shooting fish in a barrel."

"Always see them by the reserve," Richard muttered. "Poor kids . . . I'd give them a ride but I only seem to see them . . . when I'm going the wrong way. Or it's night, you know . . . you don't pick up people at night . . . "

"That guy was a sicko, though," Leslie announced, clearly trying to pull Tom's attention back to her. I had met girls like her before, girls who needed to be the focus of all the males in a room, regardless of whether she was interested in any of them. It was almost as if some women only came alive when a man looked at them. I felt a tiny bubble of jealously as she patted Tom's arm, but I knew I was being ridiculous.

"Why?" Tom asked, smiling nicely at Leslie and watching her gulp down more wine.

"He strangled her and then he undressed her. It seems pretty twisted," Leslie said, her mouth pressing into a grim line.

I felt my dinner churn in my stomach. It was such a hideous prospect to think of behaving like that. I found myself wishing fervently that I would never experience what Helen had felt.

"We never found her clothes. The police think he undressed her before he carried her into the woods," Leslie continued, spinning out her ghoulish story like a campfire tale.

"Was she . . . you know, raped?" Tom asked hesitantly. I could tell by his grimace that he wasn't relishing this twisted question-and-answer period either.

"No." Leslie took another swig of her wine. "She died a virgin. Bit of a surprise, actually. You hear all those stories about Native girls . . ."

"Don't be a cow," Richard muttered. He made eye contact with me across the table and rolled his eyes drunkenly. "Leslie's from Caledonia, down south. They hate the Natives down there."

"For good reason," Leslie murmured, tipping more wine into her mouth. I bit my lip and glanced at Tom for help. We wanted information, not racist tirades.

"The whole case sounds terrible," Tom said sympathetically, artfully bringing the conversation back to safer ground. "It must be hard for you to work on such brutal murders."

I had to stop myself from rolling my eyes. She was an administrative assistant! It wasn't like she was out in the field doing CSI work.

"Yeah, it was," Leslie said emphatically. "I'm glad they've decided not to shift their resources away from finding the Shaughnessy girl. She's the priority."

"What do you mean, the priority?" Tom asked, leaning toward Leslie. I bit back a groan. He was doing everything but bat his eyes at her. The disgusting thing was that it was working!

"Well, this is a small police force. And evidence is pretty scarce in both cases, so finding any leads will be difficult. Tough choices had to be made. Obviously, if any new evidence arises in the murder case, they'll look into it, but that case has gone on the back burner."

"But how will they get new evidence if they're not working on it? And surely a murder is more important than a disappearance?" I asked. Leslie looked surprised. I swear she'd forgotten I was at the table.

"That's just the way it is. Have you read the newspaper lately? Everyone in this town is worrying about the Shaughnessy girl. She's from a good family and the whole town is scared for her," she said with a shrug.

"So just because she's rich, the cops care more?" I asked.

"Well, it scares people more when a kid from Blueberry Hill disappears than it does when something happens to a kid from the reserve. They feel like it could have been their daughter," Leslie said, as if I were a moron who needed educating. Then, suddenly, I saw her expression change. A glint of recognition widened her eyes as she pointed at me, still clutching a sloshing wine glass. "Hey . . . wait a minute, I know where I know you from."

"Yeah?" I asked quietly. I knew what she would say but found myself still hoping that her wine-sodden brain wouldn't make the connection.

"You're the Shaughnessy kid's best friend. I remember logging the interview tapes the police did with you."

"Uh, yeah, I am," I said softly, unsure whether I should use the past or present tense for my friendship with Chloe. Something passive, resting between the two, would have been best.

"They really find you uncooperative. That's why they keep interviewing you; they know you're not telling them stuff. Why are you lying to them?" Leslie asked accusingly, her drunken face crumpling into an exaggerated frown.

"I'm not!" I said. Tom was staring at me in confusion.

"Oh, come on. Your best friend just disappears one day and you don't know anything that could help? You *must* know something, something to help understand what happened."

"I don't," I said firmly. "I don't know anything."

Leslie looked at me in disbelief, and even Richard looked perturbed, but what I found most disturbing was the expression on Tom's face. He looked as if he was seeing me in a new and unpleasant light.

After dinner, Tom's dad and Leslie disappeared upstairs. Leslie gave us a drunken wink and mouthed, "Be good." Her frustration with me had apparently evaporated with her next glass of wine.

Tom led me back to his room, saying that we should talk about what we had learned. But I wasn't interested in talking. As soon as he shut his bedroom door, I leaned against the wall and grabbed him, kissing him feverishly. The whole scene felt exciting and illicit, mashed up against a wall making out with a boy I barely knew. We kissed furiously until I felt Tom pull away. I grabbed his hands, trying to drag him in, but he stepped back forcefully.

"Jenny? What are you doing?" he asked.

I leaned against the wall, my head rumpling a few of the

pictures he had taped there. I was breathing heavily and trying to pretend I couldn't see how he was looking at me. Throughout the end of dinner, he had stared at me as if trying to understand what he was seeing. It was the same sort of disappointed look you get when you find an ice cream container in the freezer only to discover that it's been used to store soup.

"What? I thought I was pretending to be your girlfriend," I said lightly, but my heart thumped painfully against my ribs.

"This isn't about that. This is about you trying to avoid the Chloe thing," Tom said accusingly.

"There is no Chloe thing," I retorted. "What? You think I'm hiding some big secret, just like everyone else? Or maybe you think I killed her?"

"I don't know what to think," Tom said, staring past me to the Pink Floyd poster on his wall.

"Don't act like you give a fuck about Chloe!" I snapped. "It's bad enough that you're pretending to care about Helen!"

"At least I'm not running around acting like some northern Nancy Drew so I don't have to deal with shit!" Tom retorted. His words stung, and I looked away so he wouldn't see the confusion on my face. And not just because I was nothing like Nancy Drew. I mean, Nancy was rich and had a father.

"This is real," I whispered. "Helen was *real*. I thought you understood that."

"Maybe I don't," Tom said quietly, a surly expression that he usually reserved for school stealing over his face. I felt a crushing sense of disappointment. Tom was turning out to be so different than I had hoped. He was supposed to help me through all of this. Not only was he failing, but I was pretty sure that I was failing him as well. I didn't even know what he wanted from me, but I didn't think he was getting it.

"Glad to know where we stand then," I said briskly. Then I grabbed my jacket and left. Tom didn't try to stop me.

For a fake relationship, it sure felt like a real breakup.

⌒

I climbed into my car feeling deflated. I hadn't realized how excited I'd been about dinner at Tom's until I felt the weight of my regret. The whole night had been a waste of time. I'd watched two adults get drunk, been accused of obstructing justice by a police employee and then fought with my only friend. The high point of the evening had been learning that I liked cannelloni. Unfortunately, I could have made the same discovery at an Italian restaurant without dysfunction for dessert.

Beyond my car lay the pitch-black night. It was the kind of darkness that lingered around the autumn and spring, when the snow began to melt and grow dirty. You didn't realize how much light the snow was lending you until it disappeared. I crouched over the steering wheel, grimly concentrating on the section of winding road illuminated by the weak beams of my headlights.

The only important thing I had learned was that the police were no longer investigating Helen's case. It felt like racism, but a subtle kind backed up by other excuses. The whole thing left me exhausted because there was nothing I could do. I couldn't change Canadian culture; I couldn't stop people from murdering teenage girls; and I couldn't talk to Tom about Chloe.

He barely knew her. Tom needed to understand how Chloe always read her magazines from back to front. How she'd made a wind chime out of old CDs she painted with nail polish. How, if you shared a pint of Ben & Jerry's Half Baked with her, you had to stop her from strip-mining it of all the chunks. He would certainly need to eat her killer French toast with bananas. Tom would have to admire the confident way she painted daises on her fingernails with a toothpick. He'd have to listen to her whisper in the darkness of a sleepover about how she didn't want a life like her parents'. Tom would need to understand how Chloe was the person I was closest to, and that her memory had become sacred to me. Tom would need to know that I lived my life now as if I were composing a letter to her, doing everything while simultaneously describing it to Chloe in my head. And I knew that all of that was impossible. Tom couldn't do those things, and I couldn't explain what Chloe meant to me.

I was close to town when my car ran out of gas. I had just climbed a steep hill called Tower Drive and the only comfort was that I hadn't stopped halfway up. The car coasted to a stop on the shoulder.

Sitting in my silent car, I felt like a complete idiot. When was the last time I had even looked at the gas gauge? It was as if I'd decided that the requirements of daily life didn't apply since I was so consumed with bigger things. When something really bad happens, you somehow expect everything to stop around you, but the laundry piles up and your grades go down. It can feel like another injustice, the way life refuses to acknowledge what you've lost.

When I realized that there was no cell service, I felt my frustration boil to the surface. I punched the steering wheel, a huff of anger whistling through my teeth. I didn't need any of this on a night that I was looking forward to ending. I just wanted to crawl into bed, fall asleep and try again tomorrow.

I was parked on the dirt shoulder beneath a sweep of tall evergreens. Tower Drive was sparsely populated. It consisted of summer cottages nestled among long stretches of uninterrupted bush. There were no street lamps, and the only light came from the sliver of moon above and the occasional lantern at the end of a driveway. But I had no choice. I had to walk toward town until I got cell service.

I was already shivering in my thin jacket. I had wanted to look good, so I'd worn something cute instead of something warm. It had seemed reasonable when I thought I could compensate with the car heater. Now I found myself in a wet and chilly night. March nights could be worse than January because there was more moisture in the air. March cold was the kind that seeped into your bones and took up residency in your marrow.

I locked up the car and began to walk down the road. Tower Drive was utterly quiet, the only sounds coming from a tree shifting in the wind or a clump of wet snow falling from a branch. The light from a driveway elongated my shadow across the wooded expanse, and I irrationally wished that it wasn't there to call attention to me. Still, I felt a pang of loneliness as I walked farther away from the light and my shadow was enveloped back into the darkness.

I tried to calm my racing heart, but I couldn't shake the feeling that I was being watched from the woods. It was all too easy to imagine being stalked down Tower Drive until I arrived at a particularly secluded section, where I would be hunted like prey. Someone in Thunder Creek was capable of killing teenage girls. A killer had been here, and while I didn't know if he still was, I had the sensation that he knew where I was right now. I could almost see him in the woods, stealing between the trees, mirroring my movements. I tried to look away, scared that imagining him too vividly would make him appear, but I couldn't tear my eyes away from the dangerous forest pressing down on the road.

Waves of anxiety rose in my throat. I knew that when they reached my brain, they would be transformed into white-hot panic. I would end up sprinting down Tower Drive, wide-eyed and sure that the footsteps I could hear behind me were more than just an echo of my own. I needed to distract myself from that fear.

Quietly, I began to sing, lifting my face to the shadowed trees and singing the songs I had learned in Girl Guides and elementary school. I sang relentlessly as I walked toward town, trying to ignore the cold in my bones, the flickering of my shadow among the trees, the lonely noise of one set of feet crunching through snow.

By the time I reached an area with service, my voice was hoarse and my limbs were numb, but I felt a crushing relief as I waited for my mom to pick me up. I had survived the harrowing night alone.

Chapter Fifteen

March 2, 2006

The next morning, I woke up still feeling chilled. Even the woods I had dreamed about were covered in ice and snow, the chairlifts making endless loops on the hill while tiny figures in ski jackets hung in the air exposed to slicing winds. There was a core of ice inside of me that refused to melt. The hot shower warmed the surface of my skin, but no matter how long I stood there, the heat didn't spread down into the coldness beneath.

I checked my phone but Tom hadn't texted. I considered texting him but I wasn't sure what to say. Chloe and I had never fought; she was the leader and I followed, so there was no disagreement. Besides, things were more complicated with Tom. I had never wanted Chloe to kiss me.

I stood in my room and stared longingly at my bed. All I wanted to do was fall back into oblivion, but my mom was going to be home all day. She might have been too busy to hover over me, but even my mother would notice if her teenage daughter was home on a school day.

I walked down the stairs with a heavy gait, every step feeling like an effort. I was wrapped up in a thick fleece sweater but I still felt chilled. I could feel the after-effects of the night before lingering in my body. I now had zero friends and a lingering case of frostbite. Things were going well for Jenny Parker.

"Morning," my mom said. She was sitting at our table eating

toast and coffee. The table was littered with mail, scraps of paper, old phone books and a fruit bowl full of oranges. It was a large table and there were only two of us, so we used the rest of the space for storage.

"Morning," I said, pouring a bowl of Corn Flakes in the kitchen. I sat down next to my mom and watched her blearily sip her coffee. She was wearing the shabby green terrycloth housecoat that she'd had for my entire life. I could tell she was exhausted and would probably go back to bed after breakfast. She'd been working nonstop for days, and I felt bad that I had likely woken her up the night before when I called for help.

My mom had brought a canister of gas and drove me back to my car. We'd filled it up and then she'd escorted me to the closest gas station to finish the job. I doubted it was how she'd been planning to spend a rare night off.

"You're fine to drive to school, right? Your car doesn't have any other problems?" my mom asked. I nodded.

"No, honestly, it's been running fine," I said.

"Just pay more attention to the gas, sweetie. I mean, you could have gotten hypothermia out there, and, you know, it might be dangerous to be out at night alone—"

"Mom, I *know*," I said, interrupting her. I was surprised by the edge in my voice. I was grateful to her for helping me, but I didn't need reminding about the dangers of being a teenage girl in Thunder Creek.

"Well, I thought you knew," my mom said, sounding frustrated. "What were you even doing out there?"

"I was just seeing a friend," I said. "A new friend." My mom stared at me, waiting for me to explain further, but I didn't say anything else. I didn't want to tell her about Tom because I didn't want to have to go into what we did together and the

Helen investigation. It was easier to keep a whole secret than half of one.

"Well, just be smarter from now on," my mom said, her voice hurt. She knew I was keeping things from her. "I guess you'd better get a move on so you're not late for school."

"Yeah," I said, chalking up another secret I'd have to keep from her. Now I just had to figure out where I could go to kill time before school ended.

I found myself at the Thunder Creek Public Library, sitting at the computer banks in the basement. The only other people around were two librarians, an older woman in a floral sweatshirt flicking through back issues of *Cottage Living* magazine and a guy in his twenties who was picking at his skin and rocking in his seat as he scrolled through music websites. He looked like a drug addict, and I made sure to discreetly pick a seat as far away from him as possible.

Helen's death had made me want to learn about the kinds of things we weren't taught in school. I searched variations of "Native girl murder" and started scrolling through the results. There were thousands, and my eyes flicked past story after story from Amnesty International and Human Rights Watch. The articles painted a very different image of my country than the friendly one I was used to. I read about the pig farmer in British Columbia who killed Native prostitutes. By the time they caught him, he had racked up an obscenely high body count because he chose victims the police didn't care about. I read about bodies found in Winnipeg dumpsters and a girl named Helen Betty Osborne who was murdered simply because she was a Native girl trying to get an education in a white town. I read about wrongful convictions of First Nations men on the East Coast, and the grim living conditions of the Inuit in the Arctic. I read that Aboriginal women were seven times more likely to be murdered, and that their murders were significantly more likely to remain unsolved. All of the facts were disturbing, but Helen wasn't just a statistic in a grim report on Aboriginal women. There were no statistics if you were looking closely enough.

Just when I didn't think I could handle any more sadness, I found an article about the Highway of Tears in northern British Columbia. I read about Native girls going missing after hitch-hiking. The crimes remained unsolved, but most people believed that a serial killer was working as a trucker in the area. I had read a number of articles before I noticed the obvious fact: the Highway of Tears only became famous when a white girl went missing on the road. Before her disappearance, the murders were just a local story, but after her, the story went nationwide. People got worried when a white girl disappeared. If she was blond, it was a national emergency.

Most newspapers didn't even bother reporting the Native victims' names, as if those people couldn't possibly hold the reader's interest. The pig farmer case, the Highway of Tears— all of the focus was on the killer and the crime scenes, not on the people who had existed before and then suddenly didn't. Conversely, white victims got full-page articles about their per-sonalities, their achievements and their dreams. They were vic-tims. Aboriginal women were only bodies.

I felt all of this hate and pain so intensely that I had to rest my forehead against the screen. I wished I could talk to Tom and share what I had learned with him. I didn't know if I could do this alone, but I wasn't sure what other choice I had. I couldn't stop asking questions just because I didn't like the answers I was being given.

—

After school, I found myself waiting for Bobby in the parking lot, hoping to catch him before he got on his bus. Everything I'd learned over the last few days was humming madly in my brain and I needed to talk it through with someone. The irony of the fact that I had skipped school all day only to show up at quitting time didn't escape me. I was secretly hoping I might run into Tom as well, though I had no idea what I would say if I did.

I hadn't spotted Tom by the time a tall, black-haired boy crossed the front lawn and walked toward a school bus. Without thinking, I tumbled out of my car and ran toward him, yelling, "Bobby!" He turned around, but so did the hordes of students milling nearby. I must have looked like some red-eyed girl begging her teenage boyfriend not to go.

"Uh, hey, Jenny," he said, clutching the thick handle of the trumpet case. I could tell he was embarrassed, that he was the kind of boy who prided himself on slipping through days unnoticed.

"Look, I really need to talk to you," I said, uncertain of what he would say.

I needed him to listen, needed to know that everything I had discovered wasn't just in my head. I wanted to bring answers to those who needed them, but since I didn't have any answers yet, I wanted to tell them I was at least asking questions. And maybe I was looking to boost my friend count in light of my fight with Tom.

"Uh, well, I need to catch my bus . . . ," he said, looking genuinely pained as he glanced back and saw the door of the bus fold shut like a paper fan.

"Don't worry, I'll give you a ride," I said firmly. Bobby bit his lip and then nodded.

We started walking to my car. I could see how unsure Bobby looked. He couldn't know that I had been investigating Helen's death. To him, I was just a girl who had given him a ride in a snowstorm and was now acting like we were best friends.

"So, what's up?" Bobby asked, sliding into the passenger seat. His legs were bent awkwardly in front of him, and I couldn't help thinking that they looked like the limbs of a daddy longlegs.

"Uh, well, I just wanted to tell you that I've been . . . kind of . . . looking for answers about what happened to Helen," I began awkwardly as we pulled out of the parking lot.

I told him what I had learned. About how I had talked to Jake and our theory that Helen had gone somewhere else that night. About the fact that she might have been meeting someone, and that the police had stopped investigating her case. The entire time I was talking, Bobby sat ramrod straight and stared dead ahead. As we cruised down the highway, I began to worry that he was furious at me for treating the death of his cousin like a game of Clue. Maybe he thought I had no right to even mention Helen's name, much less go pawing through her life.

"So, that's what I know," I finished lamely as we pulled into the reserve.

I remembered which house was his and parked the car in front. The place looked rundown in the late afternoon light. The siding was missing sections and the roof had been patched a number of times. But I had to remember that my house was no prize either. Hell, the only reason we even had a house was because of a government subsidy program.

Bobby sighed and examined me, his eyes searching my face. Finally, he reached over and quickly patted my shoulder, his hand depressing the pillowy material of my ski jacket.

"Thanks, Jenny," he said, avoiding my eyes as he unbuckled his seatbelt. "And look, I didn't know when you picked me up that you were Chloe Shaughnessy's best friend. I understand why looking into this is so important to you. The thing is, I don't know anything that can help you. Helen was pretty private; she was really more of a listener than a talker. But I do know I'm not the one you should be talking to."

"Who should I be talking to then?" I asked.

"Helen's mother. I think she works today but she usually has Fridays off, so you could come back tomorrow," Bobby said, pointing at the house next to his. It was a smaller home with floral curtains closed tightly against the street.

"I don't know, Bobby. She's grieving. Why would she want to talk to a total stranger?" I asked.

Bobby shrugged and got out of the car. He leaned over and poked his face back through the open passenger door. He bit his lip, and I was reminded of how young he was, just a few months into high school but somehow already so world-weary.

"I think the worst thing about all of this is that no one seems to care. It would probably comfort her to know that other people are thinking of Helen, and that you lost someone too."

"Can you warn her first?" I asked. He nodded.

"I'll tell her tonight, so you'd better come back tomorrow," Bobby said firmly. I swallowed hard, trying to quell the nausea I could feel rising. I wasn't sure I was ready to meet a grieving mother, to understand just how real this person had been. I hadn't known what to say to Chloe's parents, and I'd known them my whole life. What would I say to a stranger?

But I owed it to them, to Helen's family. I just had to trust that Bobby was right.

"I'll be there," I said.

I was almost out of the reserve when I noticed the keys. After braking at a stop sign, I happened to glance over at the passenger seat. There was a set of keys on a red lanyard crammed into the crevice of the seat cushion.

I parked my car back in front of Bobby's and walked up the drive. The lanyard swung in lazy circles at the end of my fist, the keys moving together as one lump. I knocked on the door, expecting Bobby's anxious face to turn thankful when he saw me.

Instead, a middle-aged woman opened the door. Her heavy eyebrows pushed down on dark eyes that flashed with suspicion. She was wearing a bright pink sweatshirt that seemed almost comical in contrast to her stormy face.

"Yes?" she asked, her voice hovering dangerously above a snap.

"Oh, hi, my name's Jenny. Bobby left his keys in my car and I just wanted to return them," I said.

"Why exactly would my son be in *your* car?" she asked. I felt my cheeks go red. Did she think I was some older woman, preying on her freshman son?

"Oh, it's not what you think! We're just friends. I just gave him a ride home because, you know, it's so far on the bus . . . ," I trailed off lamely. The woman's expression only grew fiercer.

"There's nothing wrong with the bus. Bobby's never minded the bus before!" she muttered. At that moment, Bobby appeared at her shoulder.

"Hey, Mom. Look, I can handle this. You go inside," he said quietly, his hand gently guiding her down the hall. I saw her glance back at me once, but then she disappeared around the corner, still muttering darkly.

"Sorry about that. I didn't want to cause any trouble. You left your keys in my car," I said weakly, pressing the lanyard into his hand.

Bobby closed the door behind him, forcing us to stand on his porch. He smiled awkwardly at me.

"Thanks. I appreciate it," he said.

"I think your mom thinks I'm like, molesting you or something," I mumbled. Bobby laughed, his white teeth flashing against his tan skin.

"Oh, no, don't take it personally. My mom just doesn't like white people," he said, as simply as if he was announcing his mother's distaste for seafood.

"Oh, okay . . . ," I said, momentarily taken aback. "So, she doesn't know I drove you home the day of the storm?"

Bobby shrugged. "Well, no. It never came up. I'm sorry, I don't want you to feel bad," he said. "My mom, she just doesn't trust whites. I mean, she's not racist or anything. She just feels like the whites have betrayed a lot of their promises to us."

I nodded slowly. There was no denying that Natives had plenty of reasons not to trust white people. I had naively assumed that oppressed minorities were somehow above that kind of generalizing. But suffering didn't sanctify people or raise them above the petty impulse of prejudice. It occurred to me that this was the first time in my life that my race had made someone dislike me. The headline was almost painfully ironic: "White girl experiences discrimination; concludes: 'Racism hurts.'"

"Is this going to be a problem with Helen's mom too?" I asked. "Bobby, are you trying to get me to talk to someone who's going to hate me on sight?"

"No, Aunt Pat's always telling my mom to be more open-minded. You'll like her, I promise," Bobby said earnestly. "Honestly, don't worry about my mom. She just had some bad experiences with whites growing up."

"I understand," I said, remembering that Jake had made the exact same apologies for his father. It was strange to think of Helen navigating between all these ingrained prejudices. Why had she bothered hanging out with Jake when he kept her a secret? She must have thought it was worth the trouble to have him as a friend.

"Just a question, in case it comes up tomorrow . . . uh, what do I call you guys? Like, First Nations or something? I say 'Native,' but I don't know if that's okay . . . ," I finished awkwardly. Bobby laughed.

"Native is fine. A lot of my older relatives still say 'Indian,' but I don't think you should; it might sound bad coming from a white person. I mean, 'First Nations' is nice and all, but I've never heard anyone say it in real life. It's like what politicians say when they're trying to convince people they care about reserves. A lot of my friends say 'Anishinabek,' or 'Nish,' for short," Bobby said, still smiling.

"Okay, just checking," I said. I looked at Helen's house, which was farther down the block. "You know, sometimes I wonder why everyone doesn't think like your mom. I mean, you guys really do get the shit end of the stick."

"Yeah, maybe you're right," Bobby said with a shrug. "Maybe we would have been better off if the people here had just killed the first Europeans instead of trying to cooperate. But I think it's hard to hate people up close, to hurt them for no reason."

I couldn't stop staring at Helen's house. My knowledge imbued the house with a certain tragedy, but it was more depressing to acknowledge how ordinary the home looked. Grief was so violent but so utterly intangible. You almost wished it would tear walls and collapse staircases, just so you could see a physical representation of the loss that bloated every cell of your being.

"Some people are better at it than others," I said.

Chapter Sixteen

December 29, 2005

After that terrible night at the party, the teenage Creekers proclaimed Chloe a whore. Everyone had decided that Chloe had broken the rules and must be punished accordingly. Unfortunately, Chloe seemed to subconsciously accept their verdict. She began to punish herself by giving away what had previously been taken from her.

All winter, Chloe drank as much as she could and hooked up with any boy who asked. It was a strange series of events. No one ever said anything explicitly cruel to her face. On the contrary, they kept inviting her to parties. I would go with her, and even the girls would smile and drunkenly chat with her across crowded kitchen tables. But those smiling faces were connected to watchful eyes, to whispering mouths, to minds that gloried in every failure. It was enough to drive a person insane. Everyone was so superficially nice, but there was a MySpace page and a website, each with hundreds of different comments about how she was a slut. It was written on the bathroom doors. It was in notes that we only half glimpsed as they went tumbling back down a line of desks. Above all, it was in the inalterable archives of teenage cautionary tales. To Chloe, it must have been maddening because it would have seemed like she was imagining everything. How could you reconcile the poison you felt with the familiar kids who waved at you in the hall?

One night, just after Christmas, Chloe called me. I was

already in bed, drifting off to sleep, but I still answered. I always answered.

"Hey," I said, flicking on my lamp and rubbing my face.

"Hey," Chloe said, her voice bubbling with repressed tears.

"What's up?" I asked, looking at my watch. It was 1 a.m. The diner was short-staffed, so I'd promised my mom I would take the early-morning shift. My experience during the previous summer had taught me that 5 a.m. came painfully early. Still, I let Chloe talk.

"Oh you know, just bored . . . ," Chloe said. "God, it seems like we haven't hung out in ages."

"Yeah, not since Tuesday!" I said. It was Thursday. A year before, it would have been me badgering a loved-up Chloe to hang out. I had always felt so desperate, thinking of the texts that went unanswered as she and Liam became consumed with each other. Now, Chloe wanted all the time I could give her.

"Do you want to sleep over tomorrow night? We could hang out, get drunk," Chloe asked hopefully. I rolled my eyes. All Chloe ever wanted to do now was get as drunk as possible as fast as possible.

"Yeah, sounds great!" I said, staring out the window and waiting.

"Jenny?"

"Yeah?"

"I found another one of those websites about me. They, like, Photoshopped my head onto porn stars. What if people think it's real?" Her voice broke, the tears beginning to flow on her side of the phone. I sighed.

"They won't. People know you wouldn't put naked pictures of yourself online."

Chloe began crying in earnest. She was gasping and heaving into her phone, trying to muffle it with her hands. I recognized all of the sounds; Chloe had called me at night a lot in the last few months.

"When is this going to end?" she asked, her words wet and heavy. "When will things go back to the way they used to be?"

"Soon," I said soothingly. "People around here just love drama. Look, if you want, I'll do something to distract them. I could, like, date a teacher or try to assassinate the school president," I said, trying to get Chloe to laugh.

"You could start cooking meth," Chloe suggested finally. She was still crying, but I took the joke as a good sign.

"I could, but I should probably pay more attention in chemistry," I said.

"We'll come up with some more ideas tomorrow," Chloe said, her voice growing stronger. "And let's rent a cheesy romance and make, like, a drinking game out of it."

"Sounds good," I said. I would have agreed to anything that made Chloe feel capable of getting from today to tomorrow.

"Well, it was good talking to you," she said, yawning. "I should probably get to sleep."

"I'll just stay on the phone," I said. "We can, like, fall asleep together."

"Sounds nice," Chloe said, her voice already softening. "You're such a good friend. I love you."

"Me too," I whispered, knowing that she was likely already asleep. Chloe had always been able to fall asleep in mere seconds. She would curl up in the back seats of cars or in reclining chairs at parties and sleep deeply.

Conversely, it took ages for my steady heartbeat to overpower the thoughts spinning through my head. At childhood sleepovers I was always the last to drift off, lying in a stuffy room listening to the rhythmic breathing of the other girls.

Now, I waited until I was sure Chloe was truly asleep before I hung up. It comforted me to think of her being momentarily at peace, spirited away from her daytime anxieties. But I knew comforting Chloe before she went to bed wasn't enough. My best friend was drowning and I didn't know how to save her.

I kept my word that I would hang out with Chloe the next day. In all honesty, after working an early-morning shift and then running errands, I wasn't particularly excited to spend a late night at Chloe's. After showering at home, I resisted the urge to lie down in bed because I knew I wouldn't get up again. Chloe needed me, so I packed a bag, bought a Red Bull, and started the drive to her house.

It was already dark when I left. The week between Christmas and New Year's had the shortest days and the coldest nights of the year. The radio was playing softly, but it was obscured by the sound of my ski jacket crinkling as I shifted in my seat. That noise was the soundtrack of our movements in the winter months, and it made the unencumbered quietness of a body in summer all the more glorious.

I pulled into Chloe's driveway and turned the car off. I could see Chloe in her upstairs bedroom, the lamp silhouetting her body. Her shoulders were shuddering and I knew she was crying quietly, her arms pressed across her mouth to muffle the noises. I didn't know what had set her off, but the truth was my best friend didn't need a specific reason anymore, not when her life had become so unmanageable. The last few months had made her almost unrecognizable, and I wasn't looking forward to another night with the new Chloe.

Chapter Seventeen

March 3, 2006

There was no sign of Tom at school on Friday. He might have skipped class, or maybe he was avoiding me. I looked for him in the halls, feeling awkward as I walked between classes alone, trying to ignore the whispers and the stares. It was hard to listen in class, the words sliding out of my head, replaced by thoughts of Chloe and Helen, of meeting a dead girl's mother after class. How could French verb conjugations compete?

After school, I found myself standing on Helen's doorstep. I was trying to get my nerve up to knock when the door flew open. A short woman in her early fifties was standing in front of me. She wasn't large, but she had wide hips and broad shoulders. Her hair was thick and reached her waist, black waves glittering with gray like stars reflected in a lake. Her eyes were a deep mahogany, but I noticed that they were puffy from crying, and dark circles sat like bruised moons beneath the edge of her glasses.

"Are you Jenny?" the woman asked bluntly. I nodded.

"I don't know why I'm asking," she said, smiling ruefully. "It's not like a lot of white girls knock on my door. My name's Pat."

I shook her hand and pretended not to notice that it was trembling. Pat led me inside. The narrow hallway was lined with Helen's school pictures, and my heart sunk as I watched her age, the pictures ending abruptly with the one taken last

September. There would never be another picture. Helen would never be older than sixteen.

Pat's kitchen was small. It had a dented stove, cupboards painted to look like wood and a card table lined with placemats. She opened the fridge and pulled out two ginger ales. I watched her slowly fill glasses with ice and pour the drinks, not wanting to disturb her as she took a moment to calm herself.

"Thanks," I said, taking a sip as she sat down at the table. Pat made eye contact with me over her glass, her eyes fixed intently on mine.

"So, Bobby told me who you are and what you've been doing," she said. I nodded, and she glanced at the kindergarten picture of Helen on the fridge. It was framed with painted Popsicle sticks, glitter scraped on haphazardly with a child's hands.

"I'm sorry about your friend," Pat said quietly.

"Thank you," I said, uneasy at the idea that Pat might have agreed to talk to me only because she believed we had a criminal in common.

"Jenny, I don't really know how I can help you. Obviously, if I knew something, I would have told the police," she said.

"I know, I just . . . I just want to know . . . what was she like?" I asked finally.

Pat smiled, a wide tremulous smile that made my heart hurt. She'd been waiting for someone to ask her. The words began to pour out of her, as if she'd been subconsciously writing the news article that had never run, the respectful obituary that no one requested.

"She was a wonderful daughter. Helen was always a quiet girl, but she had such a big heart. I always thought she would be a mother someday—even as a kid she was always watching over her little cousins. My husband died of brain cancer when

116

my daughter was eleven. After that, Helen helped out a lot. She didn't like school that much but she stayed in it because she wanted to work in a hospital someday. Seeing her dad so sick made her want to help people like him."

Before, Helen had just been a blurry photo, a crime scene, a shared school building. But as Pat talked I could feel the image I had of Helen deepen and flush with detail. I could imagine her as a kid, keeping Bobby and the other cousins in line. I could see her sitting in the hospital with her father, impressed by the professional people who eased his pain. I saw a girl who was special to the people who knew her, but invisible to and overlooked by the rest of the world.

It would have been so much easier if she'd been a terrible person.

"I wish I had met her," I murmured. Pat smiled wistfully.

"You would have liked her. She was shy, but there was so much good there. She had a doll that looked like you when she was a little girl, and I can remember her telling me that some-day she wanted blond hair just like it. One time, she even tried to color her hair yellow with a highlighter!" Pat said, a laugh escaping her lips.

"That's funny," I said. We fell into silence, and I could feel pressure building inside my head. I knew I needed to tell her what I had found out from Leslie. She deserved to know every-thing about her daughter, but it seemed unimaginably cruel to tell a mother that the police were no longer investigating her daughter's murder.

"This is really hard to tell you, but you have a right to know. I . . . uh . . . met someone who works at the police station recently. She said they don't have any leads and are . . . putting the case on the back burner," I said, choking the words out.

Pat flinched and stared down at the table. Her shoulders slumped and she gave a great, shuddering sigh, as if trying to stop herself from crying.

"Let me guess, they're focusing on the missing white girl?" she asked, and then cringed. "Oh, I'm sorry, Jenny. I know that's your friend, I didn't mean—"

"It's okay," I interrupted. "I find it weird as well. I mean, this is a murder and they're doing nothing!" I said in frustration. I was slamming up against a major limitation in life: how the people who care the most about something almost never have any power over it.

Pat sighed and pushed her wire-rimmed glasses up, exposing dents where they had rested on her fleshy cheeks.

"That's what you don't understand. You trust the police because you know if you needed them, they would help you. We don't see them like that."

"How do you see them?" I asked.

"Cops are always there to arrest a Native but never there to protect one," Pat said matter-of-factly, as if I had asked her the weather forecast.

"But surely . . . " I paused, not sure how to force all of my roiling frustration into words. I knew almost nothing about politics and history, but my gut told me I was feeling around the edges of a grave injustice, something I didn't quite understand.

"Jenny, you seem like a nice girl. But why are you here? I understand that you lost a friend, but why come talk to me?" Pat asked, not unkindly. She was examining me from across the table. I swallowed hard. That was the million-dollar question. Why was I doing any of this?

"When your daughter passed away," I began, feeing queasy about using such a gentle term for an inherently violent death,

"I think it made me notice some of the stuff that had always been there, the ugly side of this town. Now, I just want to know the truth."

A long silence passed. I began to regret how selfish my words seemed. Here I was, bothering a grieving mother with my petty thoughts about how the death of her daughter, a person I had never even met, had made me feel bad. Pat took her glasses off and rubbed her face hard with the heel of her hand. Then she put them back on and looked right at me, her dark eyes steady as they met mine.

"You know, I was in a residential school," she said quietly. "They told my parents that by law they had to send my sister and me to St. Mary's, but my parents wanted us to stay with them, to grow up learning about hunting and camping on the trapline. When the police took us away, my mother fell to the ground and wept. I was six years old and it was the first time I saw my mother afraid."

"Do you mean St. Mary's Mother House?" I asked. "The convent by the lake?"

"Yeah. We were kept there. The nuns were our teachers. On the first day, my sister and I were told we couldn't speak Anishnabe, only English. We were told that our beliefs about the Creator were wrong and that our parents had raised us to be useless Indians. It was a terrible school. They beat us constantly, and we were always cold and hungry. I felt ashamed all of the time, terribly ashamed of who I was and how bad I must be to end up at such a school."

She took a deep breath before she continued. "My sister was always weaker than me. She died of pneumonia the first winter we were at the school. No one gave us warm clothing. When she died, my father came to the school. He told them that they had killed one of his daughters and he wanted the other one back. They refused. They told him he was an unfit parent and that I was better off without him. My father begged but they wouldn't listen, so he asked for the body of his other daughter back. They refused him that as well. I saw him at the gate of the school; I wasn't allowed to go down and see him. He waved and I waved back, but it was hard to see him so broken. They took everything from him and he was never the same."

"But why wouldn't they give him his daughter's body?" I asked, feeling like I was going to throw up. I couldn't believe this was Pat's life story, that all of this had happened in Thunder Creek.

"Because each school had to account to their religious leaders, they had to keep records of the souls they had saved, and those records were used to allocate funding. If a child was buried at the Catholic school, the church got to count them as a soul saved. At the residential school, we were all just numbers, and a dead Indian was worth just as much as a live one."

I felt tears gather in my eyes but I blinked them back. I didn't feel I had a right to cry.

"Did you ever tell anyone about this?" I asked, imagining Pat in a courtroom or a police station, forcing people to atone.

"Who would I tell? The people who care don't need to hear it because it happened to them too. We couldn't go to the cops. The police were the ones who made sure we went to residential school. The police would have caught us and brought us back if we ran away. They didn't care what happened at the school or who died, because we were Native. And we knew it could always be worse. Have you ever heard of a starlight tour?" Pat asked. She was speaking rapidly now, and I got the sense that she had suppressed these words for too long, aching to let them free.

"No. Is it a Native tradition?" I asked.

Pat laughed mirthlessly. "Far from it. It's what cops do in the Prairies. They pick up Natives in the winter, especially if they're drunk, and drive them out to the edge of town, take their jackets and leave them to freeze to death. The last one I heard about was three or four years ago."

"Why? Why would they do that?" I whispered. Pat shrugged.

"Probably the same reason Americans had slaves and Nazis killed Jews—because they don't see us as people, and they don't believe we deserve to live in the first place."

"And that's why you think the cops stopped looking for Helen's murderer?" I asked hesitantly, afraid to even mention her name out loud. The righteous fire in Pat's face immediately disappeared. She looked like an old woman, her features blurred and worn down by a life of hardship.

"They didn't investigate why my sister died. Why would I expect them to do anything for my daughter?" she whispered, her eyes brimming with tears. "Someone took my daughter on her own starlight tour that night. And she didn't deserve it. My daughter was a beautiful person and she didn't deserve to be treated like trash."

"You're right," I said. "She didn't."

We sat there in silence in the tiny kitchen. The ticking of the wall clock seemed to fill the space between us as feathers of snow fell past the window. There wasn't anything else to say.

The road out of the reserve took me down the highway and then along the shores of Fisher Lake. Eventually, I saw the iron silhouette of the St. Mary's cross looming above the treetops.

I felt a chill as the three-story brick building emerged from the woods. In the flurries of snow by the gate, I could almost see the figure of Pat's father begging for his daughters, one dead, one living.

I had been in St. Mary's countless times. Chloe and I had done children's plays there. I was always a chorus member, but Chloe was a born star. When we were young, the bigger parts always went to the preteens. But Chloe would manage to transform her few lines of dialogue into something so wonderful that even the lead actresses would covet her part.

The play practices were in the evenings, and sometimes Chloe and I would sneak away to explore when we weren't needed. We would climb stone staircases bathed in the jaundiced light cast by dusty bulbs. Or we would sneak into the little chapel and inspect old storage rooms stacked with school desks. Or run down shadowy hallways hung with wooden crucifixes and terrify each other by telling ghost stories about the people who might have died there. The sick irony of that last memory was now palpable.

No one had ever told me that St. Mary's was a residential school. I didn't know much about residential schools at all; the topic had been barely covered in history class. I knew that Native kids had been taken against their will and that the goal was to eliminate their culture by "killing the Indian within the child." It all seemed so hypocritical. We had been taught that Canada promoted human rights both at home and abroad. That was true except when it came to Natives.

It seemed like you were still allowed to be racist against Natives; you just had to practice a different kind of prejudice. The new racism lay in a shoddy investigation, a buried newspaper article and a willingness to move on without any sort of resolution. Maybe the message from our history had never changed. Maybe even now a Native life wasn't worth the same as a white person's. The death of one was a sad inconvenience, the other an unjustifiable tragedy.

As I watched the tower of St. Mary's recede in my rearview mirror, I felt a deep sense of shame. I had helped raise money for the convent's new roof as a child. I had skipped over the short sections on residential schools in my history textbook. But it was more than that. I felt ashamed that little Aboriginal girls grew up in their homeland wanting blond hair like mine, blue eyes like mine, pale skin like mine. I thought of Helen trying to color her hair yellow with a marker and felt sick.

Chapter Eighteen

March 6, 2006

I spent the weekend alone, watching TV and trying to make sense of everything I'd talked about with Pat. I was walking down the hallway on Monday when someone tapped my shoulder. I whirled around, expecting to find Tom standing there ready to apologize and carry on. I would have taken him back in an instant; the fight we had already seemed insignificant. Instead, my heart sank when I saw it was Joseph Pitreault.

Joseph was Thunder Creek's very own official nerd. He and Liam McAllister always had the best grades in school. Everyone loved Liam because he wore his success with an easy comfort that belied the effort required to be an academic and athletic star. But Joseph committed the cardinal teenage sin of letting people know how much he cared. Unlike Liam, Joseph had never learned to hide his ambition, and it gave him a slimy, grasping air. He had been the boy in elementary school who snatched the test out of your hands to compare scores. Now, Joseph made no secret of the fact that he was going to overachieve his way out of this school and into a top university. I'd seen Joseph corner teachers in the hallway to talk extra credit. I almost felt embarrassed for him when I heard those same teachers make snide remarks to their colleagues once he'd left.

"Hey, Jenny," Joseph said, clutching the handle of his generic laptop bag. He glanced at his watch. Clearly, the inefficiency of small talk was silently destroying him.

"Uh, hey, Joseph," I said. "What's up?"

"Well, as you probably know, I'm head of the yearbook this year . . . "

"No, I didn't know that," I said. Joseph paused, as if waiting for me to congratulate him on this great achievement, but he continued when I remained silent.

"Anyways, we'll be adding a page to the yearbook honoring Chloe. We have pictures from her parents and some stuff from the drama club. Since you were her best friend, we were hoping that you would write something. We don't have much room. Maybe a haiku or one of those acrostic poems with her name?"

"Like what? Her name has five letters," I said flatly. "That would be kind of a shitty poem."

"You can write whatever you want," Joseph said, checking his watch again. "Just keep it under a hundred words, and I'll need it by next Monday."

"What about Helen?" I asked. Joseph frowned. "You know, the girl who was murdered? Does she get a page?"

"Yeah, we're going to put something in there," he said dismissively, waving his hand. "We can't afford another page, not after the Spirit Day costumes were *so* good this year. But maybe we could Photoshop a frame around her school picture and write 'In memory of' on it."

"Why can't Chloe share a page with Helen?" I asked. "Just get rid of my writing and put some stuff about Helen in."

Joseph frowned, his body all but vibrating with stress. He had clearly thought this would be a thirty-second errand, and I was stubbornly running over time. It irked me how seriously he was taking the yearbook. If high school was mostly meaningless, then surely the memorializing of it must be even more trivial. Then again, it was easy to mock the yearbook when I was never going to be voted "Most Likely to Succeed." I only prayed that I wouldn't be named "Most Likely to Organize Their Sock Drawer on a Friday Night," the unofficial Loser of the Year award at our school.

"We have *nothing* on Helen," Joseph said through gritted teeth. "Chloe starred in all those plays; she had a real presence in the school. Helen didn't appear to be in any clubs or sports. I combed through three years of yearbook files and I can't even find a picture of her other than her class photo."

"So, you're punishing her for not being a joiner?" I asked, perversely enjoying the way Joseph's face was turning tomato-red. I was pretty sure my new bad attitude had also disqualified me from "Most Likely to Be a Walmart Greeter," an admittedly dubious honor. "She gets murdered and she doesn't even get a memorial from her own school's yearbook?"

"Yes," Joseph said shortly. "How can we remember someone that no one even noticed in the first place?"

"That sounds like a question better suited for the head of the yearbook," I said, turning to leave. "Oh, and Joseph?"

"Yes, Jenny?"

"The only way I'll ever write you a poem is if I can find a rhyme for 'Fuck you, Joseph.' You're the genius—let me know if you come up with one."

I left him standing there with his jaw hanging open. It was one of the only moments from my eleventh grade year that I actually wish *had* ended up in the yearbook.

———

After blowing off Joseph, I realized I could no longer stand to be fighting with Tom. I barely talked to anyone, and I noticed how close I was to being totally alone. I spent the day at school in a trance. My ideas about Helen were growing stagnant in my head because I couldn't trust anyone else enough to talk about them. I missed the secret life Tom and I had shared.

Was it love? I didn't know. I had been told by a host of teen romance novels that my life would be inexplicably changed when I met my first love. He was supposed to somehow fill the cracks in my personality like mortar and provoke dramatic pronouncements about eternity. I didn't really feel that, but I did find Tom pushing out the other thoughts in my head. I liked to daydream about things we could do together someday, concerts down south, road trips out west. They were pipe dreams, but they filled me with a jittery kind of excitement. I needed to make up with him.

I started to hunt for Tom between classes. His truck was in the parking lot but he wasn't at his locker and I didn't know his schedule. It was a strange feeling to roam around the school between classes, looking for one person in a sea of students.

I finally spotted him at lunchtime on Tuesday. He was outside smoking with a few friends at the curb. It was an intimidating group of guys all dressed in black. Socially, Tom was hard to categorize. The people he hung out with were mostly punks or hard-core partiers. They were the people who made the pastel preps nervous by showing up at parties with goateed friends long out of high school.

Tom saw me before everyone else. He exhaled a ribbon of smoke as he watched me walk over. I saw a flicker of a smile and I knew in that moment that he had missed me too. I suddenly felt better than I had in days, a warm flush washing over me.

"Hey, guys, this is my friend Jenny, she's a grade below," he said, shifting over so I could join the boys.

A guy with three rings in his eyebrow waved at me, and another with a shaved head offered me a cigarette. I declined. I had never smoked before, and I certainly wasn't going to try it in the cold light of day. Nice girls usually only smoked at parties. They waited until everyone was so drunk that no one would remember how trashy they looked.

Still, it was strangely exciting to stand out here in the smoking area with underage guys flagrantly breaking the law. Their confidence somehow prevented anyone from challenging them. It made me wonder what other rules were capable of flexing if you pushed against them.

"Hey. Good to meet you all," I said.

"How did you guys meet?" Eyebrow Rings asked me. He was smiling encouragingly. These guys didn't seem particularly intimidating, and I felt guilty for judging them without ever talking to them.

"Uh . . . pretty much like this," I said. I made eye contact with Tom across the group and smiled. He smiled back, his dark eyes shining from beneath his bangs.

"And here I thought you were going to say chess club," Eyebrow Rings said, jokingly punching Tom on the shoulder.

"Yeah, that seems likely," Tom said, rolling his eyes.

"Guys, would you mind if I grabbed Tom for a second? I just need to talk to him," I asked.

The guy with the shaved head laughed, his voice surprisingly warm.

"Of course you do. Man, why does Tom have all the luck with girls?" he asked. The other guys laughed as well, but Tom only rolled his eyes again.

"Because I'm the only one who showers," he said. "And I don't have that much luck."

"All it takes is one good-looking girl!" Eyebrow Rings interjected, jerking his chin at me. I felt my cheeks go warm, but it was a pleasant embarrassment. I wasn't the kind of girl who had been told she was pretty so often that she took it as a proven scientific fact. I knew that the "tall girls with freckles" appreciation society was small, so it was always gratifying to discover a new member.

"I guess you're right," Tom said. He was talking to his friend but he was staring at me. I shrugged and walked away. I heard his footsteps behind me.

We followed the trail behind the school, picking our way past a mosaic made of flattened cigarettes and the crumpled soda cans that kids used as makeshift pot-smoking devices. I sat down on a bench overlooking the creek and the woods that cradled it. The creek was still covered in a sheen of ice, though I could hear water gurgling beneath the surface, staging a quiet revolt against winter. Despite the snow on the ground, it seemed as if winter had begun its long, slow bow.

"They seem nice," I said, trying to gloss over the awkward silence with small talk.

"Yeah, they're good guys. I like people who don't worry what other people think of them," Tom said. I wasn't sure if that was a veiled judgment of me, or whether I was just committing the cardinal sin of teenage girls—overanalyzing what boys said to find hidden subtext.

"So, what's up?" Tom said.

"I just wanted to say I was sorry."

"About what?" Tom asked, feigning innocence. I sighed. He wasn't going to make this easy.

"I'm sorry, just for, you know, being an asshole the other night," I said finally.

"Yeah, I'm sorry too. I said some things to you that I really didn't mean. I do care about what happened to Helen. I also can't pretend to understand how you feel about Chloe being missing," Tom said. We sat in silence for a few moments before I replied.

"Look, Tom, Chloe disappearing has been the worst experience of my life. Everything's so recent—this all happened just a month ago. And I feel like if I don't keep moving forward, if I look back even once, everything will fall apart," I said anxiously.

Tom stared pensively out at the creek, his head nodding as he listened. Finally, he responded.

"You know, my first year here, my mom invited me back to Vancouver for Christmas. I'd only been in Thunder Creek for a few months and I hated it. I missed B.C. so much," Tom said, lighting another cigarette. He was still staring straight ahead, and I couldn't help admiring the lean angles of his face as the cigarette hung off his full lower lip.

"What was it like going back?" I asked.

He shrugged. "I didn't go. She's tried over the years, inviting me out for holidays or during the summer, but I always say no," Tom said. He turned and looked at me. His words ached with scarred-over loss, and I felt my heart clench.

"Why?" I asked quietly, even though I already knew the answer.

"Because I'd see what I've lost. And then I'd have to come back here. It would be like losing everything all over again." Tom's voice was neutral, but I could hear it waver. "I won't leave here until I know I can leave for good. But anyways, I get it, Jenny. You'll talk when you can."

"In the meantime, I do have some stuff to tell you about Helen," I said hesitantly, unsure of whether I should break the fragile reconciliation we'd created.

"Good. I'm listening," Tom said, inching closer to me on the bench. I smiled and began to talk, because I knew it was true. He wasn't Chloe, but maybe he could be the next best thing.

Chapter Nineteen

That afternoon, I was hurrying out of English class when I ran right into Liam. I dropped my binder and papers exploded everywhere.

"Oh, Jenny . . . ," Liam said, smirking. He grabbed my binder and a fistful of papers and held them out to me.

"Go away," I hissed, snatching the papers from him. "I don't need your help."

"Oh yeah, you seem like you really have your shit together. People are saying you're dating Tom Grey now. Is that true?"

"How is that your business?" I said, shoving my binder into my book bag and picking up the last of the papers.

Liam shrugged. "It's not, but I've also seen you hanging around with some freshman from the reserve. Maybe you're following in Chloe's footsteps?" He smirked.

"You really are an asshole. That freshman is just a friend. His cousin was the one who was murdered," I said. "Not that you'd give a fuck about that."

Liam glanced at his watch, clearly bored by this turn in the conversation.

"It's messed up, but I didn't know her," Liam said. "Maybe you should keep a lower profile. Everyone's talking about you already. Don't give them any more reasons."

"Yeah, like you really care about me," I muttered, stalking away. I couldn't wait until he graduated and left Thunder Creek.

I got to my locker and opened it with shaking hands. Seeing Liam always reminded me of the last night I saw Chloe and filled me with a combination of anger and helplessness. I was so jangled by his presence that I knew I couldn't face the rest of the day at school. Besides, lately school had felt like an unjustifiable waste of time. I couldn't imagine going to my grave regretting that I didn't understand titration formulas or the origins of Quebec separatism.

I felt a hand on my shoulder and jumped.

"Whoa! It's just me," Tom said. I smiled in relief.

"Hey," I said. It was comforting to see a familiar face in a school that seemed more foreign every day.

"Hey! So, I don't know how committed to education you're feeling today—"

"Minimally," I interrupted, thinking of Liam. Tom smiled and jokingly pumped his fist.

"That's what I was hoping for! Look, I realized there's something we haven't done yet," Tom said.

"Oh?"

"Yeah, we've been investigating this crime for a few weeks now and we've never gone to the crime scene. That's pretty important, don't you think?"

"Yeah, but are we even allowed?" I asked, grasping for a tangible reason why we should absolutely *not* go to the scene of a murder.

"The cops are done there, so I'm sure it's abandoned," Tom said.

"You're right," I said, nodding slowly.

"Do you think that would be too hard for you?" Tom asked quietly, his eyes concerned.

I shook my head. I knew Tom was thinking it might upset me to think that someone might find Chloe's body dumped in the woods soon, but that wasn't what was bothering me. The whole idea seemed unsettling, as if we were tourists rubbernecking our way through famous murder spots. I had never been interested in the gory side of life, and visiting a corpse-dumping site seemed grotesque. Still, you couldn't really investigate a crime if you didn't visit the scene.

"No, it'll be okay," I said finally.

"So, let's go," Tom said. "I can drive."

The winding highway led us east out of town. We passed the last gas station and the final Tim Hortons coffee shop, both of which stood like sentries at the gates of Thunder Creek. Then there was nothing but the occasional home to interrupt the monotony of the forested hills. I passed the time by scanning the sides of the road, looking for a pink and blue mitten. Chloe'd had no reason to come out here, but you never knew. Maybe she'd taken the mitt off to thumb a ride. It seemed implausible, but so did everything else this winter.

Neither of us said much on the drive. We listened to music and stared out at the wilderness as Tom's truck looped around endless turns. I wondered what we would find out there. I was becoming more invested in the case by the day. Meeting Helen's mother had made everything so vividly real that I felt I owed it to her to try to find the truth. And I hoped that, somehow, I would figure out more about Chloe along the way. I wasn't very good at facing up to tragedy, but maybe investigating all of this would make me stronger.

Tom knew how to find the crime scene. He had managed to wheedle it out of Leslie that it was on an old snowmobiling trail. Once we found the trail it was obvious we were in the right place. The snow was tramped down there, a parade of heavy boots in a now-forgotten flurry. We followed the tracks down the path. It was a longer walk than I would have expected. My boots slid around in the soapy spring snow.

Tom walked ahead of me. I knew we were at the right place when he stopped abruptly and glanced down. I took a deep breath and stepped around him.

There was nothing. It was just a wide circle of snow. Endless sequences of footsteps had packed its surface as hard as cement. Beyond the circle, an untouched crust of snow stretched toward the tree-thickened horizon.

A life had ended here. I found myself slowly sinking down onto the ground and felt the ache of hard ice against my denim-sheathed knees. I shut my eyes and tried to imagine what Helen had been thinking in her last moments. Was she afraid? Was she in pain? The knowledge that Helen—who loved historical movies, who volunteered at the hospital, who had a mother, a cousin, a friend and a million ideas and memories—had been wiped out here was overwhelming. The finality of this place made me afraid of death and all the things that I would lose. I wished someone had saved her. I wished *I* had saved her.

The trees rose above me, the white birches slicing pale cuts across the rich blue of an afternoon sky. No birds were singing in the silent woods. In fact, the only sound I could hear was the crinkle of my jacket against my chin. I stared at the snow in front of me, wondering if Helen had died where I was sitting, wondering how so much craziness could be contained in so little time.

"So, what do you think?" Tom said, squatting next to me and clasping his large hands. I shook my head, trying to dissipate the animal-instinct panic I felt in this place. I told myself that this patch of woods was as safe as any other, but I couldn't shake the paranoid feeling that the killer was nearby. I imagined what we looked like from his perspective, two defenseless teenagers in the woods. It made me wish that I wasn't quite so good at imagining things.

"There's not much to see," I said finally.

"Yeah, this is dumb to admit, but I thought there'd be police tape and, like, a chalk outline or something," Tom said. I nodded.

I felt guilty just for being there, for coming in the first place. I'd thought I was secure in the rightness of my purpose, but now I wasn't sure.

"God, Tom," I sighed. "What the hell am I doing?" From the corner of my eye, I saw him pull his cigarettes out. I heard the mechanical click of the lighter and the deep, even sound of him inhaling.

"I don't know, Jenny. Maybe you're looking for Chloe," he said slowly.

"Maybe. But then, why are *you* doing this?" I asked. I wanted to know that this mattered to him, that the time we spent together was meaningful and that maybe I was important to him too. In that moment, I needed to believe that there were things bigger than death and the loneliness of an abandoned crime scene.

"I guess maybe it's something different. Something other than what I usually do," Tom said.

I felt a flicker of disappointment that it was just a bit of entertainment for him during his last year of high school. I wondered if he saw me in a similar way. Maybe this was his senior fling with the kind of strange girl who wouldn't hold his interest for long. It hurt to think that he might not care, but I tried to push the feelings to one side so that I didn't start crying at a murder scene.

"Have you ever lost anyone?" I asked, turning to look at him. Tom furrowed his brow, the cigarette smoke curling up into the canopied lattice of branches.

"I suppose I lost my mom. But not like how you mean. I lost her when she got a new boyfriend who didn't want me around," he said calmly, as if the story was so familiar to him that all of its emotional edges had been worn away.

"Is that why you moved to Thunder Creek?" I asked.

"Yeah. He moved in, I was pushed out," Tom said, taking one last drag before tossing the cigarette down into the snow. It lay smoldering in the icy heelprint of a boot.

"Huh. When you came here, everyone said it was because you were getting into trouble in Vancouver," I said. Tom rolled his eyes.

"I guess everyone just assumed that all thirteen-year-olds in big cities get into trouble. Honestly, I never skipped school or failed classes until I moved here," he said.

"I guess they got it wrong," I said as he stood up.

"They usually do," Tom said, pulling me to my feet.

"What about your dad? Is he in your life?" Tom asked. I was walking in front of him, so the question, casually lobbed at the back of my head, took me by surprise.

"Uh . . . that's kind of complicated," I said, keeping my eyes fixed on the path ahead. I wanted to share things with Tom but he kept picking uncomfortable subjects. Still, it beat talking about Chloe.

"Like a bad divorce?" Tom asked. I laughed.

"No, my mom's never been married. Look, I don't have a dad," I said. "I mean, it wasn't Immaculate Conception or any-thing, but I never actually met him."

"Oh, okay. Does your mom know who it is?" Tom asked. I bristled at the implication. How many guys did he think my mom had on the go?

"Yeah, of course. When my mom was nineteen, she started dating this guy from down south. He was up at the college doing forestry. They only saw each other for a couple months and then they just drifted apart. He got a job in Kenora and was gone before she ever realized she was pregnant," I said, bundling the words into a tidy package. It was easier to say it all at once.

"She never told him?" Tom asked. I shrugged and focused on the slippery path in front of me.

"No, she didn't. She felt like she didn't want to make a life with him and so she didn't want him to feel like he owed her anything."

"That must have been a hard choice for her," Tom said.

"I think it was. I mean, she had me so young, it really froze her life."

"Do you ever think about finding him?" he asked.

I frowned. I hated when people tried to encourage me to build a relationship with my father. It was almost like they thought one parent wasn't enough, that somehow a father I had never met was equally important as a mother who had been there every single day of my life.

"Look, I don't have a connection to him, other than the fact that he gave me his height and freckles. Besides, I know where he is," I said, trying to keep the edge out of my voice.

"Where?" Tom asked. I sighed and stared at the tips of my boots as I walked.

"When I was a baby my mom saw a newspaper article. There'd been a really bad car crash near Kenora. A drunk driver drove into oncoming traffic, killing a family with three children. The drunk driver died a day later in the hospital. The article had an old picture of him, and as soon as my mom saw the freckles, she knew."

"Jesus Christ, that is grim," Tom said with a whistle. I turned back and met his eyes. Something in my stare must have surprised him because his features settled into a quiet expression.

"Only if I think of him as my father," I said flatly. "If not, it's just a story about a drunk driver who killed a family sixteen years ago in a town over six hundred miles from here. That's how I think about it—just another stranger in the world doing something terrible."

Tom and I were almost at the truck when I stopped and glanced back down the trail. I had been thinking about how far we had driven out of town just to tramp around the woods like murder groupies. Then it dawned on me. The important thing wasn't the crime scene but the drive.

"Tom, do you realize we're east of town?" I asked, pointing at the highway stretching in front of us beyond the last few feet of trees.

"Uh, yeah . . . ," Tom said, looking at me in confusion. "I did just drive here . . . "

I was too excited to care about his sarcasm.

"Everyone assumed that Helen hitched a ride from Birch-Bark Village, right? But Jake didn't think she'd hitchhike."

"Yeah . . . "

"Well, at first I thought maybe someone picked her up, but what if she was meeting them somewhere else?"

"But how did she—"

"There's a bus that runs from my area out here. It ends about half a mile up the road. A couple of years ago, I fell asleep on a bus to the mall and ended up at that stop."

We had reached the pavement now and Tom's truck was in front of us, parked on the edge of the slushy road. Tom frowned and glanced from side to side down the serpentine highway. All we could see was rocky cliffs and tightly knit forest.

"But why the hell would she take a bus out here? There's nothing around," he said.

I shut my eyes and tried to remember my accidental bus trip. The driver had woken me up by telling me it was the last stop and that the route was done for the evening. I had climbed off the bus feeling disoriented, unsure of where I was. The stop was just a small sign by the highway. I had checked the hours and realized that this bus stop, like many of the areas on the fringe of Thunder Creek, was only a partial-service stop. The buses were done for the day, and as was the case in so much of Northern Ontario, my phone had no service here. What had I done then? How did I get home?

"There's a bar," I said faintly, pointing down the highway, the opposite way from town. "You can see the sign from the bus stop."

Tom smiled triumphantly. "Okay! So, we know Helen said she was meeting someone. And didn't Jake say her friend worked in a bar?"

"You're right!" I gasped. "That makes perfect sense! She takes the bus out here to see him. The bus stops running in the evening, so she must have expected a ride back and . . . "

"And then . . . then he kills her," Tom said slowly. I froze, realizing that in the challenge of solving a puzzle, I had forgotten how this game finished. It ended on the snowy trail right behind me; Helen dying with the knowledge that she'd been betrayed by the boy she had trusted.

"We have to go to that bar," I said.

Chapter Twenty

The Trapper was a one-story bar cobbled together out of the scraps left over from home renovation projects. The original building was flanked with sunken additions that must have been ambitiously imagined on a Friday but then sloppily finished in time for a beer and *Hockey Night in Canada* on Saturday. The structure was completely surrounded by snowmobiles and a handful of trucks. This was prime snowmobiling weather: warm enough that being outside was a treat, but still enough snow that you wouldn't get bogged down in slush.

My mom would have been horrified if she knew that Tom and I were at a place like the Trapper. There were dozens of similar bars in the outlying areas of Thunder Creek—all rough establishments catering to men looking for cheap booze after a day outside. There were plenty of clean-cut, outdoorsy people who snowmobiled in Thunder Creek, but they didn't come to these bars.

These bars were dangerous because of the men who congregated here. They were men who had lived hard lives on the fringes of legality, hunting past their quota, fishing in protected areas and cooking meth in isolated shacks. Or at least that's what I had heard, since a teenage girl would be insane to ever step foot in a place like the Trapper. Well . . . *most* teenage girls.

"This place looks really rough," Tom said as he parked the truck. I was glad we had taken his truck; it blended in better than my sedan.

"Yeah," I said, anxiously chewing on my fingernails.

"There's one thing I don't understand," Tom said. "We've maybe figured out a connection to Helen, but what about Chloe? How would she know someone who worked here? Is this the kind of place she might go to, you know, meet guys?"

"You don't really think that Chloe would come *here*, do you?" I was incredulous. Even the thought of Chloe venturing out to the boonies was laughable. Thunder Creek was already too country for her, and she never ventured farther west in town than the movie theater. It was clear that Tom thought Chloe's disappearance had something to do with Helen's murder. I didn't agree.

"I just meant, maybe if she wanted to meet a guy but didn't want other people to know?" Tom said carefully.

"Tom, you say that like she's some kind of . . . whore." My voice sounded strained as I confronted the word. I felt my anger rising but I had to defend Chloe. "She'd *never* come here!"

"Okay, okay, sorry. I didn't mean anything by it—but maybe they crossed paths in town or something? Look, this place does look pretty sketchy. Are you sure you want to go in?"

"I think it'll be okay," I said, my heartbeat slowing as Tom moved the conversation away from Chloe. "I mean, it's early evening. It's not like we're going when the bar's in full swing."

Tom stared through the windshield at the crowded parking lot and nodded.

"You're probably right. I mean, it's just a bar. It's not like they'll shoot us for walking in."

"Exactly," I said. "Besides, all we need to do is scope out the place and try to figure out who Helen might have been seeing."

With that settled, we got out of the truck and weaved through the ring of snowmobiles surrounding the entrance.

Although the door looked new, there was already a cracked glass pane in the upper-left corner. And clearly no one had measured the frame first, because there was a gap at the bottom between the door and the splintered step.

I pushed the door open and heard hard-rock music, the clatter of pool cues hitting balls and a rumble of male voices shouting over each other. I could smell stale beer and cigarette smoke. The air was so smoky that my eyes began to water. I wondered how the place had managed to evade Ontario's regulations against smoking indoors. It was an ominous sign that anything could happen here, as normal rules didn't seem to apply.

The inside of the bar was wood-paneled with the usual Northern assortment of mounted fish, newspaper clippings about hockey and cheaply framed group pictures of guys in leaf-patterned camouflage. Men were clumped around the pool tables and bar, hunting knives hanging in sheaths from their belts.

A group of men turned around when they heard the bell on the door chime. They looked suspicious when they saw a teenage couple instead of a familiar buddy who had gone out for a smoke. The men ranged from their late twenties to sixties, but they all seemed like relics from the past with their thick, bristled moustaches, close-cropped hair and fleece sweaters advertising boat companies and local businesses. And they all shared a dazed look, as if they'd been living in this bar for so long that a reminder of anything different was shocking.

I heard Tom light a cigarette behind me and I arranged my features into a look of bland indifference, one I hoped mirrored the look of any other person who spent their time in the Trapper on a Tuesday night.

I walked up to the bar, aware of the fact that I was in the minority here. There were a few women mixed in with the men, but they were all at least forty and had crunchy peroxide perms and oversized Harley-Davidson T-shirts. A woman with a Minnie Mouse tattoo was working the bar, and I sat down on a stool and watched her joke with the locals. Her blue eye shadow almost covered her pencil-drawn eyebrows. She was too short for her jeans, and the edges had begun to degrade under the heels of her boots.

"Uh, can I help you?" she asked, a note of suspicion evident in her voice.

"Yeah, I was wondering—" I began, but she interrupted me, throwing a dirty rag in the sink next to her.

"I know you're not legal so don't bother ordering," she snapped.

"No problem," I said, feeling Tom's hands settle on my shoulders. It was comforting to know that he literally had my back, although we wouldn't be much of a match for a bar full of drunken hunters. "I'm just looking for someone."

"Yeah? Who?" she asked.

I bit my lip. I didn't want to mention Helen; I sensed this place didn't take kindly to crime talk. Helen's killer might even be here, or there could be more than one person involved. For all I knew, this whole bar was in on covering up Helen's murder. It seemed unlikely but not impossible.

"Uh, I'm looking for a young guy who works here. He's a friend of a friend," I finished vaguely, hoping she wouldn't ask too many questions.

"Oh, you're looking for Alan—he's the only young guy working here," the woman said, her face softening. I felt my stomach unclench. I nodded, hoping that Alan was actually the right person. I doubted this woman would let me play Guess Who with all of the Trapper employees.

"I think he's on his smoke break. You can go out back if you want. Just walk past the bathrooms," she said, pointing down a long corridor. She gave me a small smile, and I wondered why Alan's name had miraculously changed her perspective of us. Maybe it just accounted for our presence.

Tom and I walked down the narrow hallway, past a dank bathroom to an outside door that was propped ajar. A Native guy who looked like he was in his early twenties was leaning against the building, smoking a cigarette.

The guy jumped when we opened the door wider. He looked like the kind of person who startled easily. He had a wiry build, and I could see the ropy muscles in his arm flex as he ashed his cigarette. He had a buzz cut that made his black hair look as soft as velvet.

"Uh, are you Alan?" I asked.

He frowned at me. He was undeniably attractive, but I noticed the tattoos first. They bloomed up his neck and down his forearms, interrupted only by the thin cotton of his sweatshirt. The tattoos were mostly words—blurred Gothic script entwined with song lyrics.

"Who wants to know?" he demanded, raising his arm and tossing his cigarette away as if aiming at an invisible target.

"So, that's a yes," Tom said drily. The guy rolled his shoulders and sighed.

"Yeah. What do you want?" Alan asked.

"Uh, we wanted to talk to you about Helen," I said, figuring that there was no point dancing around the topic.

Alan's eyes widened with shock before collapsing into furious slits. His whole demeanor changed, his body tensing into action.

"I don't know what the fuck you're talking about but get the fuck away from me," he snarled, backing away from us so quickly that he looked like a video running in reverse.

"But—" I began, but he had already turned around and sprinted away.

Tom and I ran to the edge of the building and peered around it. Alan was running across the parking lot, dodging snowmobiles on his way to a beat-up red truck. He got in, gunned the engine and peeled out of the parking lot without ever looking back. Tom and I watched the truck fishtail around a corner in the highway and disappear beyond the woods.

"That went well," Tom said.

I couldn't help but laugh. Our attempt at an interrogation had been a complete failure. I turned around and looked up at Tom, who was laughing as well. His face was rendered more youthful and handsome by the smile. I stretched up and kissed him, reveling in the laughter on his lips and the warmth of his cheek against my hand. It was just an impulse, but I felt him return the kiss, the strength in his neck tipping my head back. For the first time since Chloe had disappeared, I felt truly happy.

Chapter Twenty-One

March 10, 2006

A few days after our trip to the bar, I was leaving school when I saw a cop car cruising by the student parking lot. I recognized Trudeau and Bragg immediately. Trudeau waved as the car slid to a stop in front of me. I sighed. I'd already had to slog through a full day at school and now I had to talk to the cops? Honestly, it was moments like this that made me want to shut my bedroom door and never come out again.

"What a coincidence. Hello, Jenny," Trudeau said, rolling down the window to talk.

"Hi," I said, shifting from foot to foot, the slushy sidewalk making my feet cold. I should have stuck to boots; it was too early in the year for sneakers.

"We had another chat with Liam McAllister yesterday," Trudeau said, staring at me. I resisted the urge to look away, refusing to lose some childish staring contest.

"Oh?" I said, scanning the parking lot in case I saw him. This would be a bad time to run into him. He was paranoid enough about me talking to the police.

Students were pouring out of the school and a lot of people were watching me curiously, nudging their friends and pointing at the cop car. I rubbed my eyes tiredly. This was going to do wonders for my reputation. Everyone already thought I knew something about Chloe's disappearance, and now the rumors would start flying that the cops were watching me.

It was official. No one would be asking me to prom next year.

"He claims that he took Chloe out for pizza as a friend, and then dropped her back at your house," she said. I nodded.

"Yep, that's right," I said. I hated that I was inadvertently covering for Liam. But I didn't know how to tell the truth when I'd already told so many lies.

"What do you think about him? Is he a good guy?" Trudeau asked. The question took me by surprise.

"No," I said, before I'd thought it through. "I don't think he's a good guy. But he's rich and he's good at hockey, so in high school, I guess it doesn't matter," I finished, the bitterness creeping into my voice. Trudeau frowned, still staring at me under furrowed eyebrows.

"It matters to me," she said.

"What about Helen?" I asked. "Does she matter to you?" Trudeau looked away. Bragg, who had been sitting silently in the driver's seat, piped up.

"That's not our case, Jenny. We're investigating Chloe's disappearance," he said gruffly.

"Yeah, well, I heard that it's no one's case anymore, that you've shelved it," I said.

"Who told you that?" Trudeau asked, her voice hardening. I shrugged.

"It is true?" I asked.

"That's really not my business. Any decision to allocate resources to a particular case is made by my superiors. I'm sure they had their reasons," Trudeau said, not meeting my eyes.

"Yeah," I said, walking away from the car. "That's what I thought."

I thought they might call me back, but they didn't. Maybe they didn't have any more questions for me or maybe they were sick of me asking questions they didn't want to answer. I just wished that someone would give me answers. I'd never felt so confused in my life.

A few days later I decided to try talking to Alan again. I didn't mention it to Tom because I wondered if maybe the two of us had intimidated him. We'd gone to lunch the day before and I'd considered telling him then but held back. It was hard to keep it from him, though, as I was constantly trying to dream up reasons for us to hang out. Hopefully, Alan would be more open to talking to a single girl. I knew Alan was our most important witness, either because he was the last friend who saw Helen or because he was her murderer. I should have been more scared at the idea of confronting him, but it seemed so inconceivable that any person could kill another that I couldn't fathom talking to an actual murderer.

I drove through the parking lot of the Trapper, searching for Alan's truck. I couldn't see it, but I convinced myself that he might still be there. Maybe his truck was in the shop or he'd lent it to another employee for a supplies run. I had driven this far; I might as well check inside.

I tried to calm my nerves as I entered the bar. Admittedly, it was a seedy place, but I was coming to realize that it wasn't the bar full of strangers that you needed to worry about; it was the town full of people you knew.

Inside, the same waitress was working the bar. She frowned at me as I approached. I tried not to wrinkle my nose at the smell of stale sweat and beer that oozed out of every porous surface in the room.

"I'm still not going to serve you," she said. "I don't care if you're Alan's friend."

"It's fine," I said. "I was just wondering if Alan is around."

"You know, he really should be working when he's here, not just visiting," she said, her prim sentences at odds with the low-cut tank top that revealed breasts wrinkled from decades of tanning bed sessions.

"I know. I'm sorry to keep bothering you," I said. "I just really need to talk to him."

My apology must have worked because her face softened. She began to wipe down the counters, studiously working around my area, swiping the rag in lazy loops.

"I'm sorry. I wish I could help you, but Alan doesn't have any shifts today. He may swing by anyway—he hangs out here a lot—but I can't make any promises."

"Oh, okay," I said, glancing around the bar. It was already getting crowded, but most of the guys in the place were decades older than Alan. Would this be a night that he showed up, or would I be wasting my time hanging out in this sketchy place?

"I can get you a Coke, if you want to wait," the waitress offered, gesturing at the soda dispenser as if it was an exciting prize on a game show.

"It's okay, I'll probably just take off," I said. I didn't feel safe in here, not when I so obviously stuck out. I knew the men would only get drunker, and I didn't want to be around when they began to hit on the few females scattered around the bar.

"Probably for the best," the waitress said, scanning the room. I admired the tough way she squared her shoulders and began to fill beers to bring to tables. It was obvious that she wasn't afraid of the repressed chaos of a rough bar. I wondered if that kind of strength came from past experience with worse things or whether some people were just born brave.

When I walked outside, I noticed that the sun had already set. Dusk had washed the sky in a rich and velvety blue. The Trapper was starting to fill with people looking to party hard, weeknight be damned. I could hear the front door slam behind me, and snatches of guitar music slipped outside with the patrons. The parking lot felt strangely tranquil compared to the heaving energy of the bar.

I climbed into my car and started the engine. A sensible girl would cut her losses and leave now. The waitress had offered only the slimmest of suggestions that Alan might show up later. My social calendar wasn't jam-packed, but surely I could find something better to do than aimlessly wait around at a sketchy bar.

But sensible girls didn't investigate murders. They did their homework and spent their free time improving their yoga poses and learning Italian from a Rosetta Stone program. Sensible girls dated cross-country runners, baked muffins and never snuck food into the movie theater. I was obviously nothing like those girls.

So, instead of leaving, I just moved the car into the darkest part of the parking area. I chose a space under a copse of trees that jutted into the irregularly shaped lot. I backed in and made sure I had an unobstructed view of the front and back doors.

I undid my seatbelt and reclined my seat. Then I grabbed the half-eaten box of Ritz crackers that had been bouncing around in my backseat for weeks. They were stale, but not even the soft texture could kill the buttery flavor. It was official. I was on my first real stakeout. There was something undeniably cool about the way I was sitting here like a spider, waiting for Alan to wander into my trap. It would have been more badass if I were planning on arresting him instead of just pestering him to talk to me. But TV and real life inevitably parted ways somewhere, and it was generally when the TV detective pulled out a gun.

The novelty of the stakeout lasted for five minutes at the most. Then it just became sitting in my car alone watching people have more fun than me. To make it worse, I had nothing to distract myself from my boredom. I couldn't listen to the radio because I was worried about running my battery down, and I couldn't read a magazine because I needed to watch the bar. Selfishly, I wished that I had let Tom in on my plans. The time always flew by when we were together.

At some point I drifted off to sleep, lulled by a quiet car and a sleep debt that had been steadily accumulating since Chloe went missing. The next thing I knew, I was being startled awake by a loud knocking noise.

I woke up to two men hunched over in the black night, peering into my window. When I looked at their shadowed faces, they waved, and I reluctantly rolled my window down.

"Hey there," one of them said. They were both burly men in their forties, wearing flannel jackets so grubby that dirt had warped the plaid pattern. Both had patchy facial hair (one blond, one dark) and leathery faces, undoubtedly from a lifetime of working outside and disregarding sunscreen.

"Uh, hey," I said uncertainly. The dark-haired man leaned into my window, and I could smell the sour scent of whiskey on his skin.

"I'm Jerry, and that's my buddy Roy. What's your name?" he asked. Jerry smiled, unveiling yellowed and rotten teeth. Roy leaned against my car and lit a cigarette.

"Uh, Taylor. My name's Taylor," I said quickly.

"Well, Taylor, we saw you in the bar earlier, and I said to Roy, 'What's a hot little piece like that doing here alone?' So when we came out here and saw you, I knew I had to say hello," Jerry said. He lifted his bushy eyebrows meaningfully and waited for his compliment to sink in.

"Oh, uh, thanks but I-I'm actually waiting for someone," I stuttered. It was scary to think that they had watched me in the bar and then found me out here. The parking lot was dark, and I realized how many terrible things could happen here without anyone noticing.

"Well, you might as well wait inside with us. It's not safe for a girl to be out alone. We'll take good care of you, won't we, Roy?" Jerry asked.

"Yep, good care," Roy said, smiling at me through the windshield. The light of his cigarette distorted his features and made him look like a leering jack-o'-lantern.

"And we'll get you drinks. You're probably underage, but Roy and I can keep a secret," Jerry said, oozing confidence like a salesman on commission. I swallowed hard, my stomach a pit of knots.

"Oh, honestly, that's okay—" I began, but Jerry interrupted me.

"You ever had Malibu? It's real sweet. You mix it with Sprite; it's nice. Any drink you want, I promise." The way he said it gave me the queasy feeling that he'd said the same words quite a few times. How many girls had taken him up on the offer? And what had happened to them after?

"Really, I can't. It's a school night and my dad is probably waiting for me at home," I said lamely, the word "dad" tripping artificially over my tongue.

"Come on, one drink. We're fun guys! You'll have fun with us," Jerry said more forcefully, his smile dimming.

"Maybe another time," I said weakly.

"Oh, what? You think you're too good for us?" Jerry snapped. "Here I am, trying to be friendly, and you're being a little bitch."

In that moment, I was very aware of my own fragility. You go through life trying to pretend that girls can do anything, that they're just as strong as men. But I couldn't reconcile that Girl Power sentiment with the reality of two large men in the woods just a short walk from where a girl my age had been murdered. In that moment, it seemed as though I had floated through life unmolested only because I hadn't yet crossed paths with a man who'd decided to hurt me. I felt light-headed as I realized how stupid I'd been, hanging out at a bar like this at night.

"No, I don't, please—" I began, noticing how Jerry's hands were curled around my window, the dark hair on his knuckles visible against the strained whiteness of his grip.

"You little sluts are all the same. You act like you're better than us when you're all just looking for a lay!" Jerry ranted. I really believed right then that he was about to drag me out of the car and hurt me. I felt like I represented every girl he had ever hated.

"Or they're little teases," Roy said gruffly.

"Look, I would hang out, but I came here to find my boyfriend, Alan," I said desperately, trying to come up with something plausible. "He works here and I thought he was on tonight. But he's not, so I'd better go, because he gets real jealous."

"Who's Alan?" Jerry said to Roy. Roy threw his cigarette on the ground.

"Aw, it's that Indian who works behind the bar. He was in jail with my brother."

Jerry looked at me and frowned. I held my breath and slowly inched my hand toward the key in the ignition.

"Guess we better not shit where we eat then," Jerry finally muttered.

"I like this bar. We've already come too close to losing it to a piece of pussy. This one's not worth doing it again," Roy said.

"Shut up, Roy," Jerry said. He slapped the window of my car and walked away. Roy cast one backward glance at me, as if he was considering changing his mind, and then he left.

I exhaled, the tightness in my chest easing as I realized how long I'd been holding my breath. I peeled out of the parking lot as soon as they disappeared back inside the bar. I couldn't believe that my lie had worked. I still didn't know if Alan was a murderer, but tonight he had unknowingly saved me.

I drove home with my eyes fixed on the rearview mirror, sure that at any moment those men would appear and run me off the road. My heart didn't stop racing until I walked in the front door and saw my mom curled up on the couch watching a cooking competition on TV.

"Hi, baby, how's it going?" she asked, making room on the couch for me.

"Pretty good," I said, tucking my feet under the blanket she was wrapped in.

"What were you up to tonight?" she asked. I shrugged.

"Just studying in Twiggs, lost track of time," I said. Twiggs was the local coffee shop, kind of like a Starbucks but with better food and amazing cheesecakes. They were open late and a lot of high-school girls liked to meet up there.

"Mmm, sounds good. I wish I'd known. I would have asked you to pick me up a slice of their Turtles cheesecake," my mom said with a smile. She wasn't suspicious at all, and it scared me how good I was getting at lying.

"Next time, I promise," I said. The TV had switched to a

commercial, which gave me an opportunity to jump up and check that the outside door was locked. I did that every time I got up for the rest of the evening.

Lying in bed that night, I thought of Chloe and how her confidence had crumbled like spun sugar after those boys hurt her. I thought of the waitress in the bar and how she dealt with men like Jerry and Roy every day. The inequality in life was clear. Men treated the world like an extension of their living room, a safe place where they could do whatever they pleased. Women spent their entire lives on guard against rape or abduction. We walked home with our house keys cutting indents into our palm because a streetwise cousin told us to. We looked back constantly to make sure that every person and car that passed us at night kept going. And like everything else that bothered me this year, this wasn't likely to change. Life would always be a playground for men and a survival course for women.

But all of those feelings just made me want revenge even more. I wanted to make sure that the people who hurt Chloe and Helen suffered too. I wanted Helen's killer stuck behind bars for the rest of his life, and I wanted Devon, Mike and Liam to never forget the pain that they had caused. Thinking of revenge made the weakness and fear that Roy and Jerry produced disappear. When I was finally calm, something Roy had said re-emerged from my memory. He'd said that they had already come too close to losing the bar to a piece of pussy. Could they have been talking about Helen? Roy and Jerry could have been leaving the Trapper that night and spotted her. They clearly weren't above hitting on a teenage girl. What if Helen had rejected them and they'd snapped? It certainly seemed possible.

The thought that I might have met Helen's murderers in a dark parking lot and narrowly escaped being their next victim forced me out of bed two more times to check that the front door was locked. It was a long night.

Chapter Twenty-Two

March 20, 2006

It took me a week to get my nerve up to pursue the Jerry and Roy lead. I couldn't forget how unsafe I had felt in that parking lot. The realities of investigating a murder had become all too clear, and part of me wished that I could abandon the case. But walking away simply didn't feel like an option. If I gave up now I would have no answers, and I would feel worse than before. I had failed Chloe. I didn't want to fail Helen too.

But I wasn't stupid enough to face Jerry and Roy alone. I needed Tom, which meant that I had to tell him about the parking lot incident. He wasn't going to be happy.

"So, let me get this straight. You went back to the bar we both agreed was the sketchiest place we had ever been in, but this time you went *alone?*" The volume of his voice through the phone made me wince. I was in my bedroom, pacing the small space as we talked.

"Yeah . . . I'm sorry, Tom. I really don't know what I was thinking," I said meekly, feeling like a total idiot.

"Jenny, you could have been killed! Even if they aren't killers, those guys sound really dangerous!"

"I know, I know," I said, trying to sound suitably contrite. I knew it had been a stupid thing to do, but being lectured by Tom was getting old quickly. "But do you think there's something here?"

Tom was quiet for so long that I thought the call had dropped. I stooped down to pick a loose sock off my floor and was in the process of looking for the match when he finally spoke.

"Yeah, it's possible. I mean, there's a lot of sketchy people at that bar, but those two do sound like suspects," he said grudgingly.

"So we need to find out more," I said, trying to keep my voice calm as my heartbeat sped up with nerves. "We need to know if these guys had anything to do with Helen's death."

"And how exactly do we do that?" Tom asked sarcastically. "Should we just walk up to them in the bar and say, 'Excuse me, but did you kill any teenage girls this year?'"

"No, we follow them," I said. "We follow them and hope we get lucky."

So far, this hadn't exactly been my year. Maybe I was due a bit of luck.

⁓

"I can't believe we're doing this," Tom said, starting his truck. "Seriously, this is the stupidest thing I've ever done."

"Me too," I said, watching two familiar figures cross the Trapper parking lot and climb into a dusty old van. We had been sitting here for hours, waiting for our favorite murder suspects to leave. I was better prepared for this stakeout than my last one, bringing a plethora of magazines and snacks. We had also managed to steal a few kisses, our eyes remaining firmly fixed on the bar so as not to miss our chance.

The van turned out of the parking lot, and we waited a beat before following. It was nighttime, which was both a blessing and a curse. Jerry and Roy would be less likely to realize they were being followed, but we would have to be extra careful not to lose them. We also didn't know how much they had been drinking, so keeping a safe distance was a particularly good idea.

As we headed farther out of town, the streetlights became more and more infrequent. Soon, our only light came from Tom's headlights as we kept our eyes fixed on the dusty old taillights up the road. Our headlights caught a large deer pausing a few feet ahead on the side of the road, and the sight made me shudder. It was so dark out here that if an animal jumped out in front of us we wouldn't see it until it was too late to brake.

The road wound around rock cliffs that loomed like the prows of ghost ships and steep inclines where a car coming the opposite way on the horizon could blind you with its high beams and send you veering off the road. The thought of anyone hitchhiking on this highway chilled me. It was such a dark and inhospitable road, so far from the civilizing effect of convenience stores and cop cars, security cameras and pay phones. People can be on their worst behavior when they don't think anyone is watching, and out here, you could be assured that you were miles from prying eyes. You could disappear so easily, a life wiped out as easily as tearing the last pages from a book.

The van finally turned off the road by a faded yellow sign advertising "Lazy Days Tent, Trailer and RV Park." We watched the taillights disappear in the trees as we drove past, slowing down as much as we could without looking suspicious.

"Okay, so they probably live there," Tom said, turning the car around on the shoulder so we could head back into town.

"At least one of them does," I said, examining the cartoon sun on the trailer park sign and the block letters proclaiming that they accepted rent weekly.

"So, what do we do now?" Tom asked. I patted his leg, my hand lingering on the coarse denim of his jeans.

"We go back tomorrow and try to figure out which trailer belongs to them. And then we hope that they go out long enough for us to find something that connects them with Helen's murder," I said. Tomorrow was a school day, but this seemed much more important than *Lord of the Flies*.

Tom nodded and we lapsed into silence. I stared out at the inky silhouettes of trees against a dark sky, trying to gather my muddled thoughts. The sleepless nights must have finally caught up with me because the next thing I knew, the overhead lights in the truck were on and Tom was leaning over to unbuckle my seatbelt. The stuffy warmth of the car and his presence made me feel safe. I found myself wishing that he would carry me upstairs and tuck me into bed, but I knew that was silly. I wasn't a kid anymore, and Tom couldn't protect me.

Chapter Twenty-Three

March 21, 2006

Tom and I left school at lunch on Tuesday, picking up Subway sandwiches and a bag of cookies for the mission. The day was bright and blue, and the highway seemed mundane in the sunlight.

At the faded yellow sign, Tom pulled the truck off the highway. Soon, we were bouncing along a rutted road with cracked asphalt and deep puddles filled with equal parts ice and mud. Tree branches brushed against the windows of the truck; the road was so narrow it felt like we were tunneling through the forest. There was no room to pass, and it was only luck that kept us from meeting another car coming the opposite way.

Fifteen minutes of slow, ponderous driving later, we emerged into the open. Lazy Days was a bigger park than I expected, with trails to campgrounds and lake beaches jutting off like spokes from the hub of the central offices. Some of the camping was seasonal, but there were a surprising number of trailers and RVs visible through the trees. Lazy Days seemed like a town, hidden away from prying eyes, and I could only hope that people kept to themselves and didn't worry about outsiders prowling around. Things could get dangerous if Jerry and Roy found out we had followed them.

"I'll walk around and see if I can spot their van. You get down," Tom said, pointing at the foot space of the passenger seat. "I don't want them to see you."

"Really?" I asked. "Don't you think hiding is a bit dramatic?"

"Hiding from two potential murderers who you've already pissed off? No, I don't think that's dramatic," Tom said, arching his eyebrow.

"Fine," I grumbled, pushing my seat back and sliding down onto the floor with my knees pulled up to my chest. "If you insist."

Tom got out and shut the door, leaving me alone in the truck. I put my face down on my knees and shut my eyes, trying to ignore the silence that engulfed the car. Hiding somehow made me feel more afraid, and I couldn't stop imagining looking up and seeing Jerry's face in the window of the truck, just like at the Trapper. Jerry would glance down at me and then I'd feel a gush of air as I was pulled from the truck. The image seemed so real that I promised myself I wouldn't look up, because I just might lose it if he was really there.

After what felt like ages, Tom returned and started the car.

"I found the van. It's parked outside a trailer down the road a bit," he said. I braced myself as the truck lurched down the trail.

"So now we just have to wait for them to leave," I said. Tom nodded and parked the truck between some snow-covered vehicles half shaded by the tree line. He slipped off his black hoodie and pulled an old baseball cap out of the glove compartment, bumping my head in the process.

"Here, wear this in case they spot us. They shouldn't recognize you from far away," Tom said, as I heaved myself up. I slid the large hoodie on, marveling at how warm it was from his body heat alone. Then I tucked my hair under the hat and glanced in the mirror. I looked like a freckled boy, plain and unremarkable. I tried not to regret the fact that I looked even less attractive than usual. Why couldn't my disguise be an evening gown and hair extensions?

"Where's the van?" I said, stretching my arms and grabbing a cookie from the bag.

Tom pointed at a large trailer a few houses down. The van was parked behind it, giving us a clear view of the trailer door. It was an old model that looked like it had seen better days, but it was surprisingly large, with additions built on the back and side. This trailer clearly wasn't moving anywhere. I smiled and considered the permanent trailers on the site. It was almost a philosophical question: At what point is a mobile home rendered so immobile that it just becomes a house?

"Now we wait," Tom said, shoving a chocolate chip cookie in his mouth. I nodded and methodically began to pick the M&M's out of the cookie I was holding. Chloe and I used to complain about being bored on a regular basis, as if that was the most insufferable condition known to humankind. Lately, though, I seemed to be getting a lot of practice waiting. I'd have given anything to spend one more boring day with Chloe.

An hour later, Tom shook me awake. "They're leaving!" he whispered, his hand still on my shoulder. I rubbed my eyes, surprised that I'd fallen asleep in the middle of the day.

"That's them," I said with a nod.

Jerry and Roy were shuffling down the steps in heavy workmen's boots, lighting cigarettes and swigging Red Bulls. Jerry grabbed the keys from Roy, there was a brief argument over who would drive and then they went around the back of the trailer to where the van was parked. A moment later, the van drove away. Neither of them even glanced in our direction.

"Okay," I said, pulling Tom's hat off my head and opening the door of the truck. "You keep lookout and I'll search the trailer. Text me if you see them coming."

"Wait! Why am I the lookout?" Tom asked.

I shrugged and hopped out of the truck. "Because you don't fall asleep on the job," I said, shutting the door behind me. The real reason was that I knew more about Helen's murder than Tom did, and I didn't want him to miss any key pieces of evidence. But I knew that pointing that out would only cause an argument.

I meandered over to the trailer, casually glancing around to make sure no one was watching me. Then I ambled up the steps and pushed the door open. In a stroke of luck, the door was so old and warped with moisture that it hadn't closed properly.

I slipped inside, closing the door behind me. The trailer was dank, and I was immediately assaulted with the overpowering smell of stale cigarette smoke and wet mold. There were empty cans of beer and overflowing ashtrays everywhere, and the floor was littered with graying socks and crumpled jeans. I quickly scanned the floor for the missing mitten, just in case, but of course it wasn't there.

The addition held a card table covered in empty bottles and sticky playing cards. Beyond that was a couch, which had been half made up with sheets and blankets. It was possible that both men lived here, then, which made searching for evidence easier. If they had killed Helen, and there were clues to be found, they would probably be in this trailer.

I began to search the cabinets, finding nothing but shot glasses and mugs from Bass Pro Shops. I didn't really know what I was looking for. Helen had been dumped in those woods naked, so any women's clothing would be important. I also had an inkling—probably from watching too much TV—that some murderers kept trophies or took pictures of their victims, although I didn't relish the thought of finding grue-some photos. Still, one couldn't be picky about their murder evidence.

The trailer contained surprisingly little stuff, and I quickly exhausted the kitchen cabinets, the clothing on the floor and the storage area above the bed. I found evidence that these men were big drinkers (the empties everywhere), horny (a couple of boxes of condoms and a stack of *Playboys*) and major fans of hard rock (the Iron Maiden T-shirts on the floor), but nothing to prove that they were killers.

I opened the closet between the bedroom and the kitchen. Inside was a box full of hunting knives and two crossbows. They were hunters, of course. I knew all of this stuff could be completely innocent, but it did seem like a lot of weaponry. I glanced at the knives and wondered if they'd been carrying them when they found me in the parking lot. It wasn't a comforting thought.

I was searching through the box, gingerly pushing past the crossbows, when I spotted it. A small black leather satchel shaped like an envelope. I extracted it from the box and opened it. Inside was a slim stack of pictures, taken in the summer, judging by the sparkling lakes and denim booty shorts on the girls. The trailer I was standing in wasn't in any of the shots.

The pictures all featured girls in various states of undress partying with Jerry, Roy and some of their friends. The girls looked like teenagers, even though their heavy makeup seemed a bid to look older. I flipped past shot after shot of naked girls passed out on beds and topless girls with heavy-lidded eyes perched on Jerry's lap. The girls all had glassy expressions and sweat-dampened hair. I flashed back to the offer the men had made to me in the parking lot. They clearly had some experience getting underage girls drunk. I thought of Chloe and that terrible night when Matt and Devon had sex with her at the party. That night, Chloe had looked just as helpless as these girls.

I felt nauseous, but I made sure to examine every picture, looking for Helen. She wasn't there. None of these photos seemed recent, although some of the indoor ones could have been taken at any time of year; there was no way to tell. I was just tucking the envelope back into the box when my phone buzzed.

"They're back!" Tom's text read. But it wasn't necessary. I could hear the car door slam and voices arguing. I froze for a second, my feet rooted to the spot as I considered what the men would do when they found me with their box of weapons and collection of incriminating pictures. The sound of feet thudding up the steps snapped me out of my paralysis and got me moving faster than I would have thought possible.

I stepped into the closet and shut the door quickly, my calves brushing against the hunting box behind me. The closet door folded in the middle, and I could see through the crack between the hinged panels. At first, I could hear nothing over the sound of my own rapid pulse in my ears. The fear made me queasy, and I felt my stomach clench as I realized how serious this situation could turn. I was trapped in the trailer of two dangerous men in the middle of nowhere. Tom was outside, but what could he do against two men defending their property? It would take a long time for the police to get out here. Too much time.

Jerry and Roy came shouldering into the trailer carrying multiple cases of beer. Tom and I had assumed that they were going to the Trapper and would be out of the house for hours. Instead, they'd been on nothing more than a beer run, a quick jaunt into town before settling in for the night. I really wasn't having much luck lately.

"Just leave them on the counter," Jerry said, hefting his two cases up with a grunt. I could see the men's plaid-flannel backs moving around in front of the door crack. They were barely two feet in front of me. I tried to slow my breathing, afraid that some hunter's instinct in them would sense the presence of cornered prey.

"Want one?" Roy asked as Jerry moved toward the couch.

"Yeah, and grab the weed too," Jerry said.

I watched Roy grab two cans in his meaty paws and pull a baggie of weed out of a kitchen cabinet. I shut my eyes as he turned around, scared he would notice the watery blue eyeball staring at him through the crack in the closet door. I held my breath as he moved past, his shoulder brushing the door and causing it to rattle.

The men sat down on the couch, leaving me with a view of nothing more than their forearms and the edge of the card table. I watched two sets of hairy arms crack open beers, the sound like a belch slipping from an embarrassed dinner guest. Then one set of hands began to roll a joint, the large fingers clumsily dropping the rolling papers.

I took the time to text Tom, my hand shaking as I shielded the light of the cell phone from the crack in the closet door. "I'm hiding," I wrote. "I don't know what to do." I felt completely vulnerable, just a stupid teenage girl in over her head. I slowly reached behind me, feeling for the box of weapons while trying not to make any noise. My fingers brushed across the handle of a knife. Slowly, almost painfully so, I pulled it out of the box. I was terrified that the weapons would all clank together, or, even worse, that I would inadvertently set off the crossbows. I didn't start breathing again until the knife was in my hand and a glimpse through the closet crack proved that no one had heard me. I wasn't sure if the hunting knife really made any difference—it was hard to imagine me stabbing anyone, and a lot easier to imagine me being attacked by one of the hunters—but it was comforting to hold.

"The girls coming over?" Roy asked.

"Yeah, any second," Jerry said. "I can't wait to see her. She's so fucking worth it, Roy, I don't care what you think."

"But what if her old man finds out? He'll have us fucking killed; he'd just ask one of the bikers that hang around that place."

"Jesus, he owns a bar, not the Mafia. I'm not gonna be scared shitless by a bartender," Jerry said. The joint was ready and I heard a lighter click.

"But there's plenty of other pussy at the Trap. Why does it have to be her?" Roy asked, his voice tight as he held in the smoke.

"She's something else. No girl's as hot, or as much of a freak in the sheets," Jerry said.

This scintillating conversation was interrupted by a knock on the door, and then two women were shuffling into the trailer. I balled my hands into fists and mouthed obscenities. I needed fewer people home, not more! What was next, a kegger?

My phone vibrated, and I carefully checked the screen. Tom had texted: "More people arriving. Hang tight, I'll figure something out." I clenched the hunting knife harder, trying to quell the waves of panic rolling through me.

"Hey, babe," Roy called from the couch. "Help yourself to a beer."

The two women moved in front of the closet, and I realized with surprise that I recognized one of them. It was the waitress from the Trapper. Suddenly, I understood what Jerry and Roy had been talking about when they said they didn't want to ruin the bar because of a piece of pussy. Jerry was dating the waitress, who was also dating the bar owner. I tried to tell myself that none of that meant they weren't Helen's murderers, but it certainly didn't strengthen the case against them.

I didn't recognize the other woman, but she looked like all of the other females I'd seen in the Trapper, middle-aged with bushy hair and a Harley-Davidson tank top revealing drooping bra straps. I watched Roy amble over to her and give her butt a lusty squeeze. She laughed and I rolled my eyes. I wondered if these women would like Jerry and Roy so much if they knew the things they did with teenage girls.

Everyone went back to the couch and passed the joint around as they drank. I stared hungrily at their beers, my mouth as dry and papery as a hornet's nest. I also needed to use the bathroom and knew that if I didn't get out of this closet soon, I was going to have to wet myself. The thought of silently peeing myself in the closet was a depressing possibility. Detective work really was getting less glamorous by the day.

"Fuck, I really missed this inside," Jerry said, finishing his beer and cracking open another one.

"Yeah, no booze, no pot, no girls. It's bullshit," Roy said.

"What, you guys didn't like prison?" the waitress said sarcastically. "That's the point, fuckhead!"

"Hey, fuck off," Jerry said, his voice turning dark and serious. "You don't know what the fuck you're talking about so why don't you shut your mouth?"

"Okay, chill," the waitress said nervously. I gritted my teeth, suddenly concerned for her. Jerry seemed like he had a vicious temper, and I didn't know what the others would do if he lashed out at her. Jerry sprang up from the couch, and I watched him pace back and forth in front of the others, my vision still obscured by the angle of the closet.

"Don't tell me to fucking chill! You've got no fucking idea. A bar fight gets out of hand and suddenly we're locked up for six months? September to March, Roy and I are stuck in that shithole?"

"But we're out now," Roy said, trying to placate Jerry. "First of March, we walked outta there and we ain't going back ever."

I considered the photos of underage drunk girls and prayed that Roy was wrong. Those pictures had all been taken in the summer. Was the only reason they stopped because the two of them had been in jail? I could only hope they would find themselves back inside soon.

My cell phone buzzed and I glanced down, forgetting to shield the screen. The text from Tom said, "Get ready to run." When I looked back up, I saw Jerry standing in the kitchen, a strange look on his face. He had cocked his head and was staring at the closet. I felt everything in the world grow still as I realized, with frightening certainty, that he had seen the light from my phone. He may not have understood what it was, but he was about to find out.

Jerry slowly walked toward the closet, his footsteps as heavy as my heart, which was pounding painfully. I could hear his breathing, spitty and rattled from all the smoking. I could even smell the cigarettes and pot smoke on his skin. Jerry rested his hand on the closet door and I gripped the knife tighter, desperately trying to decide how I could get out of this situation, how to avoid the inevitable.

Suddenly, there was a loud smashing sound outside, followed by the noise of a car alarm going off.

"What the fuck?" Roy asked, getting to his feet and looking out the back window. "Jerry? It's the fucking van!"

Jerry swore and all four of them ran outside, their feet thundering down the steps. I stood in the closet for an extra second, trying to catch my breath. I didn't know how long they would be behind the house, or whether any of them would spot me coming out the front door. But I didn't have a choice; they wouldn't be outside forever, and I couldn't stay in this closet any longer. Eventually Jerry would remember to check in here, and then I would be stuck.

Saying silent prayers, I lurched out the open front door and quietly moved down the steps. I could hear them talking angrily behind the house, and I could even see the back of the waitress, who was standing much closer to the road than the others. There was nothing to do but run to the next trailer across open ground, hoping she wouldn't turn around or walk back toward the front of the trailer.

I put my head down and ran, any conscious thoughts blotted out by the white heat of terror. I waited for the inevitable shouts as they noticed me, but they never came. Then I was behind the next trailer, and I could see Tom's truck parked down the road. He must have moved it before he created the distraction. I ran over to it and climbed in, my hands scrabbling to shut the door as Tom drove away. I had never been happier to see anyone in my life.

"Did they see you?" Tom asked as we bounced down the rough road that connected to the highway.

"No, I don't think so," I said, my voice high and wild with adrenaline. "What did you do?"

"Pitched a rock through their van window and ran like hell," Tom said.

"Not exactly a master plan, but it worked," I said, rubbing my sweaty face with the sleeve of his hoodie.

"What's that?" Tom asked, pointing at my lap. I glanced down and realized I was still holding the hunting knife.

"Oh . . . I grabbed it when I was hiding. I didn't realize I was still carrying it. But I'm not going back to return it," I said with a laugh.

"Is it, like, proof or something? Did you find anything in there that connects them to Helen or Chloe?" Tom asked as the truck pulled onto the highway. He punched the accelerator and we took off down the road, my heartbeat dropping as the miles between me and Jerry and Roy increased.

"They didn't do it," I said quietly, realizing the implication of what Jerry and Roy had said to the women. "They couldn't have done it."

"Why?" Tom asked.

"They were in prison all winter," I said. "They're scumbags, but they didn't do this."

"Damn it. So this was a big waste of time," Tom said mournfully. I glanced at him and couldn't help noticing how good he looked in profile. He had saved me today, and I found myself briefly fantasizing about how I could thank him. I blushed and averted my gaze, staring at the hilt of the hunting knife.

"Not a total waste," I said, waggling the hunting knife at him. "I'm now totally prepared in case the zombies come."

Tom laughed and I turned on the radio. We listened to music in amiable silence until I felt him reach out and take my hand. It was funny. I was holding a giant dagger in my right hand and Tom's hand in my left, but I knew which one made me feel safer.

Chapter Twenty-Four

March 24, 2006

Soon it was Friday. I couldn't have been more relieved. It had been a crazy week and I wanted to do nothing all weekend but curl up on the couch and watch daytime television. I wasn't done with Helen's murder, but I knew I needed a couple of days and a good night's sleep before I'd feel capable of continuing. Jerry and Roy had been a complete waste of time. It felt like I'd taken three steps back in the investigation.

As I stood at my locker, I felt the promise of Friday afternoon in the looseness of my shoulders and the lightness of my legs. That sensation cut through the dull sluggishness of my sleep-deprived mind. I was putting myself on vacation.

Suddenly, I felt a dainty hand poke my back. I turned around and found Taylor Sullivan standing behind me. She was nervously smoothing the tips of her hair, the neurotic habit of choice for pretty girls. It was as if they were constantly improving themselves, whereas normal people's tics (like nail-biting) engineered new flaws.

"Hey, Jenny . . . ," Taylor said, elongating my name and rolling her eyes in a way that suggested she was about to launch into a long-winded explanation of something tedious. Of course, that was just her voice, rendering even the most obvious sentence ambiguous.

"Hey," I said shortly. The last time we'd talked, she'd told me about Helen's body being found. Taylor had never been a bearer of good news.

"Look, I know we haven't really been hanging out lately, but I just wanted to be a friend . . . ," Taylor began, crossing her arms. I frowned and shut my locker door.

"I don't actually think we've hung out since the fourth grade. So yeah, *not lately* . . . what's up?" I asked sarcastically. Taylor rolled her eyes again; apparently, a seven-year gap was insignificant. I could only assume the post-gymnastics Disney marathons would resume any day now.

"Jenny, we're just all really worried about you. Like, that you're losing your mind or something," she said seriously, her words reedy and clipped. I said nothing and she continued. "Ever since, you know, *Chloe*, you've been hanging out with some really weird guys. Like a freshman? From the reserve? And Tom Grey, who's totally going to, like, shoot up the school someday. And I wouldn't want you to become one of *those* girls, who go looking for attention from, like, whatever guy will give it to them."

Apparently, you could go through life invisible, evaporating bit by bit, as long as you didn't stand out for the wrong reasons. But I was starting to believe that there were no wrong reasons. Maybe everything good started with paying attention to others.

"What, like Chloe? I shouldn't be like her?" I snapped. Taylor's jaw dropped.

"Jenny! What? H-how could you—"

"Oh, I forgot!" I interrupted her, my voice dripping with sarcasm. "Now that she's gone, she's been forgiven! You only treat people like shit when they're around to be hurt by it!"

Taylor didn't say anything, but I knew we were both thinking of the same night: the party with Mike and Devon. I would never forget how Taylor had looked when we met on the stairs, how her eyes were bright and her cheeks flushed at the thought of a teenage girl in trouble. Had we lived in a dictatorship, I knew Taylor would be the sort of person who thrived on denouncing others. She was a born finger-pointer, all of her aggression sublimated into a concerned smile.

"Taylor, you don't know anything," I continued, on a roll now that I'd started. "That freshman? His cousin was the girl who was murdered. And Tom is not a psycho just because he hates this fucking town! Because you know what? I hate it too!"

"What is *wrong* with you?" Taylor cried, her voice pitching like a lopsided boat. "You're a total freak now! Look, I get it, it's been a shitty year, but you've got to move on! We all lost Chloe—"

That was when I slapped her. It happened so quickly, a twitch of the elbow governed more by reflex than emotion. I had never hit anyone in my life, so I was shocked by the feeling of another person's skin under my hand. Taylor reeled back, her hand rising to her face as she stared at me. Her mouth gaped but no sounds bubbled up.

For a moment, I felt relieved. Taylor caused so much trouble with other people that it felt right to take her down a notch. However, as we stood there, I began to feel uncomfortable with the way Taylor was staring at me. She looked afraid, as if she had no idea what such an unpredictable person might do next. I didn't feel good about hitting her anymore; the momentary satisfaction passed quickly and then the shame set in. It was one thing to be an outsider, but I had never intended to be a threat.

I was about to offer some attempt at an explanation when I felt a hand grab my forearm. It was our vice principal, Mr. Delorme. He was frowning at me, the creases starting at his black eyebrows and continuing without interruption up into his receding hairline.

"I saw that, Ms. Parker. I think you had better come with me," he said. I nodded and lowered my hand, which still stung with the force of what I had done.

As we turned the corner, I glanced back at Taylor. She was still watching me with a strange look on her face.

They called my mom, likely waking her up. I sat outside the vice principal's office while I waited. It felt strange to be ripped out of the daily routine of school. Most things happened far beneath the eye level of the staff, and I'd certainly never risen to their attention before.

My mom arrived. She was wearing her paint-splattered chore jeans and an old silver sweater that I vaguely remembered from my childhood. Her blond hair was a halo of frizz that hovered above her ponytail. It was obvious she'd thrown on the first clothes she found and rushed over.

"Jenny? What the hell happened? What did they do?" she whispered. My mother was always willing to give me the benefit of the doubt . . . even when I didn't deserve it.

"Uh, I hit a girl," I said. "I had a good reason, though."

"I'm sure you did!" My mom crossed her arms over her polyester front. "But that doesn't change how stupid it was." I nodded and didn't say anything. My mom sighed and knocked on the vice principal's door.

"Mrs. Parker?" Mr. Delorme asked.

"It's Miss Parker," my mom said tiredly. I had heard her repeatedly correct that assumption over the years. I wondered if she corrected people when I wasn't around. Maybe it was a relief to pretend your story wasn't quite so *complicated.*

"My mistake," he said, ushering us into the office. "So, I just wanted to have a chat with you about Jenny's behavior. As I told you on the phone, we had a physical incident today."

"Yes, and I'd like to hear her side of the story," my mother said, touching my arm and smiling at me. She was trying to be my champion, and it made me feel unworthy of her.

Mr. Delorme nodded and studied me over his glasses. I had never spoken to him until today. I was the kind of teenager who passed through high school, buoyed along by the momentum of the middle. I was never exceptionally talented or dramatically bad. In fact, until I became infamous as the girl with the missing best friend, my presence at school had never affected anything.

"Uh, well. I slapped Taylor. She was saying rude things about my friend Chloe," I said.

"This would be Chloe Shaughnessy?" Mr. Delorme clarified. I nodded. I felt guilty using Chloe to get out of trouble, even though I knew she would have approved of the emotional manipulation.

"Well, surely *that* is understandable!" my mom began, her hands flying off the desk like startled birds to emphasize her point. She glanced at me, her blue eyes softening.

The vice principal squirmed in his seat. He obviously preferred clear-cut disciplinary issues with bullies and blameless victims. Girl feuds, which are full of escalating acts of passive-aggression, muddied the waters.

"Well, yes . . . but there are other issues with Jenny. She has been skipping a significant amount of school. I've pulled her attendance records. In the last two months, she has been absent as frequently as she is present. Jenny's grades are dropping, and she's in danger of failing math and chemistry. I've had a chat with a few of Jenny's teachers. They say she doesn't interact in class and that she's been seen around school with a boy named Tom Grey, who may be a bad influence on her. He often gets into trouble for smoking on school property and skipping school. We also believe he's a drug user. In short, I believe Jenny is making some serious mistakes right now, and these choices could affect the rest of her life," Mr. Delorme said solemnly.

I exhaled, unaware that I had even been holding my breath. It was a damning case, a portrait of the last two months as seen through disdainful eyes. My mother wasn't smiling any longer, and she wasn't boiling with self-righteous fervor. Her lips were pursed and she was staring at me with the kind of concerned anger typically reserved for teenagers who get so hammered that they have to get their stomachs pumped. She couldn't tell if my flaws required healing or punishing. Truthfully, neither could I.

My mom and I always had an unspoken understanding about the roles in our little family of two. She would be the breadwinner, working tirelessly to keep us above water. She would crank through night shift after night shift, her smile never dimming until she got home. Then she could rest her aching feet, the cushions of which were worn down to the bone like an eroded pencil eraser by years of waitressing. In return, I was the responsible child who would go on to do better. My only limitations were the ones forged by her trust and her hopes for me. Lately, though, I hadn't been doing better; I hadn't even been trying.

"I-I didn't know all of that," my mother stuttered. "I've been working long shifts and I've always trusted Jenny."

"I understand, of course," Mr. Delorme said soothingly. "I'm sure this has been a tough time for Jenny, but something has to be done."

"I agree, but what?" my mom asked anxiously. "Please don't suspend her. There must be something that we can do that won't go on her record."

Mr. Delorme didn't say anything. He stared at me across the table. I wasn't sure what he saw.

"Jenny, I won't suspend you if you stop skipping school. And I mean zero tolerance, not a single unexplained absence for the rest of the year. And I'm relying on you, Miss Parker, to ensure that she's keeping up with her schoolwork. Are you willing to commit to that?"

Both my mother and I nodded. We didn't know which one of us he was addressing.

"Good," he said. "And Jenny? I want you to think carefully about the people you choose to spend your time with. Ask yourself if they're helping you or hindering you. Do you understand?"

"Yes," I said, hoping he wouldn't sense the insincerity in my voice. I could promise to do my homework and attend class, but I wasn't going to stop hanging out with Tom. The two of us worked, and I wasn't giving that up just to make my teachers happy.

Plus, Tom was my only friend, and beggars can't be choosers. Especially not in high school.

Chapter Twenty-Five

My mom and I drove our own cars home. She was silent when we left the office, and I knew she needed time to process this new perspective on me. My mother was much more reflective than reactive. *She* would never have slapped a girl in high school.

I spent the drive home watching the rain blur halos of headlights across my windshield. I knew that my mother would want an explanation for my behavior, but I didn't know what to say.

Sure enough, when I got home my mom was waiting in the living room. She had cracked open a dusty bottle of red wine. Without waiting to be asked I took off my shoes and sat down on the couch.

It always pained me how tired she looked, as if providing for me was sucking the life force out of her. This feeling was only magnified by the fact that tonight I had actually driven her to drink.

"So, that was pretty crazy today," my mom said, arching her eyebrow at me.

"I guess you're wondering what's going on . . . ," I said. My mother shook her head and sighed.

"I think I have an idea. Look, Jenny, I understand how terrible it's been for you since Chloe disappeared—"

"It's more than that," I said, the words gushing out. "It's like,

I can't even pretend to care about stuff like school when there are things that are so much more important."

"What's important to you? What do you do instead of school?" my mother asked quietly. The question caught me off-guard; I had been expecting my mom to give me hell.

"Well, uh, honestly . . . I've been kind of investigating the death of that girl Helen. I've been sort of talking to people about it and trying to figure out what happened. And that guy Mr. Delorme mentioned? Tom? He's been helping me. He's really not a bad person."

"You've been skipping school to investigate a murder?" my mom said, her voice strained. "Jesus Christ! Jenny, there's a murderer out there killing teenage girls! What if you actually find him?"

"I'm not really looking for him! It's more that I want to find out what Helen was like. I've mostly been talking to her friends and just trying to figure out how she spent her last day," I said. Of course, this wasn't exactly true, but my mom would have an aneurysm if she ever found out about the trailer incident.

"You promise? You're just talking to people?" my mom asked suspiciously. "Not putting yourself in harm's way?" I nodded and she sighed. "Jenny, I need to be able to trust you. I can't control what you do while I'm at work, so I need to know you'll be sensible."

"I will, I promise," I said, feeling guilty about the lies I was telling my mother. But I would try my best from now on to stay out of trucker bars and trailers owned by criminals.

"Okay. To be honest, I was expecting a boyfriend, or even drugs. But I have to say, this is a new one, Jenny." My mother took a deep sip of her wine before laughing dryly.

"Yeah, I know it's kind of weird," I said quietly, choosing not to mention the fact that maybe Tom was kind of like a boyfriend. "But everything seems so mixed up this year. First Chloe disappeared, and then Helen was killed, and it was like people cared less that Helen had been murdered because she was Native."

"You're probably right," my mom said with a sigh. "Did I ever tell you about my friend Carol?"

"No," I said. "Who was she?"

"Carol was my best friend when I was a little girl," my mom said, her eyes staring beyond me. "She'd been a foster child practically from birth. Her parents were addicts. Carol was Native, but back then, they always put Native kids with white families. I guess they thought whiteness could just rub off on people." My mom laughed darkly.

"Your best friend growing up was Native?" I asked. My mom smiled.

"Don't look so shocked! Not everyone in Thunder Creek is a racist! But anyways, Carol didn't really know who she was. She'd been in a white home since she was a baby, but the world still treated her like a Native. When we were teenagers, we started going to bars." My mom paused and wagged her finger at me. "Which, looking back on it, was a very stupid thing to do."

"I know, I know," I said. "So, you went to bars and . . . ?"

"The men there . . . ," my mom said, shaking her head. "I remember, there would be a whole group of us girls, and those men would come up and just grab Carol. They'd grab her and try to drag her away to the parking lot, right in front of us! And they'd get so mad when she refused, like she didn't have a right to say no. I remember this one time a guy started slapping her, and I had to actually get a bartender to stop him. Carol was so embarrassed and afraid. We stopped going to bars after that. None of us talked about it, but we knew we were doing it to protect her."

"Did they try and do stuff to you too?" I asked, thinking of the night I met Jerry and Roy.

My mother sighed. "No. We were white like them. It was like those men were always trying to remind Carol that she was worth less than them, that they could do what they wanted to her."

"Why is that?" I asked.

"I'm not sure." My mom shrugged. "I guess everyone needs someone to look down on, to feel superior to when they're feeling low. And Natives are a great target because they've been pushed down by white people for so long."

"That's really depressing," I said. My mother nodded and looked at me. She was chewing her lip, a sure sign that she was mulling something over.

"Look, Jenny, if you want to ask around, I'm okay with that, as long as you don't do anything dangerous. I won't lie—I'd prefer you to join the debate team or take up running. But I understand that you think the cops aren't investigating this murder well."

"You're taking this whole thing pretty well," I said, unsure when the other shoe would drop. She frowned.

"I'm a lot more disturbed by the fact that you slapped a girl, skipped school and are in danger of failing. Those things are more serious than you playing detective."

"I know," I said, trying not to bristle at the fact that she said I was "playing detective," like a ten-year-old pretending to be Encyclopedia Brown. "I can do better. I don't fit in at school, but I'll work harder."

"I don't know, Jenny. Maybe you need to think seriously about leaving Thunder Creek after high school," my mother said. "I'm not sure if you'll ever really be happy here."

"But where would I go?" I whispered. The scope of the unfamiliar world beyond Thunder Creek seemed overwhelming. How would I know where I'd belong? What if I ended up in an even worse situation?

"You'd find a place," my mom said. "You'd have to be brave. But I just don't see you being happy here, at least not after everything that's happened."

"I know you'd like me to go to university," I said hesitantly. It seemed ridiculous to discuss higher education when we had just been told that I might have to repeat the year.

"I would. I think it would give you so many options and the chance to make a good life for yourself," my mom said. "I don't regret not going, but that was because I had you. And you were the best thing that ever happened to me," she said, giving my arm a squeeze.

I swallowed hard. My mother always said I was the best thing in her life, but maybe that was because I had prevented her from ever experiencing anything better. I couldn't imagine being the best part of anyone's day, much less their entire life.

"But we don't have the money for university," I said. It felt like a betrayal to mention paying for school when my mother was slaving away to keep us above water.

"We'll figure it out," she said firmly. "There are student loans, and I'll take more shifts, and you can work full-time in the summers and part-time during school."

She tucked a strand of hair behind her ear and set her half-full wineglass on the table. The mention of my future animated her. It was as though the thought of me being happy gave her much more comfort than any dreams she harbored for herself.

"Jenny, we can make it work. You could go to a university somewhere completely different from Thunder Creek. You could meet people from all over and discover a million things to be passionate about. But you have to work much harder at school. You have to buckle down and get your grades up. Will you do that?"

"Yeah," I said finally, feeling the weight of my promise settle on my shoulders. "I will."

"Good," she said, pulling me in for a hug. I felt the familiar softness of her arms, the hard flat of her back. She smelled like cigarettes and rose-scented Herbal Essences shampoo, the smell that was embedded in every memory I had of her. "It's all going to be okay, you'll see."

I could have stayed like that forever, folded up in her arms, but there was one more question I wanted to ask. Something had just occurred to me: my mom had reacted differently to Chloe's disappearance than almost everyone else. "Mom, how come you never asked me about Chloe's disappearance? Everyone else asked me what I knew, but not you. Why?"

I felt my mother shrug, her shoulders pulling away from my head as she stroked my hair.

"Sweetie, I know that if you knew anything that would have helped find her, you would have told someone. Since you didn't, I figured you didn't know anything important."

I nodded slowly, my cheek still pressed into the weave of her sweater. I felt a little queasy as I thought of the trust she had in me. It made me feel worse about the secrets I was keeping from her.

"Mom?" I asked. "Whatever happened to Carol?"

"She's a mental health counselor in Alberta." my mom said, a smile in her voice. "She sent me an e-mail last year. She's married, has three kids and does a lot of camping in the Rockies. She sent some beautiful pictures."

"Oh. I thought you were going to say something terrible happened to her," I said, relief flooding my voice.

"Oh, Jenny," my mom murmured into my hair. "Sometimes sad stories have happy endings."

I spent that Friday night organizing my school things and doing the homework assignments that were only moderately late. I could still get partial grades, and I knew I would need all the marks I could get. It was strange to sit down and decide to care about schoolwork, almost as if I was pretending to be someone else.

I had never been particularly academic. When I was young, I used to get in trouble for daydreaming in class. I would sit by the window and watch the janitor rake leaves or a dog meander around the playground equipment, lifting its leg on the red plastic slide. Inevitably, I'd be asked something and register nothing before the question mark. Back then, Chloe called me the "space cadet." We were both dreamers. It was just that Chloe actually thought her dreams would come true.

By the time I started high school, I had accepted the fact that I was completely average. There were no hidden talents or opportunities for greatness lurking in my genetic make-up. Until this year, my grades had been an assortment of Bs and Cs. It seemed daunting to think that next year I would have to get As. Still, stranger things had happened in Thunder Creek.

I didn't crawl into bed until the slim hours past midnight, but it was gratifying to see a stack of completed assignments on my desk. It also occurred to me that I hadn't checked my phone once, and that Tom hadn't texted me. I might have texted him then but I was just too tired. The moment my head hit the pillow I felt myself tip backward into sleepless oblivion. I had no dreams that night.

Chapter Twenty-Six

March 25, 2006

On Saturday I did the week's grocery shopping. It was almost comforting to mindlessly roam up and down the aisles. My thoughts didn't run any deeper than considering whether I should buy spaghetti or penne pasta, strawberry or blueberry yogurt. Grocery shopping really was the closest I came to meditation.

But my inner peace didn't last long. I was loading my bags into the back seat when I saw the cop car through my window. I sighed and shut my door.

"Well, if it isn't Jenny Parker," Officer Trudeau said. Officer Bragg was riding shotgun, drinking out of a tall thermos.

"Yep, that's me," I said, resisting the urge to roll my eyes. "How are you guys doing?"

"How are we doing? Not good, Jenny," Officer Trudeau said, waving me over.

I jammed my hands into my pockets and grudgingly walked over. I leaned into the car and, for a fleeting moment, worried that she would smell pot on my coat. I had been wearing the same jacket a few weeks ago when Tom and I smoked a joint.

"You see, Jenny, we are really running out of leads on Chloe Shaughnessy's disappearance," Officer Trudeau said, searching my face intently.

"Oh?" I said awkwardly. "I'm, uh, I'm sorry to hear that."

"Are you sure you don't remember anything else?" she asked.

"Maybe Chloe mentioned a new boyfriend? Or someone she talked to online? Was she having problems at home?"

"No, Chloe didn't mention any of that," I said nervously. "And Chloe didn't have any problems at home."

"How lucky of her to have a perfect life," Officer Trudeau said, her voice verging on sarcastic. "But seriously, you were her best friend. Who doesn't confide in their best friend?"

"I *am* her best friend," I said through gritted teeth, emphasizing the present tense. "And I can't tell you what I don't know."

Officer Trudeau's eyes bored into mine. I felt an irrational urge to run away. I could even feel the muscles in my legs flex, readying themselves to evade justice. I took a deep breath and tried to quiet the quivery feeling in my chest.

"It's what you *do* know that I'm worried about, and whether you might be stopping us from catching a criminal before something else happens. I will find out what you're hiding. You can be sure of it," she said. With that, she put the car in reverse and I stepped away from the window.

I stood there and watched them drive away. The white car slid across the gray parking lot, passing salt-stained minivans full of haggard mothers negotiating with their children about breakfast cereal.

I didn't feel safe even after they disappeared over the horizon. I knew they were out there, watching and waiting for me to slip up. But I wasn't going to let go of my secrets that easily.

Even the secrets I didn't want to keep.

⌒

Tom texted me that afternoon as I sat at the kitchen table studying. The message said: "Want to hang out tonight? My dad's out of town so you could stay over. We could talk about the Helen thing."

That second sentence set my heart racing. The thought of spending so much uninterrupted time with him was alluring but terrifying. What if he realized I was boring or totally inexperienced with guys? The thought of a whole night alone made me sweat. There would be no reason to stop anything.

Still, I couldn't say no. If I did, I knew I would spend the night at home alone, wondering what might have happened and wishing I'd been brave enough to find out. I would have gone to bed aching with loneliness and trying to imagine what lying next to Tom might feel like. I wished he hadn't texted me, but now that he had, I couldn't ignore the new possibilities it presented.

I wrote a note to my mom explaining that I was staying at a new friend's house for the night and that I would have my cell phone if she wanted to get ahold of me. I left the note on the kitchen table under the saltshaker and then I texted Tom back: "Sure, see you at eight." I did it not because I was brave but because I was lonely and because Tom seemed like the only person who could help me through this terrible year.

Chapter Twenty-Seven

I t was still light as I drove to Tom's. Spring came so quickly to Northern Ontario. As I drove along the twisting road, I could see that the ice was breaking apart on the lake. It had become dark and waterlogged, splitting into jagged sheets that floated freely in the frigid water. Within a couple of months, the lake would be warm and the beaches would be clogged with sunbathers and kids in water wings. Tonight, though, the darkness of the open water and the half-submerged ice seemed menacing.

I pulled up to Tom's house, feeling even more nervous than the last time I'd been here. It was almost as if I was taking another step away from who I'd always been and becoming someone different. I used to have the same feeling when Chloe and I would get ready together for house parties. I could remember straightening my hair in her bathroom mirror, confident that somehow tonight would change *everything*. This would be the night that one of the boys I had gone to school with for ten years would morph into my personalized Prince Charming. This would be the night that my terminal quietness would evaporate and the thunderous pressure of words in my head would become easy conversation. My optimism was fueled by the countless teen movies that promised viewers that somehow, a disappointing adolescence could be redeemed by one crazy night at a house party.

Inevitably, Chloe and I would come home late with aching feet and teeth covered in the sugary film left by Bacardi Breezers.

The boys hadn't changed overnight, and my flaws still existed. We never regretted going, but only because we had no other ideas on how to spend a weekend.

Tom must have heard me arrive because he stood in the doorframe and watched me walk up the drive. His hair was rumpled and came to a point high above his forehead. He was wearing a dark green sweater that bulked up his slim frame. Standing there, he looked somehow older than seventeen, and it occurred to me that in a few months he would be done high school. I felt an ache at the thought of him leaving someday, at the idea of being at Thunder Creek High and being even more alone than I was right now.

"Hey," Tom said, turning his body so I could slide past him and into the house. My hip brushed his hand and that was enough to make my stomach bubble with nerves.

"Hey," I said. I dropped my backpack to the floor and glanced over my shoulder at him. Tom smiled at me, and the look in his eyes, warm and knowing, made our silence seem heavy with significance. The world shrank to the size of the two of us. The thought that I might have chosen to stay home alone now seemed ridiculous. It occurred to me that Tom probably hadn't heard about the incident with Taylor, which was just as well. I wanted to forget all about it.

"I was thinking we could order a pizza," he said. "I don't know if you've had dinner yet . . . "

"No," I said, relieved that we were talking about something as ordinary as pizza. "Pizza would be great."

"Cool." Tom shuffled into the living room. "I'll be honest, I like really weird pizza toppings, so if you want to do half-and-half I'd totally understand."

"Yeah, that'd be best. I just like plain cheese," I said.

Tom laughed. "Of course you're a pizza purist. That fits you!"

"I guess," I muttered. I watched him call a takeout place and request a large pizza, half with cheese and half with sausage, pineapple and olives. I felt instantly proud of the fact that I wasn't the kind of girl who let a guy order for her, because Tom's choices sounded repulsive.

"Anyways," Tom said as he hung up, as if continuing a conversation we had already started. "Want to get high before our pizza comes?"

"Uh, yeah, sounds good," I said. He handed me a can of beer and I followed him into his room.

Tom's room was cleaner than the last time I had seen it. His laundry was all contained in a basket and his desk was tidy. He had made his bed, and somehow, the queen-sized expanse of mattress made me nervous. It seemed so adult to have such a large bed; from what I could see, he didn't have faded Disney sheets like I did. I found myself tipping half my beer down my throat. It was a cliché, but booze was called "liquid courage" for a reason, right?

Tom rustled around in his closet before finally extracting a blue and white bong. It was at least two and a half feet long and the glass was decorated with painterly swirls. I stood awkwardly in the center of his room, unsure if I should sit on his computer chair or the bed. Sitting on the bed might seem too forward, but sitting on the chair would be overly distant. Why couldn't I be the kind of girl who parked her ass without analysis? It was strange how I felt simultaneously so awkward and so comfortable around Tom. Teen romances never told you that happiness could have an undercurrent of nausea, but maybe that was just me.

Tom sat on the bed and waved me over. Decision made. I sat down next to him and watched him grind pot and pack a bowl. I desperately wished that he'd pulled out a joint or a pipe. I had never used a bong before. I'd never wanted to be the person at the party who had a choking fit and tipped dirty bong water onto a bedspread. More important, I knew that bongs were complicated, with holes that you needed to cover with your thumbs and metal bowls to be pulled out at the appropriate speed. The intimidating process made me feel, not for the first time, as if my peers were pulling ahead of me in terms of life experience. I sat on Tom's bed, a virgin who couldn't use a bong, feeling supremely uncool.

"Do you want to go first?" Tom asked. I shook my head.

"No, go for it," I said.

I watched him hunch over the glass, flicking his lighter and making the bong bubble with his breath. The chamber filled with milky smoke before Tom slowly pulled it into his lungs, the muscles of his back contracting with his breath. Tom sat up, his face tight before he finally exhaled in a great gasp of relief.

"Don't you worry about your dad finding your bong?" I asked. Tom shrugged.

"I think he probably knows but chooses to look the other way. He's like that about my smoking too."

"He doesn't mind your smoking? But isn't he a surgeon?" I asked. Tom flopped back on his elbows and drained the last drops of his beer.

"He smokes too. You'd be surprised how many surgeons do. Their jobs are super-stressful."

"Huh," I said, finishing my beer. "You do smoke a lot for a teenager, though."

"Yeah," Tom sighed. "I've been smoking for three years now. Sometimes I think I should quit. I'll quit someday. Smoking's lame when you're middle-aged."

"True," I said.

195

"Feel free to smoke a bowl," Tom said, tipping his chin toward the bong on the floor.

"This is sort of embarrassing to admit, but I've never smoked out of a bong. I'm not really sure how to do it," I said.

"Oh, wow, okay." Tom looked genuinely surprised. "Well, that's no problem. I can help you."

He sat up on the bed and pulled the bong up, careful to support the base so he didn't break it. He tilted the bong toward me and tapped a small hole on the back.

"Cover that with your finger," he said. "I'm going to light this until you say stop. And don't worry, I'm holding it in case you drop it." I felt his hand brush my leg as he wrapped his fingers around the base.

Tom lit the bong and I inhaled, transforming the weed into a glowing coal. The bong bubbled furiously. When I realized how much smoke was in the chamber, I urgently flapped my hand at him to stop.

"That's a big hit," Tom said nervously, but it was too late; I sucked it all up. Instantly, I was aware of the contours of my lungs, expanded and full of the reeking sweetness of weed. My chest strained until the smoke finally came gushing out of my nose and mouth.

"You didn't cough," Tom said with admiration. That comment made me feel strangely proud, as if the ability to hold in smoke was a great life achievement.

"Thanks for helping," I said, leaning back on the bed. My head felt completely disconnected from my body, floating far above its skeletal confines. My thoughts were so fluid that I wondered if they would come leaking out of my ears.

"No worries. You just chill. I'm gonna go get another beer. Do you want one?" Tom asked after taking another hit.

"Sure," I said absentmindedly. I folded my arms across my chest and stared at Tom's ceiling. The effects of the pot hit me in increasingly stronger waves, making it hard to understand any moment that wasn't purely in the present. And yet, there was relief in momentarily forgetting the past. The past was what made me a girl with a missing best friend. In the present, I was just a girl on a bed. The mattress was so cushioned that my muscles ached with pleasure.

Tom returned with the beer after what felt like a lifetime but was probably only a minute. He flopped down next to me and passed me my drink. I cracked it open and dribbled it into my mouth without sitting up. The liquid soothed my smoke-raw throat, and before I even realized it, the beer was done.

"You chugged that," Tom said with a smile, tossing my can into the garbage without getting up.

I turned my head and looked at him. It was hard to make sense of his face when I was so close and so high. Tom was looking at me too, his eyes slowly roaming over my features. I felt our world contract even more, to just the inch of space between our faces.

"I never noticed your freckles. But there they are, beneath your makeup," Tom said. I blushed.

"I try to cover them up. I think they look terrible," I whispered. Occasionally, I would glance in the mirror and feel mute horror at the spots that covered my face, neck, shoulders and back. In my head, I didn't picture myself with them; they inhabited no part of my self-image. I might have always had freckles, but I still viewed them as aggressive colonizers that had occupied me by force.

"No, they're unique, just like you," Tom said. I couldn't help snorting.

"Me? Unique? I'm, like, the most ordinary person ever."

"No, you're quiet, but not ordinary. The problem is that some people don't know how to tell the difference," he said, his voice full of the arrogance of a boy who believes he understands the world.

"But you can?" I asked, a hint of teasing entering my voice. Tom stared back at me, his eyes so steady and calm that I felt pinned down by his stare, like a butterfly in a natural science exhibit.

"Yeah, I can. Probably because no one thinks I'm quiet or ordinary," Tom said, his eyes crinkling as he smiled. This conversation felt incredibly right in our hazy state. It was like we were peeling back the superficial stuff to see the whispers beneath our skin.

"You're just cool," I said. "I wish I was as brave as you. You've never cared about fitting in. Even in middle school, you showed up and you didn't care if you made any friends. That's pretty badass."

Tom laughed, his face so close to mine that I felt his breath on my shoulder.

"That's the farthest thing from brave! I'm awkward anyways, but I was actually trying not to make friends because I was terrified that I would end up fitting in here, and somehow that might stop me from going home. It was honestly me just being stupid."

"Wow," I said. "You *really* didn't want to live here. Like, willing to sacrifice quite a lot just to prove that."

His wry smile showed that he didn't totally regret alienating his entire class. "Jenny, that's why you're the brave one," he said. "Some people need to fit in. I needed not to. But it doesn't seem to matter to you."

"Maybe it should," I said, a smile tugging at my mouth. "Maybe if I cared more then I wouldn't have slapped Taylor Sullivan.

Maybe if I cared more then the cops wouldn't think I was hiding something, and everyone wouldn't think I was so weird."

"Maybe, but you wouldn't be as interesting," Tom said firmly. There was a slight pause as the entirety of what I'd said sank in. "Wait, so, you slapped Taylor Sullivan?"

"Yeah, but she deserved it," I said.

"I'm sure she did. Probably more than one." I could hear the smile in his voice.

We lapsed into silence, a heavy pause that filled my ears with the sound of my own heartbeat. Tom was still looking at me but in a different way. His eyelids were heavy and his lips were slightly parted. Something in me shifted. Despite the heavy veil of weed and alcohol swimming around my brain and my empty stomach, I knew exactly where this was going.

Tom leaned over and kissed me. Instead of treating the kiss as a single act, a one-off, I decided it was just the opening overture. When he leaned back, I leaned forward, my mouth a question that he answered with his own kiss.

With nothing to stop us, things escalated quickly, fueled by the recklessness that substances invoke. Hands began to slide up and down each other's backs, the kisses coming harder and faster until our faces stayed together. I felt a hand on my back, firmly pressing me toward Tom. I knew what he wanted, could sense it in the way he shifted his body. I slid on top of him, glorying in how risqué I felt straddling a boy, even if our clothes were still on. Tom looked up at me and smiled lazily in a way that told me he'd had a girl on top of him before.

I leaned down and kissed him, aware that I was the one in charge. My hands grazed his jaw and I could feel the rough rasp of his stubble. My hands traveled down to his chest. Tom wasn't particularly built, but I could still feel the firmness of muscle under skin, which reminded me that at seventeen, Tom wasn't far from being a man. He did adult things like shave, have sex and smoke bongs. That thought should have terrified me, but in that moment, it was exhilarating.

Tom's hands traveled up my back as I curved over him, his fingers rumpling my shirt. They moved down to the hem of my top and then slipped beneath it. I held my breath as I felt his warm hands on my skin. He was watching my face, waiting for me to stop him, but I didn't. I just kissed him again.

His hands slowly slid up my spine, fanning out on my rib cage like wings. The new sensation was almost overwhelming, but I focused on kissing his neck, my head cocked to the side as if I was telling him a secret. I felt his fingers alight on the clasp of my bra. I could feel him hesitate. I reached my hands behind me to unhook it, light-headed at my own nerve. Tom's eyes widened but he didn't say anything as I fumbled with the clasp.

It was at that moment the doorbell rang. The sound was so unexpected that I nearly fell off the bed. Tom sat up and grabbed my hips.

"It's the pizza," he said, kissing me one last time as he pulled me off him. "They really have the worst timing."

When Tom came back, he was carrying the pizza. I realized that I didn't feel hungry anymore. I wasn't the kind of girl who lost her appetite easily, but tonight food seemed like the least satisfying possibility. Tom casually threw the pizza on his desk, like it was more of an inconvenience than anything else. He picked up his pack of cigarettes and lit one, his eyes watching me over the burning tip. The mood created by our brief flurry of lust had been broken, and I wasn't sure if that was it for the night.

I was still sitting on his bed, my hair messy from the hands that had run through it. Tom's hair was even more tangled, and his cigarette made him look especially deviant. I remembered what the vice principal had said about Tom being a bad influence. I wasn't sure if that was true; I knew there were worse people at that school. I'd watched a lot of "good" kids in Thunder Creek hurt Chloe, and Tom was much sweeter than I'd imagined.

Tom finished his cigarette before either of us spoke. Then he smiled at me.

"Do you want another beer?" he asked.

I shrugged. "Do you have anything harder?" I only noticed the double entendre after the words were out of my mouth. To Tom's credit, he didn't make a joke.

"My dad's got a packed liquor cabinet. What would you like?"

"Vodka Sprite?" I asked.

"No problem," Tom said. He was back in a moment holding my drink and a tall glass full of ice cubes and whiskey. Tom took a deep swig, his mouth involuntarily puckering.

He sat next to me on the bed and handed me my drink. It was strong but sweet. I drank deeply as I watched him take another bong hit and chase it with whiskey.

"Do you want one?" he asked. I nodded, knocking back more of my drink as he arranged the bong for me. I'd reached that level of high and drunk where you're consumed with an overwhelming need to smoke and drink more—almost as if the substances inside of me had formed a personality with an agenda all its own. Later, you look back on the night and wonder why you didn't stop three drinks earlier, but at the time that would have been inconceivable. This night had a momentum of its own, and I didn't think it would ever stop.

I had a hit and then Tom smoked another, and before we realized it, Tom had to refill our drinks. I couldn't believe he was knocking back straight whiskey. It was such an adult preference that it seemed like an affectation for a teenager.

Tom and I split one final bong hit. We sat there in a haze of booze and pot. The air in the bedroom seemed thick and overly warm, like a wet blanket smothering us.

"Do you want any pizza?" Tom asked. He was sitting pressed against me even though his bed wasn't exactly crowded.

"No," I said, without breaking eye contact. "Do you?"

"No," he said, staring back. I could smell the whiskey and cigarettes on his breath, a foreign aroma for a teenage girl.

Then we were kissing again, except this time the pace was accelerated. We had already laid the groundwork before our interruption, and within seconds I was back on top of Tom. The vodka filled me with artificial confidence and propelled me past my very real insecurities.

I was high enough that my spatial sense was confused. Tom and I bumped noses and pasted sloppy kisses on chins and the corners of mouths. But I liked how my intoxicated state made me feel as if I was melting into Tom's skin, our molecules mixing beneath the surface.

I guided Tom's hands under my shirt and placed them on my bra strap. He sat up and wrapped my legs around his waist. I felt him lean in to kiss my neck while he effortlessly undid my bra. I held my breath as a wave of heat washed over me, filling me with a longing I had never felt before. The band loosened around my chest and Tom's hands slid up my bare back. I was still wearing my shirt, but there was something undeniably exciting about his hands being in a spot usually covered by clothing. I felt incredibly alive. How was it possible that I'd held myself back from such experiences before?

In a burst of confidence, I pulled Tom's sweater up and over his head. His T-shirt went with it and I found myself kissing a shirtless boy. A half thought passed through my head—*I wish I could tell Chloe about this*—but it was absorbed back into the ether before I could feel any emotional reaction.

I was standing on a steep precipice and knew that I was getting closer to the edge. I couldn't tell if the substances were giving me fake courage or merely sweeping aside the inhibitions I'd created to stop myself from becoming like Chloe. But in that moment, as I straddled Tom, I felt true lust for the first time. Without another thought I pulled my shirt off and slid my bra down my shoulders.

My breath caught in my throat as I pressed my chest to his. The only people I had been naked in front of were my mother and Chloe. Both had entailed a sort of distance: either because of my younger age or through the chaste averting of eyes. I had never been so close to another human being, with only skin separating our heartbeats.

Tom's hands roamed over me, and eventually we kicked our pants off beneath the covers. We were dangerously close to having sex, two pair of underwear being the only things standing in our way. And yet, while our fingers breached the cotton barriers, neither of us moved any further.

Instead, we began to slow down. Our hands wrapped around each other in static hugs. Long pauses bloomed between our kisses, the furious pace now a distant memory. I began to feel sleepy from the alcohol, and I could tell that Tom was having trouble keeping his eyes open. Finally, we stopped. I lay on top of him, the room quiet except for the sound of our breathing. Our bodies fit together easily, and it surprised me how comfortable I felt even though it was my first time going beyond a kiss.

"Do you want the light out?" Tom asked, his voice slurring.

"Sure," I said, my shoulders shrugging against the pillow.

Tom staggered as he got to his feet, his lean arm grabbing the desk to keep him upright. I watched him flip off the overhead light, leaving a small bedside lamp on.

"I'm drunker than I thought," Tom muttered, crawling under the covers.

"How romantic," I said. We were lying next to each other, and I could feel his skin on mine, a connection that began at our shoulders and ended at our ankles, with only our underwear interrupting it.

"I never said I was," Tom said. I could feel him examining the side of my face, but I kept staring at the ceiling. Finally, he put his arm around me and cuddled up. My face lay nestled in the soft skin between his collarbone and bicep.

"Jenny, I just want to tell you, you're amazing, and if I was sticking around, I'd ask you out properly but—"

"You're finishing school, I know," I interrupted. It was a nice sentiment, but ultimately, it meant nothing. I hated when people called other people "amazing" or "fantastic." Those words were meant for the truly jaw-dropping—like seeing a giant waterfall or an incomprehensible magic trick. Teenage girls like me weren't generally that awe-inspiring. I felt my heart drop into my stomach. For a moment, I'd let myself believe that somehow this night had changed things between us, but Tom seemed more clinical about it.

"Yeah, day after grad, I'm going to backpack Asia. I'm finally going to use those guidebooks," Tom said. He was trying to sound calm, but I could hear the excitement bubble up in his voice. I frowned.

"What? How do you have the money for that?"

"Over the years my mom sent me money for birthdays and Christmas and stuff like that. I never spent it. Then my grandpa died last year and he left me an inheritance. It should be enough if I live cheaply. Honestly, I've been dreaming about this for years. I can't believe it's going to happen," Tom said, his eyes shut as he whispered. I could hear the smile in his voice.

"Wow," I said. I was jealous, and that bitter fact wedged a distance between us. I also felt a measure of embarrassment about what we had just done and how little it seemed to mean to him. "Guess it's good I didn't fall in love with you."

Tom didn't say anything. I glanced up and realized that he had fallen asleep. I sighed and turned off the lamp. Only moments before I had felt so powerful. Now I was just a silly girl again, reading too much into a hook up. There had been a tenderness in our night together, but maybe I'd misread that as something bigger. All I felt now was ashamed of how much more he mattered to me than vice versa.

It hurt me somehow to think that Tom was rushing out of Thunder Creek right after graduation, that all of my fantasies about summer road trips and concerts had never even crossed his mind. I knew that he was following his dreams but it still stung. How could he claim that I was so special when he didn't want to spend even a single extra moment with me once he was free?

I laid my head on his chest, hating myself for feeling so addicted to someone who saw me as nothing more than a pleasant distraction. I would have salvaged my dignity and left right then, so that my heart wouldn't hurt when I saw Tom in the morning and remembered that he was leaving me, but I was in no shape to drive. All I could do was lie on the bed, mad at myself for savoring the warmth of his skin and the way his breath gently rustled the hair on the top of my head.

I fell asleep wishing that I could be stronger.

Chapter Twenty-Eight

March 26, 2006

I woke up in a panic, as if someone had clamped a pillow down on my face. It was the middle of the night and the room had become unbearably hot. I knew that if I didn't get fresh air I was going to puke on Tom's floor. I had an image of us in our underwear, scrubbing the ground while I apologized wildly. That kind of humiliation was too horrifying to even imagine. I slipped out of bed and pulled on my clothes, then quietly left the bedroom.

I stepped out the back door and paused on the deck of the house. It was dark, but the full moon illuminated the silver lake and a path leading from the deck to the shore. The sky was bursting with stars, hanging above me like stationary snowflakes frozen in time.

Suddenly, another wave of sickness passed through me and I ran to the edge of the deck. I retched over and over until my stomach was empty and I could taste bile in my mouth. I found myself staggering down to the shore, afraid that my violent vomiting would wake Tom. I didn't want him to see me like this.

I broke into a run on the path, hopping down uneven ground as I gained momentum. When I reached the beach I tore down the shoreline. My feet sank in the frozen sand, which glittered with ice crystals. I turned away from the shore and sprinted across a field. It was crazy to be out at night in my current condition, but the idea of finding my way back to Tom's and my normal life made my heart sink. I passed through the woods until finally I stopped, gasping for air. It occurred to me that I was now officially lost.

I was in a small clearing surrounded by trees. It was full of mud that had frozen as solid as cement. Drifts of snow still clung to the bottom of the trees as if left over from a lackluster spring cleaning. I hadn't been this drunk in a long time, and I found myself sinking to my knees as my vision tipped and churned. The night sky was dark, the milky moon full, and the stars glimmered dully behind a hazy veil. My vision slowly tilted toward the tree line, where I realized that I was staring at the tower of St. Mary's.

At that moment, the wind began to pick up, shaking loose a raspy noise from the trees. The wind grew more and more ferocious, tearing at my hair and wrapping it around my face and neck. The shifting of the trees became a fearsome noise, rising to a roar like an ocean wave crashing over my head. The snow began to fly, swirling around me and obscuring the tower and the looming trees. I was glad to watch Thunder Creek disappear for a moment.

The wind grew even stronger and the snow stung as it hit my face, but I stared directly into the vortex of swirling white. Before me, shapes appeared in the snow. Human figures began to emerge from the cacophony. I felt a gasp tumble from my mouth, snatched away by the winds, as I realized I was seeing children. They looked as if they had been sculpted from the snow, ghostly apparitions in thin dresses and short pants. They were all Native, and their faces were small and sad, their eyes boring into me with dread. My gaze slowly traveled down their forms to the ground in front of me. These woods were on the grounds of St. Mary's. I heard Helen's mother's words in my head, about the children who died at the school. Some of them probably ended up in the graveyard, but that was a tiny cemetery. Maybe the rest were hidden where no one could ever find them.

These children were beneath the ground, with no one to visit them. I felt tears sting my eyes as I curled my fists into my legs and cried at all the horror this world brought and all the pain we inflicted on each other. "I'm sorry! I'm sorry! I'm so so sorry!" I screamed over and over into the wind, never hearing my own voice reach my ears. Finally, I slumped over and pressed my forehead against the cold ground. I wept and wept, the wind scoring my back with icy blasts.

I felt the chill in my body as it shook from the ice and snow. Then the wind stopped as suddenly as it had started. The air became calm. Slowly, I opened my eyes and sat up, unsure if any of this was real or if I had finally lost my mind.

I looked across the clearing and felt my heart momentarily stop beating. Chloe was standing on the other side. Her eyes were fixed on me with concern, but she was smiling in her secretive way. I stayed as still as I could, afraid that any change would make her vanish. She was standing between two trees, wearing the clothes she'd had on the night she disappeared: a blue wool coat over a teal dress. I noticed she wasn't wearing mittens.

In that moment, Chloe began to fade away. My tears fell harder as I begged her, "NO! Please, stay! Please stay!" But she only gave me one last smile before turning away, her figure dissolving into the shadows. I stayed there for a long time, hoping that she might come back but knowing she wouldn't. Finally, I stood up, shuddering at the knowledge that I was on a mass of unmarked graves.

I slowly walked out of the clearing, carrying the heavy knowledge that at only sixteen, I had already lost so much. And yet, somehow, I felt less alone.

Chapter Twenty-Nine

I managed to find my way back, picking across frozen patches and examining the silhouettes of the houses looking for Tom's place. I spent the rest of the night lying in bed next to Tom, listening to him sleep as I stared at the ceiling. The next morning I was gone before he woke up. I felt like a criminal sneaking around his room as the first rays of light set the Venetian blinds aglow. I wrote a hurried note, explaining that I had to get home before my mother came back from her night shift. It wasn't true—my mother had been home the night before and was probably about to leave the house for her morning shift—but it was plausible.

Every turn of my neck made my head ache. The hangover I was nursing only became more lethal when combined with smoke-raw lungs and bruised knees. My whole body felt stiff and sore from my time outside, and I knew that I couldn't discount what had happened as a dream.

Before I left the room, I paused at the door and examined Tom. His face was turned toward me, and yet sleep somehow made it unfamiliar. The muscles were slack except for the smallest of frowns puckering the skin between his eyebrows. He looked younger asleep, but nowhere near as special. I realized that Tom had fairly average features; it was his personality that animated them, molding them into something more exotic and appealing.

It was strange to think that even though we hadn't had sex, physically no one had ever been closer to me. I wondered if the morning would have felt different if we'd actually had sex. I already felt changed, but I knew that had more to do with what I had seen in the clearing than getting to third base. I was glad, though, that I hadn't gone further with a boy who already had one foot out the door. I didn't know how many people I could handle leaving me, or whether it was worth getting involved with someone when you knew you would get hurt. It was hard, not wanting to be alone but also not wanting to depend on other people. I was pretty sure I was failing on all fronts.

I got into my car and drove away, rubbing my tired eyes and biting back a yawn. The lake gleamed like molten gold beneath the sun and made my eyes water. I would go home and sleep, secure in the knowledge that I could be alone until early evening. I couldn't bear the idea of spinning yet another confection of lies for my mother. It would have dissipated the newness that lay on my skin. I had witnessed something wildly profound, and I wanted some time to myself before the mundane details of life contaminated everything with doubt.

I slept until 2 p.m. When I woke, I couldn't help luxuriating in a quiet house, sun-warmed blankets and the pleasurable half-awake consciousness of afternoon naps. My phone showed a missed call and a couple of texts from Tom. I didn't feel up to talking to him yet.

I curled up in bed and read the texts. The first said, "Hey, I saw your note but why'd you leave without waking me up? Hope we're cool." The second had come an hour later. "Are you mad at me? Everything okay?" I sighed and texted back. "Don't worry, everything's cool! I just didn't want to get caught by my mom." I hoped he wouldn't text back again. I needed some time to think.

After a quick shower, I slid into my car, unsure of where I was going. Now that I had promised my mother that I would treat school as a daily (as opposed to weekly) requirement, I wanted to use what remained of the weekend productively.

Without even realizing it, I found myself heading out of town. I drove past where they found Helen, the snow now completely gone from the wooded path. It made me think of what I had seen the night before, and I felt a chill pass through my body.

I ended up back at the Trapper. I had to try again to talk to Alan, no matter how dangerous my last attempt had been. This time, I had come earlier in the day, and I had no intention of trying another stakeout. But I couldn't leave this aspect of the investigation unfinished. Alan had to know something useful. I just hoped he wasn't dangerous.

There were only a few cars in the parking lot, a logical result of spring chasing away the snowmobile crowd. The bar looked pitiful, squatting in a clearing full of churned-up mud. As I walked toward the building, I spotted Alan's rusted truck nestled up against the side of the bar. Instead of going inside, I headed to the back, hoping Alan smoked as frequently as Tom. I had a flash of memory: Tom smoking a cigarette in his bedroom last night. I felt myself flush as I thought about hooking up with him. It had been such a strange night, and I wasn't sure what confused me more: ghosts or boys. I did my best to push Tom out of my thoughts. I needed to focus on Alan.

I saw Alan standing there and couldn't help smiling. Today was my lucky day . . . or Alan's unlucky one, depending on the perspective. Alan was wearing a thin sweatshirt, the cotton rubbed raw from continuous wear. He was obviously cold; he had wrapped his free arm around himself as he rigidly brought the cigarette to his mouth.

Alan saw me and tensed, ready to run again. It was almost laughable, a twentysomething guy running away from a girl like me. I wondered if Jerry or Roy had mentioned that I was allegedly his girlfriend. I doubted it.

"Wait!" I said, throwing my hands up. "I know you didn't do anything wrong!" I didn't know that, but I figured if I shouted, "I think you're a murderer" there was no chance of him sticking around to talk.

"What?" Alan asked suspiciously. "Who the fuck are you?" He was still in a running stance, poised to startle at any moment.

"I-I-know about Helen," I stuttered.

"Don't know nothing about that," Alan muttered, turning away. Without thinking, I grabbed his arm. His free hand twitched, as if he was going to strike me. Our eyes met, and I saw the wildness in his face, the anger he was wrestling to control.

"Sorry," I said, releasing his arm. "Please, please just talk to me for a second. I know you were friends. I know you didn't hurt her. I-I just want to know about her last day," I finished softly.

Alan's shoulders fell and he slumped against the wall. I watched him ash his cigarette between his battered white running shoes. He wasn't saying anything, but the fact that he wasn't leaving was promising.

"Why the hell do you care?" he asked. He didn't seem angry, just curious.

"I just do," I said finally. "I've learned stuff about her and I just want to know how it ended."

"What'd you learn?" Alan asked suspiciously. I bit my lip and tried to form a few inklings into a coherent thought.

"I know that she was a good person. I know"—I flashed back to Jake talking about meeting her in the hospital—"that Helen always took care of people. Especially the people others didn't notice."

A tiny smile shifted the cigarette on Alan's lips.

"Yeah, that's Helen."

"How did you two meet?" I asked carefully. I was slowly feeling my way around Alan, uncertain which topics were off-limits.

"Uh . . . fuck," Alan said, running a hand through his inky hair. "Back when I was a foster kid. She was nice to me. I hung out with her older cousins, but she was just a nice kid," he said shortly, his eyes looking past me. "Foster care fucking sucks. You get beat a lot. If someone's nice, it sticks out. Uh, I fought a lot so kids were scared of me."

"But Helen wasn't bothered?" I asked.

Alan shook his head. "Nah, she wasn't scared of me."

"So you grew up together?" I asked. A shadow passed over Alan's face. I could almost see the bad memories ricochet around his skull.

"Nope. Kept moving foster homes. Nobody wanted me because I flipped out a lot."

"Oh . . . ," I said, my heart sinking as I imagined a new scenario: Alan, in an uncontrollable rage, attacking Helen in his car. He seemed placid enough now, but the ropy muscles of his arms looked like they could do some serious damage.

"Went to juvie a few times. For fires and smashing shit. Then I got sent to jail for beating the shit out of a guy."

"So when did you see Helen again?" I asked.

"When I got out, I was homeless. Almost froze to death one night. Woke up in the fucking hospital and Helen was there, talking away and happy to see me," Alan said quietly.

213

It was hard to believe that he had once been homeless. It made me look at his current lifestyle, with a truck and a job, in a much more positive light.

"Helen kept coming by after I got better. We'd hang out. She didn't tell her mom that she was doing it. I get it; I'm a fucking dirtbag!"

"She sounds like she was a good friend to you," I said. Alan's features twisted, and I knew that there was something complicated in their story, a secret that made him nervous.

"Yeah. She, like, believed I could do shit. She was so fucking proud when I got this job," Alan said, a smile trying but failing to melt the tense corners of his mouth.

"And she kept visiting you?" I asked. Alan nodded and lit another cigarette. His hand was shaking and the cigarettes in the half-full pack bounced around like jumping beans.

"Yeah, every couple weeks. She'd bus out here and hang out at the bar while I worked. Then I'd use my break to drive her to the rez."

"The bar owners didn't care that she was underage?" I asked. Alan shook his head.

"Fuck no. People do what they want out here. Everyone knew Helen was in the Trapper that night, but they weren't gonna call the fucking cops."

I nodded thoughtfully. It really was a different world in the bush. Out here, it seemed like people had receded into the forest, coming out only to drink. Some people lived off the land: hunting and fishing (often illegally on Crown property), running traplines and squatting in abandoned hunting cabins. But others made their living in shadier ways. I knew there were meth labs out here. Sometimes you spotted the ones that had blown up, leaving behind a pile of charred rubble and pine trees with scorched tips. This was where people disappeared to avoid all manner of inconveniences, from cops to child support.

Crimes didn't always get solved in Northern Ontario. People had a tendency to disappear up here without a trace. It was as if the city's hold on the land was tenuous, and every now and then a person was just absorbed back into the wilderness. A whole family had disappeared in the seventies, their dinner left half eaten on the kitchen table. A college kid from down south disappeared on the walk home from a bar. Afterward, his heartbroken father had moved to Thunder Creek and papered the city with missing posters for years. This was the sort of place where unsolved crimes lasted a lifetime, the wild landscape silent about the dark things it had witnessed. Eventually, the mysteries were woven into the lives of the Creekers. But I didn't want Helen to become just another ghost story.

"What happened that day?" I asked finally. Alan didn't say anything for a long time. I studied his face, trying to decide if Helen had been right to trust him.

"I always knew Helen *liked* me," Alan said finally. He shook his head and sighed. "But I'd have been shit for her. And, uh . . . she wasn't my type," he said, his cheeks reddening, like he was ashamed that he hadn't fallen in love with her.

If this had been a fictional story, Alan and Helen would have fallen in love. But the uncomfortable truth Alan was avoiding was that Helen hadn't been very pretty. She might have been the kind of girl who blossoms in her twenties, the kind who hides her yearbooks and experiences regret when looking at old school photos. But the sad fact was that Helen was overweight, with bushy hair and unremarkable features. Sometimes you see two people and you think how everything would have been so much easier if they'd just fallen in love. Unfortunately, chemistry isn't born of convenience. If it were, I probably wouldn't have a crush on Tom, a guy who wasn't that into me and was hell-bent on leaving Thunder Creek as soon as he could.

"Did she ever tell you?" I asked.

"Not until that day. Helen showed up, dressed kind of *slutty*, with makeup and shit. And she asked for a beer."

"Was she a drinker?" I asked, my head aching at the thought of alcohol. I had momentarily forgotten how crazy the night before had been.

"Nope. Fucking gave it to her, though. Then, when I go to drive her home . . ." Alan's voice trailed off and he grimaced as he sucked on his cigarette.

"Helen kissed me and said 'I love you,'" he said, staring at his feet. "I didn't do shit. I just sat there."

"But she wanted more from you, didn't she?" I asked. I could picture the awkwardness of the moment. Helen, dolled up in cheap makeup and a top that had sat in the back of her closet for ages after she impulsively bought it at the mall. Alan, nervous and afraid to ruin his first real friendship. It was heartbreaking from all perspectives.

"Ah . . . fuck. I shouldn't be talking to you," Alan muttered, kicking a stray soda can. I didn't say anything and eventually he continued.

"Helen wanted to hook up," Alan said, his voice dripping with embarrassment. "But I stopped her. I said she was just my friend."

"How did she react?" I asked, imagining how humiliated I would have felt in her place. Putting yourself out there and being rejected by a guy was a teenage girl's greatest fear. Most girls would rather spend years convincing themselves that no boy actually liked them rather than act on the assumption that one of them did.

"Shit . . . she started crying and saying sorry. I said it was cool but she didn't believe me."

Alan's voice began to creak and I realized that his eyes were glistening with tears. One by one, they fell on the rubber tops of his running shoes, speckling the surface like raindrops. It was surprising to see someone who acted so tough do something so vulnerable.

"I wanted to drive her but she said she wanted to take the bus. I let her go. She was so fucking hurt by me that I thought she'd be better off," Alan said quietly. He glanced up at me, wiping his tears with the ratty sleeve of his sweatshirt. Our eyes met, and I could see the bitter regret that stained his memories of Helen.

"Last time I ever saw Helen, she was walking away from my truck. She was crying so fucking hard. I went back to work and felt like shit all night."

"When did you find out that the buses out here don't run at night?" I asked quietly.

"Not till they found her fucking body," he said, tears spilling over again.

I stood there, letting him cry. Alan had been keeping all of these secrets for weeks, most likely because he was terrified the police would think he murdered her. I knew that he didn't do it, though; his story fit perfectly with everything else I had learned about Helen.

"You know, maybe you should talk to Helen's mom," I said. "She's a nice person, and I think she likes to hear from people who cared about Helen."

"Are you fucking kidding? She'd hate me!" Alan said, wiping his face with his forearm. "Helen's fucking dead because of me!"

"No, Helen's killer is the reason she's dead," I said. "You're just someone she left behind."

The sun began to set as I followed the highway back to town. My car slowly fell below the speed limit. There was no reason to hurry home when the hills were painted golden and the breeze brushed against my skin like silk. It was days like this that made me understand why anyone tolerated the winters of Northern Ontario. The glorious summers never receded far enough into their memory to allow them to leave.

But this winter had been hard, and people had died. This winter had taught me that every life mattered and that losing a person was about more than simple substitution. Every life mattered because every life contained a million connections. Each disappearance sent an incomprehensible shockwave through a web of people. We all lost something when a life was taken, even if it was only a chance to be connected to that person in the future. Helen hadn't known that she'd already had her last summer. It made me feel guilty to think that even though we'd been born in the same year, I'd already been given more time than her.

I sighed as I passed the sign for Thunder Creek. I could see Helen stumbling out of Alan's car, humiliated and sobbing. I could see her thumbing a ride, her tear-soaked face irresistible to a predator. I had similar visions of the last night I saw Chloe, and I knew they'd both suffered in their own way. Sometimes I felt like I focused on finding Chloe's mitten because it was the easiest part of the story to investigate. I wanted to find Chloe, but I was also scared of what might have happened. So I looked for a piece of her instead, some reassurance that everything was okay. Sometimes I dreamed about going away to a tropical island someday and seeing a mitten half buried in the sand. I would glance up and see Chloe walking toward me, older and more tanned, telling me that I could put all of my fears behind me because everything had turned out okay.

There was something so tragic about the acts of desperate girls. My helpless heart wished that I could write a different ending to the story, that I could have kept Chloe from disappearing and delivered Helen safely home. But trusting the wrong person wasn't the only kind of desperate act. Wishing for the impossible could break you just as swiftly. Whether you wanted someone to love you or someone to protect you, it was hard to be a girl in need.

The forest ended behind me like a sweater slipping off my shoulders. The city streetlights made the golden sky seem even more luminescent. I turned off the highway and rolled up my windows. I was almost home.

Chapter Thirty

March 27, 2006

Monday morning. I walked down the hallway to my locker, still mulling over the most eventful weekend of my life. It had been hard to sleep the night before, with Helen's story and the ghosts I'd seen competing for space in my head. I also couldn't stop thinking about Tom, no matter how hard I tried. I couldn't help wishing that I hadn't run out that morning. Alone in my room and safe from any real consequences, I wondered what would have happened if I'd stayed in Tom's bed. Would we have had sex? Did I want to?

Tom had texted me again before school, asking if I wanted to skip class and meet up, but I said I had a test that I couldn't miss. I knew I couldn't dodge him forever, but I needed a little more time to gather my thoughts. Everything was so confusing right now.

There was a clump of people milling around my locker as I arrived. They turned toward me, the middle of the crowd clearing like a set of doors swinging open. Their faces searched mine for a reaction, but I just sighed and pushed past.

Someone had written "Psycho" in Sharpie all over my locker door. The printing style and color varied, making it seem as though a number of hands had taken part. The blue and black writing bruised the yellow locker from top to bottom. In the chaos of the weekend, I had forgotten all about slapping Taylor. Now, though, that memory lapse made me feel even crazier.

I had hit a girl on Friday and it hadn't even stuck with me. Maybe I was a psycho.

What could I do? I needed things in my locker, and I wasn't about to let my audience see me skulk away. I took a deep breath and unlocked the door. I kept my expression blank as I carefully hung up my jacket and backpack. I purposefully moved slowly, and by the time I turned around, the crowd had dispersed.

I didn't hear a word of the lesson in English. At the end of the class, I handed in my homework and left. Taylor, Devon and some of their friends were standing just outside the door. The smirk on Taylor's face told me beyond a shadow of a doubt whose idea my locker art had been. She must have spent her entire weekend thinking of ways to respond. Vandalizing my locker wasn't exactly the work of a master criminal, but Taylor was nothing more than a poor man's Gossip Girl. But the fact that Devon was there made the whole thing worse. Everything had been so much better before he'd hurt my best friend.

"Oh my God, there she is," Taylor said in a stage whisper to Devon. "Be my bodyguard." Devon grinned as she pretended to cower behind him. I guess it was a nice change for him, helping girls instead of hurting them.

"Please. Having just seen my locker, I think you can take care of yourself," I said flatly.

"I don't know what you're talking about, Jenny," Taylor said innocently. "But I did warn you that people are starting to talk. And after your little freak out on Friday, maybe people are worried about your violent side."

"My violent side? It was a slap, Taylor. Calm the fuck down," I said, my voice cracking.

I had always been tall for my age, and when you're a tall girl, you worry that you are somehow mannish. You look at the delicate little things all around you and wish that you could be so undeniably female too. The way Taylor was pretending to cower made me feel like an oversized thug.

"Yeah, *that's* the kind of thing that makes people wonder," Taylor said smugly. Her friends were all staring at me intently, as if I might launch myself at them. Even Devon was frowning at me, like he was in any position to judge.

"They should be wondering how you managed to spell *psycho* right. Quite a feat for a girl like you," I hissed, turning away.

"You see?" I heard Taylor say. She was speaking to her friends, but loudly enough for me to hear. "She's a total freak. I'm just saying, maybe she got angry at *Chloe* that night . . . "

"Do you really think she would do that?" Devon asked. "Kill Chloe?"

"I don't know . . . ," Taylor drawled, her voice dripping with confusion. "I mean, we *know* she's violent. So . . . " The conclusion was left unsaid but inescapable.

I turned the corner, my heart beating so hard I could feel my pulse in my head. It was such a bizarre accusation, but I knew half the school would instantly embrace it. Everyone loves to blame a victim; it lets them believe that bad things don't happen to good people. High school sure made it hard to like people.

I spent the next twenty minutes sitting in a bathroom stall, trying to calm down. My chest felt so tight that I thought I was going to pass out. The competing pressures of my life were pushing in on me: get my grades up so I can pass; help Helen's family; make my mom proud; keep it together at school; don't fall in love with Tom; fall in love with Tom; get revenge on Taylor; forget

Taylor; be happy in high school; get out of high school. I felt as if I were being forced through a tube that was too small for me. The strain was cutting off my oxygen and making it hard to think. I gasped shallowly and tried not to panic.

The old graffiti was still on the wall. I was eye level with a note that said, "Amanda Rich steals boyfriends." To my left I could read, "Ashley Baudette is a coke-whore." Finally, on my right was the note that had become the unlikeliest memorial at Thunder Creek High: "Chloe Shaughnessy is a slut-bag." Underneath this pre-disappearance judgment, people had subsequently written "Miss you, Chloe" and "R.I.P." But no one had thought to cross out the original insult. It was maddening, but all the comments were equally false anyways. Chloe hadn't been a slut, and none of those people really missed her.

Having my locker vandalized heralded a nasty turn in my high-school career. I had been marked as an outsider, a crazy girl who might have killed a friend. I should have seen it coming. I'd struggled to connect with people since Chloe had disappeared. I couldn't care about all the meaningless things, and I couldn't seem to understand the meaning of the important ones. Maybe I really was crazy.

I knew it was only a matter of time before my name ended up on the bathroom wall of shame. But maybe it would hurt less if I didn't have to passively wait for it to happen. I pulled a pen out of my purse and proactively wrote "Jenny Parker is a Psycho"—right next to the slur against Chloe. It was strangely comforting to see my name up there with Chloe's. It made me feel closer to her.

I was late to my next class, but at least I wasn't absent.

Chapter Thirty-One

March 29, 2006

I didn't see Tom at school until Wednesday. I'd been coming up with excuses not to see him, getting progressively more nervous about what it would be like when we did meet up again. I knew it was immature, but I didn't know how else to deal with him leaving. I just threw myself into going to class and studying.

It felt strange to focus so intently on school, but it wasn't boring. I was starting to realize that school was a lot more rewarding when you thought it might lead somewhere exciting. I had always been so convinced that I would end up like my mother, scraping by in a crappy job. But I didn't believe it anymore. It made me wonder how much of our personality was negotiable, how concrete any fact about you was at sixteen. Maybe it could all be changed.

After school on Wednesday, Tom found me by my locker. He was wearing a worn-out Led Zeppelin T-shirt, and I could see the square outline of his cigarette pack in his jeans. The moment I saw him, I felt a rush of heat travel from my hairline to my toes. I knew I couldn't forget that night . . . and not just because it had ended with a snowstorm of ghosts.

"Hey," Tom said, leaning against my locker. The janitor had cleaned the graffiti off after school on Monday, but the yellow paint still seemed stained, as if particles of the word *Psycho* had been permanently ground into the surface.

Tom didn't look as relaxed as he usually did. He kept crossing his arms in different iterations and shifting uncomfortably. I tried to play it cool, to ignore my mixed-up feelings and treat Tom like any other guy. I didn't want to waste my time thinking about someone who didn't care enough to return the favor.

"Hey," I said, zipping up my backpack. "What's up?"

"I don't know, I just haven't seen you since . . . Saturday," Tom said, glancing around the crowded school. "And I was worried that you were mad at me or something."

"I'm not mad at you," I said flatly. "I've just been busy."

"Really?" Tom asked, eyes narrowed. "You're acting a bit weird."

I sighed and decided to tell him the truth, or at least a bit of it. "Tom . . . I can't have nights like Saturday if you're going to leave soon. It's just too . . . confusing," I said, trying to maintain a shred of dignity even as my cowardly heart begged for a million nights just like Saturday, even if it all still ended with Tom leaving me to go traveling. Was it braver to take the heartache now or postpone it for a few months? I didn't know.

"Oh . . . okay," Tom said. "Look, Jenny, I thought you got that with me graduating, I can't . . . I mean, I really like you but . . . "

"I get it," I said. "It's just not easy for me. This has been a tough year. Can we just focus on the Helen thing?"

"Sure," Tom said, patting my arm. "Whatever you want."

I nodded and tried to pretend that this was the end of it, that I could turn my thoughts about Tom off so easily.

"I talked to Alan yesterday," I said. A hurt look settled on Tom's face, and while my aching heart felt a moment of satisfaction, I hurried to explain. "I think the two of us were too intimidating, and thought he might talk to me if I was alone."

"Did he?" Tom asked.

"Yeah, he told me a lot," I said.

"Okay, cool. Do you want to get together later and discuss everything?" Tom asked.

"Yeah. How about you pick me up at eight? I know where we can go," I said. My mom would be working tonight so there would be no awkward questions.

My breath caught at the thought of the evening ahead. Somewhere between his arrival at my locker and this moment, I had made a decision: I was going to tell him everything, and not just about Helen. I had nothing to lose; he was going to leave me anyways. I needed to tell him everything that had happened the week Chloe went missing. It was time he knew the truth, no matter how much that scared me.

———

When I arrived home that day, there was a cop car parked in front of my house. I groaned and slapped my steering wheel in frustration. I really wasn't in the mood to be interrogated. I briefly considered backing the car out and making myself scarce for a few hours, but they were cops. It wasn't like they were going to forget about me. Better to get it over with.

I parked the car and slammed my door a little harder than necessary. In one smooth motion, Officer Trudeau slid out of her car and shut the door behind her.

"Where's your partner?" I asked flatly.

"He had something to do. It'll just be me today," Trudeau replied, giving me a sugary smile.

"Goodie," I said, unlocking my door. My mom wasn't home, but that was okay. I knew that the cops coming around worried her, and I didn't want that after she'd been so understanding about everything.

I dropped my backpack in the hall and flopped on the couch. Officer Trudeau sat stiffly in the armchair. It was like she was trying to be as uncomfortable as possible.

"So, Jenny, how have you been?" Trudeau asked, smoothing a piece of dark hair behind her ear.

"Okay," I said. "As best as can be expected, I guess." It made me uncomfortable when the cops asked that. If I said that I was good, they might think I didn't miss Chloe and that maybe I'd had something to do with her disappearance. If I said I was awful, they might think I was overplaying the devastated friend act in order to hide something. Talking to the police made me feel as if I were on a tightrope in hurricane-force winds.

"What have you been up to lately?"

"Nothing much," I said, choosing not to mention my amateur murder investigation. "Trying to get my grades up in school."

"Yes, I heard you've been having some problems in school. You hit a girl, didn't you?" Trudeau asked, her face deliberately calm. I frowned. How did she know that? Had someone called the cops on me? Or did that piece of information come through the same informal channels that Tom had used to find out about the police investigations?

"Well, she insulted me. She called me crazy," I retorted, before instantly regretting my words. I didn't need to tell her anything more about me.

"Jenny, I'm going to level with you," she said, staring at me over clasped hands. "You've been spotted hanging around the reserve and out at a bar called the Trapper. That seems a bit strange. Would you mind telling me what's going on?"

"Nothing," I said with a shrug. "I stopped at the Trapper to use their phone, and I have a friend who lives on the reserve."

I could feel my pulse quicken as I considered the fact that I had been watched without knowing it.

"Really? You just stopped at a rough bar on the edge of town to use a phone? Are you sure this doesn't have anything to do with a murder victim being dumped in that area?" Officer Trudeau asked, her arched eyebrow telegraphing how little she actually believed me.

"What? Now you think I know something about that too?" I asked sarcastically. "I'm curious, is there any crime in Thunder Creek that the cops don't think I have information on?"

"Careful with your tone," she warned, wagging a finger at me. "Jenny, for all we know, Chloe's disappearance and the murder could be connected. And we keep interviewing you because I *know* you're hiding something. We need all the information we can get."

"I'm not hiding anything," I said tiredly. "Look, I'm friends with Helen's cousin. You know, Helen—the girl who got murdered? He lives on the reserve, and that's why I was near the Trapper. He needed to see where she was found."

"Huh," she said. "Word of advice, Jenny. I would avoid crime scenes."

"Maybe if you guys had actually solved her murder I wouldn't be hanging around," I said.

"You think it's that easy, huh?" Trudeau asked, snorting with laughter. "Trust me, solving a murder is damn hard, especially when there's so little evidence."

"Well, finding evidence is hard when you're all focusing on the girl who disappeared and not the girl who was murdered," I said.

"Look, we have limited resources. Decisions about how deeply we investigate things have to be made," Trudeau said, her flushed cheeks indicating that this was not a decision she supported.

"And that decision had nothing to do with the fact that Chloe's white and Helen's Native?" I asked.

"It wasn't my decision, so I don't know," Trudeau said weakly. "In any case, we are still searching for links between the two cases. And as I've said before, I don't know why you're complaining. I'd assume you'd want us devoting every moment to trying to find Chloe."

"I think you guys can do two things at once," I said.

She rolled her eyes. "I forgot how simple everything is when you're a teenager."

"*Nothing* is simple right now," I said fiercely. "My best friend is missing and I keep being questioned by the police."

"There's an easy way to fix that. Just tell me what you're hiding and we'll leave you alone. I know you know something about her disappearance." Trudeau's voice had become soft and comforting. Was this some sort of interrogation trick to convince me that she was my friend? It would have taken a far better actor to convince me that the cops were on my side.

"Look, Chloe was my best friend, and I really hope you guys do find her safe and sound. But I didn't have anything to do with her disappearance," I said, wondering how many times I'd have to say this before they believed me.

Trudeau jumped up and began pacing in front of me. Her whole face changed in an instant as I rebuffed her attempt to play "good cop." She was breathing sharply and glaring at me as if trying to stop herself from throttling me. It was a strange situation; there really was nothing she could do to make me talk. She had no proof that I was hiding anything, so all she could do was keep questioning me, hoping that eventually I would give in.

"I'm not talking about actions. I'm talking about *knowledge*, Jenny. You know something you're not telling us. Maybe you're doing it to protect Chloe, or maybe you're doing it to save yourself, or maybe you just don't think it's relevant, but you can't make that call. It could be the thing that helps us find Chloe, and by not telling us, you're obstructing justice."

She said all of this in a flurry, her chest heaving and her eyes shining, but it didn't have the desired effect. I sat there, staring at her with an expressionless face.

"I've told you a million times, I don't know anything," I said.

Chapter Thirty-Two

When Tom picked me up that night, I told him to drive to the top of the ski hill. I'd been avoiding this place ever since Chloe disappeared, but it was time now to tell the truth. The whole truth.

The hill had shut down for the season a few weeks earlier, when the number of runs they kept open gradually dwindled down to zero. I was taking Tom to the top of the chairlifts, the place I'd shared with Chloe. It would be the first time I'd ever been there without her. It made me sad to realize that I might keep accumulating these firsts until someday I'd look back and realize that I'd lived a full life without my best friend.

Tom drove on the highway that curved through town. We passed our high school, a few cars haphazardly parked in front. I wondered if they belonged to teachers working late or drama students practicing. Maybe it was the janitors, silently pushing their brooms down granite corridors. I leaned out the window, the wind coursing across my scalp, and watched the school disappear behind me. Someday I'd leave it behind forever.

The streetlights bathed the highway in an amber glow. After I got my license, Chloe and I spent whole nights driving aimlessly around town. I always loved driving on this particular stretch of highway because the orange lights made you feel like you were in California on a summer night. It was hard to find exotic things in Thunder Creek; a good imagination was necessary.

Tom glanced over at me while we waited for a red light to change. His face was half bathed in shadow, but I could see a smile crinkle his eyes. He reached over and patted my leg.

"I wish you were graduating this year too," he said.

I shrugged. "But you're going to Asia anyways," I said. I'd been reminding myself of that fact constantly, hoping I'd stop forgetting that he was leaving, that he didn't want me. Every time I forgot, it hurt more to remember.

"You could have come," he said wistfully.

I looked out the passenger window, my mind turning over the unknown contours of that idea. I couldn't imagine Tom and me anywhere other than Thunder Creek. Our connection was so grounded in feeling trapped by the familiar and resenting our lives. I couldn't envision us being in a brand-new place together, a place we had chosen to represent freedom. It hurt to think of something so exciting when it was wrapped in the understanding that it couldn't happen.

"Maybe. I'd settle for just getting out of Thunder Creek," I said flatly, trying not to get upset over one more missed opportunity.

The light changed and Tom sped off again, climbing the road that led to the hill. When we got to the top, Tom parked in the darkest section of the lot and I led him to the ski lift.

It was terrifying to be back here, but I knew it was necessary. I spent the walk searching for Chloe's mitten and was genuinely surprised when I couldn't see it. I'd thought for sure that it would be here, a final breadcrumb to confirm my suspicions. Maybe it was silly to assume all along that the mitten was a sign.

Tom hesitated when I started climbing the ladder, but he eventually followed me. The view was especially beautiful. The moon was almost full, and it hung low in the sky like a balloon that had slipped through a child's fingers. Thunder Creek was a blanket of lights thrown across the hills, its beauty only dulled by the stars above.

"It's cool up here," Tom said, sitting next to me on the platform. It was a tight squeeze, as Tom was a lot larger than Chloe, but I didn't mind. The warm, spring-like breeze coming over the trees made my soul feel as light as whipped cream.

"I know, right?" I said. "Chloe and I came here sometimes. It was our favorite spot in town."

"Well, I can keep a secret," Tom said, smiling at me. I smiled back and then looked out at Thunder Creek.

I had considered asking Tom to bring some booze. It would have been traditional, as it had been a long time since Chloe and I had come here without a drink. But I wanted to talk to Tom, not just get drunk with him. If I had learned anything from the night I'd stayed at his house, it was that I couldn't do both.

"Let me tell you what I learned from Alan," I said.

Tom nodded and lit a cigarette. He didn't say anything as I told him about how Helen and Alan had become friends, how she fell for him, and what had happened the night she kissed him. When I finished, he stubbed his cigarette out on the metal scaffolding and whistled.

"Man, I feel bad for that guy. He rejects a girl and the next day she turns up murdered? I can see why he didn't mention it to the police."

"I believe him, though," I said. "Do you?"

Tom nodded. "I do. I mean, you'd have to be pretty dumb to kill a girl next to the place you work. Especially after everyone in the bar saw her with you."

"And I could tell he cared about Helen," I said quietly. "You know, sometimes I feel so ashamed that I never even noticed her before she died. The people who knew her say she was a special person."

"I don't know, Jenny," Tom said skeptically. "Everyone's special to the people who know them. I think no matter what you found out about her, you'd have wished you could have met her. We can't notice everyone."

"I think the world would be a better place if we could," I said.

Tom smiled and put his arm around me. "I think the world would be a sadder place. There's a lot of heartbreaking stories out there. I don't think we can handle them all." The tenderness of his hug made his conclusion feel even more tragic.

"So what's next? How do we move forward?" Tom asked. I glanced down at my feet. I was wearing a pair of ratty knock-off Converse that Chloe had decorated with Sharpie swirls. I could see the tips of my sock-covered toe through fraying holes.

"I don't think we can. I don't know what else we could learn," I said quietly. Tom frowned and pulled me closer.

"Hey! Don't give up hope. I know you need to find out what happened to Helen and Chloe, and I'm going to help you. We still have a couple months, and even when I leave, we can discuss things through e-mail."

I nodded and we lapsed into silence, staring out at our tiny section of the world. It was strange to think that Thunder Creek was just a postage stamp on the planet. I thought of all the girls who disappeared like Chloe and all the girls who were killed like Helen. I thought of millions of grieving families and terrified communities. All of those people were unique, and yet loss was so universal. I wished I could tell all of their stories and make sure they weren't forgotten. But how could I do that if I couldn't even tell Chloe's?

"Tom?" I said finally.

"Yep?" Tom said, leaning over to light a cigarette. I bit my lip, unsure if I was ready to take this step.

"I think I might know what happened to Chloe," I said.

"What? Really?" Tom pulled away so he could stare me in the face. "Are you serious?"

"I'm sorry. We should have talked about this earlier, but I think I've kind of been in denial about everything. I'm really sorry. But you said you could keep a secret. Can I tell you one?" I asked. Tom still looked surprised, but he took a deep breath and nodded.

"Of course."

"And when you're keeping this secret, please, just try to understand," I said. I knew I was teetering on a precipice, but it was too late to go back now. I took a deep breath. Then, I began to tell him about Chloe.

Chapter Thirty-Three

February 2, 2006

At the beginning of February, Chloe began to hope that her ordeal as the town whore was coming to an end. For months she had endured the phone calls, the bathroom-stall comments, the computer screen that spewed forth a never-ending stream of poison. I watched her drink herself into a stupor and hook up with more guys, distancing herself from the girl she had been before that terrible night. It wasn't easy to witness her deterioration. I had grown to expect her midnight phone calls, deciphering her slurred admissions through wrenching sobs.

Then a miracle happened—or at least the closest thing to one that you could expect in Thunder Creek. Liam McAllister, Chloe's ex, asked her on a date.

He had called her on February 1—a Wednesday night—asking her out for Thursday. The minute he hung up, she called me.

"I just can't believe it!" she said, her voice bubbling with excitement. "I guess he must regret the breakup."

"Yeah, he must still have feelings for you," I said. "I mean, you guys dated for over a year. It makes sense."

"Jenny, I know it's just one date, but if we did end up getting back together . . . God, that would fix *everything*."

"Yeah," I said, nodding even though she couldn't see me. Liam was so popular that reconnecting with him would change how people saw Chloe. I wasn't an idiot; I knew that people wouldn't initially understand the reconciliation, but over time, Chloe's transgressions would be obscured by her rehabilitated image. Inevitably, someone else would screw up, and Chloe's walk on the dark side would be yesterday's news.

"Anyways, tomorrow, can I come and stay at your house? You could help me get ready and then I can tell you all about it afterward."

Her voice had become breathy with excitement, and I couldn't help smiling. She sounded like the old Chloe. For so long, I had felt weighed down by her sadness. Now, I wanted nothing more than to witness her joy.

"Of course! My mom's on nights this week so I'd love the company!" I said. I wasn't sure who was more excited about this second chance at happiness—Chloe or me.

The next night I sat on my bed and watched Chloe bounce around my room, frenetically changing the music and holding up different outfits for my approval.

Chloe and I had never been able to satisfy a key aspect of female friendship: the sharing of clothes. I was easily five inches taller than her, and she was petite and curvy, whereas I had a medium build and was completely straight. Chloe poured herself into clothes, the fabric hugging her rounded hips and tiny waist. Meanwhile, clothes hung on me as if I were a human coat hanger. Chloe was the kind of teenage girl that rock songs immortalized with lyrics about cherry-red lipstick and tight jean shorts. Meanwhile, I looked like the kind of white-bread teenager that mothers dreamed of hiring as their babysitter. If Chloe's appearance screamed, "Put me in a music video," mine screamed, "I took all the CPR courses and I won't even drink your chocolate milk, much less invite my boyfriend over."

Even if our body types hadn't been completely contrary, our fashion senses just didn't mesh. I watched as Chloe crouched over the duffel bag she had crammed with clothes. Finally, she triumphantly pulled out a retro sailor-inspired romper.

"What about this?" she asked. I frowned at her.

"It's the middle of the winter! You'll freeze your ass off," I said. Chloe flipped her sable hair over her shoulder. She had already straightened it, and it hung down her back as glossy as a horse's tail.

"I could wear tights, but fine. What about a cocktail dress?" She pulled an emerald-green satin tube dress out. I couldn't help but laugh.

"You're going on a date in Thunder Creek, not New York!" I said. Chloe laughed and flopped down on the bed next to me. I leaned back and our heads almost touched.

"I know. I just want everything to be right tonight," she said quietly as we stared up at the ceiling.

"You really loved him, didn't you?" I asked.

"Yeah, I did," Chloe said wistfully. I glanced over at her. She had a small smile on her mouth, as if her mind was elsewhere. "But I also loved who I was when we were together. If we got back together, maybe I could be that person again."

"And if you were dating him, other guys wouldn't mess with you," I said.

Chloe sighed. "Yeah. Maybe people would start paying attention to me for the right reasons. I really hope I end up with Liam again."

"You will," I said. "I just know it."

I rolled off my bed and began to sift through the duffel bag. It was a kaleidoscope of colors and patterns, but I found what I was looking for—a teal sundress that Chloe had owned for ages. It was perfect with her hair, and I'd seen her wear it a million times when she and Liam were dating. I pulled out a pair of tights, her pink ballet flats and a black cardigan.

"Wear this," I said. "I promise you it will be just right."

Liam picked Chloe up at eight o'clock. He didn't knock; he just texted her when he'd parked his SUV outside. As she was leaving, Chloe paused at the door and turned back to give me one last hug.

"Thank you," she whispered. "Thanks for being there for me this year."

"Of course. I'll always be there," I said. I wanted to hug her longer, but she was already pulling away, her face radiating excitement.

"See you later! I can't wait to tell you everything!" Chloe crowed, zipping up her jacket. She paused when she spotted her mittens lying on the floor near the kitchen. I had knitted them for her birthday a few years ago during my short-lived knitting phase, before I became embarrassed by the lame image of a teenage girl who knits and gave it up. Chloe always made a big deal out of how much she loved them, but I could never figure out if she was being genuine or just sparing my feelings. "Oops! Almost forgot these!" Chloe said as she pulled them on and slipped outside.

Through the frosty window in the door, I watched Chloe walk down my steps, her shoes sliding on the film of snow. I felt strangely empty as I watched her climb into the dark car. The SUV's headlights were pixelated by the ice on my window, their origin obscured. Chloe had filled the whole night with light and noise, and now, without her, the house had become a vacuum, devoid of anything. I had the haunting feeling that everyone else was out in the world, spinning under starlit skies, while I stood at a door alone, waiting for someone to come home.

Later that night, I was in the kitchen washing dishes. I was already in my pajamas, though I had no intention of going to bed until Chloe came back. I wanted everything to be perfect for her, and coming home to a sleeping friend would have been anticlimactic.

I was tense with waiting as I got ready for bed. I even peed with the bathroom door open to listen for Chloe's footsteps on the stairs. As it got later and later, I felt more acutely the difference between Chloe's magical night and my lonely evening of television and aimless flicks through magazines.

When I heard the door slam, I grabbed a dishtowel to dry my hands and walked around the corner, my mouth already curving into an anticipatory smile. Seeing Chloe immediately wiped the happiness off my face.

Chloe was shaking, her jaw clattering from the cold. The skin on her face was a mottled pink. She had two circles of frostbite on her cheeks and another on her chin. The frozen patches were pure white and so arresting that it took me a moment to realize that Chloe's eyelashes were rimmed with frozen tears. I watched as fresh tears welled up, tracking circuitous paths around the icy clumps.

"Chloe! What happened?" I cried.

Chloe leaned against the door, sliding down to the floor. She cradled her head in her frozen hands and began to sob violently, as if she were splitting apart.

"Please, Chloe. Please tell me what's wrong," I begged helplessly.

Chloe's face screwed up into a mask of gritted teeth and clenched features. Suddenly, she reared back and began to smack her head against the wall. With every strike she emitted an angry grunt, as if she was trying to knock herself clear out of her own body.

"Stop it!" I shouted, grabbing the back of her head. I could feel her neck strain, trying to force my hand back. Finally, she stopped fighting and slumped forward.

"Oh God, Jenny," she said, tears running down her face as she wrapped her arms around her knees.

"Please," I said. "Please just tell me. I'm listening."

"Well, uh, Liam picked me up," Chloe whispered, wiping her face on the sleeve of her coat. "We had pizza at Catalano's and it was really nice, you know, like it used to be," she said, her voice wavering dangerously.

"Then what happened?" I asked hurriedly. Chloe's calm was as precariously balanced as a child learning to ride a bike. If I didn't keep her going, I was afraid that she would lose momentum and fall.

"Uh, he drove us to the beach," Chloe said. "Which I thought was weird because it's night and, you know, it's winter."

"Okay . . . " My heart sank as I began to suspect what lurked in the time between then and now.

"And then, then he just sort of jumped me," Chloe whispered, a new wave of tears streaming down her puffy face.

She seemed astonished that one action could so abruptly change the course of a night. "He was just touching me, you know, *everywhere*. And he kept trying to get me to touch him. And he was saying all these terrible things, like, 'You should feel lucky that I took you out for dinner first. That's more than the other guys did.'"

"Oh, Chloe, no," I said, my eyes welling with tears. I wiped them away furtively before she saw them.

"Yeah, and he was on top of me and just grabbing me. I panicked and shoved him as hard as I could," Chloe said. She was still holding her knees like a little girl, but a distant, haunted look had settled over her eyes.

"And his whole face just changed," Chloe said, staring forward into the distance. "Liam just looked so dark and . . . mean. And he said, 'It's not fair. I had to wait half a year for you to give it up, and as soon as we break up, you start giving it away to every guy who asks,'" Chloe said, reciting his words robotically.

"I felt so afraid," she continued. "I thought your first boyfriend, your first *love*, would always have this connection to you. But I was so afraid in that car. I really thought he was going to hurt me if I said no."

Chloe paused, the sobs welling up inside of her. I sighed and stroked her back. Liam's words infuriated me—that she was "giving it up" to boys who "ask." I remembered the night at the party, the night all of this had started. Nobody *asked* her that night, and Chloe was in no condition to offer anything. Afterward, guys seemed to assume that Chloe was so damaged that she'd lost the ability to say no.

"I let him touch me some more but when he unbuttoned his pants, I got out of the car and ran away," she finally said, wiping her runny nose again.

"Jenny, I was so scared when I was running. The waterfront was so dark, and I kept looking behind me because I felt like he was going to come after me in the car. I felt, like, *hunted*," she whispered, her lip quivering at the memory.

I felt chilled just thinking of that bitter black sky and frozen lake. The only sounds would have been her heavy breath and her feet hitting the sidewalk. She must have been sure that at any moment her shadow would explode in front of her, trapped in the headlights of Liam's car.

"I don't think I can do this anymore," Chloe said tiredly.

"What?" I asked.

"Be the girl everyone hates," she said. "Well, everyone but you."

"But Chloe, as crappy as this is, it will end. High school will be over before you know it."

"But all the shit that's happened to me won't disappear! I don't want to be this person anymore, but no one will let me be anything else. Jenny, I have to go to school every day and see the guys who ruined my life last September. They look like they're having so much fun, while I'm walking around, hoping no one will notice me," Chloe said, tears welling up in her eyes again.

It was heartbreaking because until this year, Chloe had thrived on attention. It never had to be purely positive; she didn't mind ruffling a few feathers or getting a reputation for being offbeat. But now, the attention she received was so toxic it seemed to deny that she was a person. Chloe had become our school's version of a blow-up doll, batted around by guys who acted like the world was their bachelor party.

"I wish there was some way I could fix all this," I said helplessly.

"I wish you could too. I just can't keep living here," Chloe said faintly, her hands shaking as she covered her face.

"This will all feel better after you've had a sleep," I said, not even managing to convince myself. I doubted heartbreak and betrayal were as easily corrected as a hangover, but I couldn't bear to watch Chloe cry any longer.

"Maybe," Chloe said, wiping her eyes. A strange look came over her face. It was almost as if a Venetian blind had been pulled down, rendering her features clear and expressionless. Usually, I could tell what Chloe was thinking, our shared history giving me a road map to her mind. But in that moment, her face was as flat as a snowy field, her eyes as dull as the muted grays of November.

"Jenny, I really think I would feel better if I slept at home. I really just want to go home," she said firmly.

"Uh, okay. I can drive you home," I said. I should have been glad that she had stopped crying, but what remained didn't feel right. It was as if Chloe had lost the last piece of herself on that cold run home. Maybe Liam's betrayal had been the final match that sent Chloe curling up into the sky like smoke around the winter moon.

———

I drove her home in silence and watched her walk up the stairs to her house. Chloe stood on the doorstep. The porch light transformed her into a dark silhouette with a halo of light on her scalp. I could see the steam of her breath rise in swirling clouds. Her body was angled toward me and I somehow sensed that she was watching me. Slowly, I raised a hand off the steering wheel. The shadowy arm on the porch gently waved back.

Chloe turned around and shuffled toward her door. I saw the teal dress beneath the shifting hem of her coat and her hair glow copper in the porch light. I put the car in reverse and pulled away.

That was February 2, 2006. I never saw her again.

At the time, I thought I was doing the right thing, leaving Chloe to fall asleep in her own bed. Now I think that Chloe never went inside the house, never did more than rest her hand on the frozen doorknob and wait for me to leave. They found her snow-covered cell phone under a porch chair. She must have left it there after I drove away.

I hope she didn't go inside. I can't bear to imagine Chloe walking down familiar hallways, examining old family photos and pausing at her parents' door to listen to familiar snores. I want to believe that she wouldn't have been able to leave forever, not after all the reminders of those who loved her. But like so many things that come up when a person disappears, I'll never know for sure.

Chloe couldn't drive, so I'm sure she left her home on foot. Maybe she hitchhiked out of town. Maybe a kind stranger spirited her away to a new life where her past was wiped clean. Or maybe she met the same kind of predator as Helen, and Chloe's last moments were spent fighting for her life. But deep down, I don't believe any of that happened. Chloe had been so desperately distraught that I can't imagine her forming a coherent plan to leave. Anyway, her problem was no longer just the people of Thunder Creek. By the end, Chloe hated herself so deeply that no trip could have helped, not unless she could somehow leave herself behind.

On the morning of February 3, before school, the phone rang at my house. I picked it up thoughtlessly. I was mentally running through what clothes I could resurrect from my dirty laundry pile, so I never even wondered why someone would call so early.

"Hello?" I asked, standing in the watery light of my kitchen window. I had been eating cereal for breakfast, mechanically spooning it into my mouth as I tried to move past a sleep-deprived night.

"Hey, Jenny, it's Linda Shaughnessy. I just wanted to ask Chloe about her plans after school. Her cell phone's off, could you put her on?"

I felt my knees buckle, the phone almost falling out of my hand. In a single revelatory moment, I knew that my best friend had killed herself. I felt the events of the last few days arrange themselves into a sickening chronology with a foregone con-clusion. She committed suicide. I knew what Chloe had gone through that year, and I also knew who Chloe was. Everything that made her special, her sensitivity and flighty emotions, also made her incapable of understanding that the present didn't dictate the future. Her suffering had narrowed her vision so profoundly that she couldn't understand that these days would soon fall away in the rearview mirror.

If it had been me, I would have put my head down and trun-dled through the indignities. But that didn't make me superior to Chloe. Maybe I was better at surviving, but Chloe was always better at living. If Chloe hadn't been betrayed, she would have led a life much more brilliant than mine.

I didn't know how Chloe killed herself. She might have taken pills or climbed through a crack in the ice to drown. She might have jumped off something tall or she might have slit her wrists. But I knew that she was likely somewhere in the woods next to the ski hill. It would have been a ten-minute walk from her house, and Chloe was so distraught that the idea of a dark and quiet forest would have been appealing. I wondered how far into the bush she'd gone. The forest up there was wide and uninterrupted for hundreds of miles.

I opened my mouth, steeling myself to tell her mother where I thought Chloe was, but the words stuck in my throat. I was sixteen years old and the responsibility of that message seemed impossibly heavy. It would take so much explanation. I would have to tell her about the bullying, the sex, the drinking and the ultimate betrayal by Liam. The truth was an unwieldy bundle of explosives, and I lacked the courage to thrust it into a mother's hands. I didn't want to shatter the cheerfulness of Mrs. Shaughnessy's voice, didn't want to be the person she always associated with tragedy. And what if I was wrong? What if Chloe had just run away and would return within a couple of days? She would hate me for exposing her secrets, and her mother would hate me for not telling her earlier.

But even then, I didn't really believe Chloe had run away. Over the years, our thoughts had become so aligned that it was hard to distinguish our memories. Now, I realized that I couldn't feel her anymore. It was almost as if I had been listening to an amazing song and someone had snuck up behind me and torn off my headphones. Where Chloe had been in my mind was now just a silent space.

"Chloe decided that she wanted to go home last night," I began, my cowardly voice cracking as I clutched the phone so hard that the plastic flexed. I leaned against my wall, steeling myself for the anxiety I was about to invoke. "I dropped her off around midnight. She's not here. She should be home."

And that was the day my life changed forever. Believing that Chloe had killed herself, I also believed that she would be found quickly and that I would never need to explain my suspicions. But they didn't find her. Of course, everybody looked. The police organized volunteer search parties to investigate the ravines, the woods, the frozen rivers and lakes. But it was slow going, wading through snow that seemed to fall continuously, obscuring every footstep and beaten-down path. It was just so easy to disappear in the winter, when a soft spot in the ice or a crust of snow hiding the edge of a ridge could catch you unawares.

By the weekend, Thunder Creek was pinned down under a snowstorm and the volunteer parties dwindled. It was the worst thing that could have happened, the snowstorm wiping away precious clues and covering everything in so much snow that the searchers could have been in the same clearing as Chloe without even realizing it. I sat at home that weekend, wondering in my more desperate moments if I should look for her myself. But I couldn't bear the idea of finding her. As long as her suicide was just a belief, I could entertain the possibility that she had run away and was living it up with a bohemian boyfriend in Toronto. If I found Chloe in the woods, the full weight of what had happened that year would crush me.

The police came to talk to me two days after Chloe went missing. Bragg and Trudeau visited my house that time. It should have been less intimidating than going to the police station, but there was something unsettling about seeing your home through the eyes of the police. You felt as if you had something to hide.

"Jenny, do you want me to stay with you?" my mom said worriedly, standing at the door in her coat. I shook my head. She'd already taken the day after Chloe's disappearance off to be with me. We couldn't afford to lose any more shifts.

"It's okay, Mom. I'm not in any trouble. I'll just tell them how I dropped her home that night," I said, my heart racing. My mom nodded.

"You're right. They're just trying to find Chloe and want your help," she said, pulling on her toque. "Bye, baby, see you tonight."

I watched her leave and then sat down in the living room. Officer Bragg was sitting in the armchair and Officer Trudeau roamed around the room, picking up framed photos and examining them.

"So, was Chloe upset about anything?" Bragg asked. I took a deep breath before giving the most sanitized version of the truth that I could muster.

"Well, she was disappointed that her ex-boyfriend Liam didn't want to get back together," I said feebly. I felt as if we were playing Twenty Questions, the cops slowly backing me into a corner by asking the right questions.

"Any other problems at school? Any reason she might run away?" Trudeau asked, stopping and staring at me.

I paused, feeling the truth froth my stomach into a churning mess. I wasn't sure if I could stop the ugly story from rising up my throat and foaming out of my mouth.

I wanted desperately to tell the police that the last few months had been hell for Chloe. I wanted to tell them what Liam had done, how he'd betrayed her that night. I wanted to tell them that Devon and Mike had taken advantage of her when she was barely conscious. They might not have realized quite how drunk she was, but I doubted they tried very hard to find out. That was the uncomfortable fact about these kinds of situations; alcohol added a level of ambiguity that made the girl wonder if she was really the architect of her own troubles. But the thoughts I had been skirting all year finally crystallized into one inescapable conclusion: Chloe had been raped.

She had never said that word out loud and neither had I. It was almost as if we thought it was better for her to decide that she had made a drunken mistake. Maybe, unconsciously, Chloe and I had both concluded that it was better to be a slut than a rape victim. But labels couldn't change what actually happened. I wondered if I had only done more damage by letting Chloe blame herself and deny the truth she must have sensed. I wondered why I had ever thought that the two of us could just shut our eyes and pretend to see something else.

And if Chloe and I weren't going to use the word *rape*, why would anyone else at Thunder Creek High? Chloe had always thought she was a bit too special for this town, and a lot of jealous hearts might have been glad to see her humbled. You could almost understand how everyone had believed the boys' stories.

I wasn't going to tell the cops that she was raped. I had no evidence and I didn't want to add to her family's sadness by tainting their memories of her last year. Instead, I opened my treacherous mouth and let the lies spill out.

I stayed home from school for almost a week, lying in my bed and pretending that the world beyond my room didn't exist. I tried to keep myself distracted by reading books, but every now and then a wave of grief would crash over me like a tsunami. I would double up in bed, in pain but unable to cry. From the moment I found out Chloe was missing, not a single tear had escaped my eyelashes. I could feel the secrets I was holding back simmering inside of me, and I wondered if that slow boil had dried me from the inside out. I felt my organs begin to cook and my arteries shred under the weight of the toxic things I knew. Nothing made sense anymore, so why should the normal rules of biology apply?

For a culture that talked nonstop about the importance of friendship and how friendship meant forever, no one ever talked about what happened when you lost a friend. There were no support groups or self-help books. We didn't have a word to describe a grieving friend, like *widow*. Apparently, "best friend" was just a motif to decorate the necklaces of little girls. Everyone expected to someday lose their parents, and most had considered the idea of losing a spouse. But no one thinks they will have to mourn a friend.

I finally returned to school the following Thursday, and that was only because my mom forced me to go. It was the anniversary of the last day I saw Chloe. It had been a decade since I'd gone a week without talking to her. The idea that I might never talk to her again made me want to climb back into bed and never come out.

That was the day I discovered how visible a person could be. Everywhere I went, I could feel a torrential wave of whispers crash over me, the phrase "she *must* know" echoing down the halls. I didn't realize at the time that it would become a constant refrain in the coming weeks, but even then I could tell that my world had irrevocably shifted. I had always been a face in the crowd, and I had been content to be invisible. I blended into the background like the freckles I covered in foundation.

I spent my lunch hour in the bathroom, annoyed at myself for choosing the most clichéd place in a high school to hide. Still, it was a relief to know that I had an hour in which no one was watching me and waiting for me to crack.

I waited until the first bell rang before I came out, hoping everybody would be too busy hurrying to class to notice me. I threw the door of the bathroom open and walked right into someone, the force of our collision sending me staggering.

"Oh! Sorry about that!" a familiar voice said, and then I heard a sharp intake of air. I looked up and Liam McAllister was staring at me, a stunned look on his face.

"Uh, hey, Jenny," he said, attempting a bargain-basement version of his usual charming smile.

"Hey," I said flatly. The muscle above his eyebrow creased, a momentary frown that took flight before I registered it.

"Jenny, actually, I've been meaning to talk to you . . . ," he began, stepping toward me. I shuffled back so quickly that I smacked my tailbone on the water fountain.

"Well, it's not mutual," I said. "I don't think I have anything to say to you."

"Hey, I don't know where this is coming from," Liam said, his voice dripping with faux outrage. "I thought we were friends."

"No, you didn't," I said, my voice as flat and unadorned as my face. Inside, I could feel an emotion other than sadness begin to emerge: anger. It was the first thing I'd truly felt since Chloe had disappeared.

Liam had barely talked to me when they were dating. I was a minor annoyance who had to be driven home from the party before he could hook up with Chloe. I was the girl he had to make pained conversation with when he picked his girlfriend up and found me hanging around. I was the bland barnacle to whom he had to be civil as long as he was dating her hotter friend.

I knew that a popular guy like Liam probably struggled to relate to girls like me. I was shy around guys because I'd never spent much time with males. My best friend was a girl and my family consisted of one other person, who happened to be a woman. I had no brothers, no male cousins, not even an assortment of guys I was proud to call my friends. I didn't know what guys talked about, since it seemed like everything that Chloe and I discussed (reality television, crushes, emotional needs) was acutely feminine. Applying what I knew about guys from television, I could only assume that boys talked about sports, cars and the challenges they had shaving their face.

In a way, I was almost relieved when Chloe and Liam started having sex, because she spent all her time alone with him. Suddenly, there were no more expectations that Liam and I hang out. It was refreshing, albeit in a lonely, wish-I-had-a-boyfriend-too kind of way.

"I did think we were friends, but anyways, it's about the cops who came to my house. They wanted to talk about the last night I saw Chloe. Did you tell them I took her out that night?" he asked. Liam was still smiling but his eyes were like black ice. Black ice was the most dangerous ice for driving; you don't notice it until you're skidding out of control.

"Yeah, I did. And you should be thankful that's all I told them," I said sharply.

"There's nothing else to tell. We got a pizza and caught up. Big whup," Liam said, forcefully pushing the words out through his teeth. He was talking as if he had rehearsed those sentences, repeated them while driving and washing his hair until their sheer familiarity evoked the sensation of truth.

"You and I both know there was more to it than that," I said bluntly. I had never talked to anyone like that. I had never had to—not when I had a fiery and vindictive best friend to fight my battles for me.

Liam's face darkened, and I saw that he was clenching his fists so tightly that his hands looked like bulbous softballs. Class had started and there was no one left in the hallway. It was strange that we were having such a dramatic conversation standing in a hall festooned in construction paper hearts. Valentine's Day was still a week away, but they always made a big deal of it at Thunder Creek High. I kept looking at the paper cupid hovering near Liam's head and wondering if, before their pizza date, Chloe had been mentally planning what they could do for their second V-Day as a couple.

The thought that Liam might have killed Chloe later that night winged through my head. It was strange, imagining the guy voted "Most Likely to Succeed" killing his ex-girlfriend and then going about his life. Still, it seemed unlikely that Liam would ruin his future by murdering someone. He would have seen Chloe as a minor character in the grand life he'd planned for himself, not someone worth getting in trouble over.

"I have no idea what you mean," Liam said, his anger inserting sharp pauses between each carefully enunciated word.

"Then I guess you're not as smart as everyone thinks. Stay away from me," I said to him. Then I turned on my heel and walked away.

I tried to keep my walk casual, but it was hard to stop myself from breaking into a run. I was at the end of the hallway before I looked back. Liam was standing exactly where I left him, his eyes fixed on me. A chill shivered its way up my vertebrae. I shoved open the hallway door and left, deciding that I couldn't be bothered to go to class.

For the entire walk to my car, I felt a weight on my shoulder blades, as if someone were watching me. But this time I didn't look back. It wouldn't do any good. Liam knew where I lived and he knew where I went to school. If he wanted to get me, he would get me.

But that meant I could get him too. Liam was going to have to spend the last four months of his time at high school seeing me and knowing that I knew his secret. That would make him nervous, but I wanted to do more. I wanted to make him pay.

⌒

On Saturday, February 11, I went to the waterfront. I wanted to feel close to Chloe. She had been there the night she disappeared. I hoped that by going to the same spot, I could maybe calm the roiling thoughts inside my head and understand how what started as a normal day could have ended so tragically.

It was 4 p.m. by the time I reached the waterfront, and the gray sky was already growing dim with night. I stared out at the frozen lake covered in snow, a white sheet beneath an ashy sky. It was bitterly cold, and I could feel a thick layer of stinging numbness settle on my face. The limited palette and oppressive silence mirrored what my life had been like since Chloe's disappearance.

I walked around the parking lot, trying to guess which of the tire tracks embedded in the hard snow belonged to Liam's car. I had hoped that coming here would give me a measure of understanding. But what had happened seemed just as incomprehensible as ever. Chloe had been betrayed twice that night—once by Liam and once by me. I should have stayed with her. Even if she'd wanted to go home, I should have insisted on spending the night. I knew how upset she was. Why did I let her go?

At that moment, my eyes caught a splash of color in the otherwise anemic setting. It was lying on the ground, half frozen against the ridge of a tire track. I crouched over and peeled it off the ice, the wool mashed into clumps of snow. I felt tears gather as I tenderly cradled Chloe's mitten, the last trace of her that I would find after her disappearance. The mitten was frozen stiff and cold in my hands, but I didn't care.

I stayed out there until my legs were numb beneath my jeans and my fingers swelled with cold. A single mitten was useless; you needed a pair for it to make sense.

⌒

And that was what things were like after Chloe disappeared. The first three weeks were the loneliest of my life. I thought of Chloe so often that I began to feel as if I was losing my mind. She was there when my consciousness snapped back between my eyeballs every morning. She remained until I tipped back into a restless sleep each night. I felt haunted by her secrets, and by my belief that Chloe had killed herself in the woods.

No one at school told the cops about how wild Chloe had become. The teenagers of Thunder Creek High closed ranks, keeping Chloe's secrets as well as their own. It wasn't an act of charity. It was more that no one wanted to give adults access to the insular world of adolescents—especially when they all knew that no one was entirely blameless in Chloe's story.

Not mentioning Chloe would have been one thing. Instead, all everyone at school talked about was how much they missed her. It was as if disappearing had absolved her of all her sins. Every day I heard people talk about how outgoing Chloe was, how funny, how lively, her stellar performance in last year's play.

It infuriated me. The Chloe they were describing had eroded in the last year. And now, it seemed, the entire school population had embarked on a grand scheme of revisionist history. The only remaining evidence of Chloe's troubles was the wall of anonymous comments in the bathroom. I hadn't bothered to cover up the newest set now that Chloe wasn't around to read them. I wondered if the girls who used those stalls shut their eyes so as not to remember how callous they had been to Chloe.

I stopped talking to people, sick of the insincere things they said about my best friend. It all felt so wrong, to mourn a girl who had disappeared long before she actually went missing.

Chapter Thirty-Four

March 29, 2006

When I finished telling Tom everything, I stared at the night sky above Thunder Creek. The stars were unfurled all around, and it reminded me of how Chloe and I had felt up here, sure that the night belonged only to us. Back then, time could slow down and you could live forever on the sensations of just one night. But this wasn't a totally happy place for me anymore. My eyes drifted sideways toward the unbroken line of forest, where I suspected Chloe had died. Had she brought the other mitten with her to the woods? I wondered if she would be wearing it if they ever found her.

"Since Chloe went missing, everyone's wondered what I really know about it. And now I've told you the whole story," I said, looking over at Tom. He was staring out at the trees, his brows furrowed.

I knew why everyone assumed that Helen's killer had taken Chloe as well; it was more than just the fact that they were teenage girls. People wanted to believe that up until the last moment of her life, Chloe wanted to be alive. Because the truth—the idea that we were all Chloe's killers, including Chloe herself—was so much more difficult to grasp.

I took a deep breath to quell the shaking feeling in my throat. It had been cathartic, telling Tom everything, but I had no idea how he'd react to the gravity of my secrets. They never covered this aspect of boy/girl interactions on television. But Tom and

I didn't exactly represent a normal love story: boy meets girl; boy and girl have ambiguous and semi-romantic connection; boy helps girl investigate a brutal murder replete with racial issues . . . I must have missed that episode of *Dawson's Creek*.

"Now I know everything," Tom said, lighting a cigarette.

He reached over and took my hand, enveloping it in a loose weave of fingers. He wasn't saying much, but I could tell by the way he was squinting over his cigarette that he was trying to make sense of it all.

"Do you want a cigarette? I know you don't smoke, but if there was ever a time to have one, it might be now," Tom said.

I hesitated, unsure what it meant if I said yes. Chloe hated cigarettes. She thought they were a disgusting habit and that the only thing worth smoking was pot. I usually agreed with her. My mother's wet coughs and the way even our tissue boxes and bath towels reeked of cigarette smoke had dispelled any ideas that smoking was glamorous. But maybe you should try everything once.

"Okay," I said, holding out my hand for a cigarette and a lighter.

To my surprise, he insisted on lighting it for me. There was something strangely enticing about the way he leaned over and cupped his hand around the flame. It was a small gesture of caring, a sign of something more beneath our months of playing detective.

I inhaled and found that smoking didn't feel like anything new. It was the same sensation I got sitting next to my mom on the couch watching TV. Still, it gave me something to do during this heavy conversation.

"I didn't realize how bad it was for Chloe," Tom said finally. "You always kind of think slutty girls are enjoying themselves. You know, maybe making some reckless decisions but living it up when they're young."

"No, she was pretty unhappy this year," I said, my mouth grimacing at how bitter the truth tasted. I could feel the tears gather in my eyes as I continued. "Everyone ground her down. They ruined her because they made her forget she was better than them. Better than me," I choked, the tears spilling over and soaking my cheeks. "And then they changed as soon as she went missing. I don't get why people care more about other people once they're gone. By then, it's too late to mean anything." I wiped my face with my free hand.

"Because it's easier," Tom said, putting his hand on my knee and squeezing. "Because when they're gone all you have is a memory that you can make be anything you want. Real people are a lot harder to understand," Tom said. He glanced down, his hair obscuring his face.

"I think you're right," I said quietly. "Do you think Chloe killed herself?" It still felt wrong to say something so wretched out loud.

Tom was silent. I took a final drag off my cigarette, my throat catching as the filter began to singe.

"Maybe some mysteries are better unsolved," he said finally. Then he stood up and grabbed my hand, helping me to my feet on the narrow platform.

"So what now?" Tom asked as we began the climb down.

"What do you mean? I think the investigation is over," I said. We would never get the full story on Helen's death, and I was worried that if we struggled for any more slivers of insight, everyone involved would be hurt, even us.

Tom helped me down off the ladder, and when I got to the bottom he kissed me lightly, his lips grazing mine as I leaned against the chairlift. When he pulled away, his eyes had a mischievous glint.

"You keep saying you want to teach everyone a lesson about Chloe," Tom said.

"Yeah, but I'm not going to, like, pull a Carrie and go crazy at prom."

"Don't be stupid," Tom said with a snort. "Look, I don't think we can get revenge on everyone, but maybe we can make Devon, Mike and Liam pay."

"I've wanted to do that all year, but I don't know how," I said in frustration. "I don't have enough evidence to go to the police, and I can't think of any other ideas."

"I can. You said the worst part about all that Chloe stuff was how it was a secret, right? Well, maybe it's time everyone knew the truth. Maybe we should make that happen at graduation," Tom said with a smile.

I nodded slowly. I had thought this conversation with Tom was my big exercise in truth-telling, but while I felt somewhat relieved, it hadn't actually fixed anything. I didn't know what his grand idea was, but I felt I owed it to Chloe to try. If the truth didn't set me free, maybe revenge would.

Chapter Thirty-Five

May 15, 2006

A month and a half later, I went to visit Helen's mother again. It was May; the longest winter of my life was finally over.

I was incredibly busy with school, throwing myself into studying and begging extra work from my teachers in order to pull my grades up. My hard work had paid off. The week before, Vice Principal Delorme had informed my mom that I was on track to pass grade eleven. He was astonished that I had managed to get my grades up so quickly, but my mom wasn't. She had always believed that I could do anything. Now I was starting to believe it as well.

Taylor had mostly left me alone after our big fight in the hall. She said the occasional bitchy thing, and she wasn't above shooting me a dirty look in class, but I think she realized she had gone too far with the locker graffiti and saying I might have killed Chloe. Taylor probably wasn't going to become the next Mother Theresa, but she wasn't evil. She just didn't understand what it was like to lose someone.

I was still spending time with Tom, though it was getting harder and harder to do. He was so incredibly excited about this trip. All he could talk about was beach hostels and overnight buses. He would be chattering away about his itinerary and all I could hear was the loud ticking of a clock marking time. Every time I saw him, another layer of my feelings for him came unstuck. It was ridiculous. I was falling for him even though I knew he was leaving, and that knowledge made seeing him painful.

If hanging out with Tom left me jangled and upset, seeing Bobby had the opposite effect. I had started driving him home after school more and more often. We didn't talk that much, we just listened to music, but I always felt relaxed afterward. When we did talk, it was usually about school and how I hoped I would pass the year. Somehow, his calmness reminded me that while failing the eleventh grade would be annoying, worse things had happened to girls in Thunder Creek.

I had also been spending a lot of time with Jake, the trumpet player who lived in my housing complex. We didn't have much in common other than proximity, but that was beginning to change. I had now seen the complete *Band of Brothers* series, and we were going to start *The Pacific* soon. I'd learned that history was a lot more interesting when HBO produced it, and this newfound interest was really showing in my history grades. Sometimes Jake and I even did homework together. It was kind of nice to have a study buddy.

Lately, I had begun to notice people in a way that I never had when Chloe was here. None of them were exactly the right fit, not the way Chloe was, but together they made me realize that although I might not have a best friend anymore, I wasn't alone.

I turned onto the road leading up to the reserve. It looked a lot nicer in the springtime. The lawns were a lush green, a stunning metamorphosis from the matted and brown grass the melting snow always revealed. I could see children crouched over chalk drawings, their faces obscured by dark hair gleaming in the sunlight. Older people sat on their porches in rickety lawn chairs with crossword books and paperback novels.

I still saw the poverty. The kids didn't have as many toys as you'd expect, and the old people had the mottled brown teeth that showed they'd never been to a dentist. Dirt-matted dogs roamed the neighborhood, mutts that lived off scraps. Rez dogs had always been a problem here. I could remember my mom making me stay in the car as a kid when she came out here to buy cigarettes. Summer softened the edges of those uncomfortable truths.

But no matter what I thought about the reserve, this had been Helen's home. Bobby told me Helen was buried in the reserve cemetery. It was a small funeral plot in the woods, peaceful and secluded. It comforted me to know that Helen would always remain close to her family. Chloe used to worry that she would end up dying of old age in Thunder Creek. We would drive by the graveyard next to the French Catholic high school and Chloe would shudder and say, "Imagine being dead and forgotten here." Chloe had always been so sure that one had to live somewhere important in order to have a meaningful life. But she was wrong. This little reserve in the woods was the only place in the world where Helen mattered.

Pat was sitting on her porch when I pulled into her driveway. I could see her sturdy legs jutting out from the nylon lawn chair. She was wearing shorts and a green T-shirt from Casino Rama, a huge place on a reserve down south. My mom went there once with a friend to see Shania Twain perform. She had come home gushing about how much fun she had on her "girls weekend." It was the only trip I could remember her ever taking.

Pat waved at me, a smile turning up the corners of her mouth as I got out of my car.

"Beautiful weather, huh?" she asked, the traditional way to open conversation in Northern Ontario.

"Yeah, what a relief after the winter we had! I thought it would never end," I replied, shaking my head in disgust. Canadians tended to take unusually long winters as a personal affront. You felt as if the seasons had betrayed you by refusing to adhere to the agreed-upon time limit.

"Bobby's just inside getting a Coke. You're welcome to one too. I thought it would be nice to sit out here," Pat said, gesturing to the lawn chairs she had arranged outside.

"Sounds good. Do you want one?" I asked. Pat shook her head.

"Nah, I'm trying to lose weight. I drink too much of that stuff," she said, slapping her thigh. I nodded and went inside.

Pat's house was hot and stuffy. The lights were off, but the small windows that kept the cold out didn't provide much air. We had the same problem in my house, and my mom was vigilant about keeping the curtains shut in the summer.

Helen's face peered out of pictures at me in the dim light of the hallway. She had been in my thoughts so much that I felt like I was recognizing an old friend. It was as if time had folded in on itself and we had become acquaintances, even though we had never actually met when she was alive.

Bobby was in the kitchen, using his finger to dig half-moons of ice out of an ice-cube tray. The spaces hadn't been filled completely to the top, so the ice slid away from his prying fingers. Bobby was as gangly as ever, but there was something beautiful in the way his spidery fingers fanned out from his bony wrists.

"Hey," I said, smiling at him.

"Hey, good to see you," Bobby said quietly.

"Likewise," I said. I watched him pour two Cokes and a glass of ice water for Pat.

"Any word yet on your grades?" Bobby asked.

265

"Yeah! I found out this week that as long as I don't fail my exams, I'll be a senior next year!" I said proudly.

"Congratulations!" Bobby said, giving me a high five. It was funny how I had pushed the bar down so low this year that passing had become an achievement. I knew that I would have to do much better next year. The idea of twelfth grade made me feel relieved. It would be a fresh start after the roiling upheavals of grade eleven.

"Thanks for being a friend," I said. Bobby shrugged, his bony shoulders arcing through the air like the handles of a jump rope.

"You too, Jenny," he said. I smiled and we walked outside to meet Pat.

I sat down on the chair and took a big sip of my Coke, trying to figure out how to start. I knew that the stuff I had found out belonged to Pat and Bobby, and that they deserved to know what I had discovered, but it was still a hard step to take. Finally, I just took a deep breath and launched in, scared that if I left it any longer I would put it off until the next visit, and so on.

I spent the next half hour telling them everything I had learned since I'd last seen Pat. I told her how Tom and I had pieced together Helen's last hours. Pat knew that her daughter had been visiting Jake, but she had no idea what Helen had done afterward. I told her about Helen catching the bus out to the Trapper. I described Alan, and she furrowed her eyebrows and nodded. She remembered him from his days on the reserve. I told her about Helen's unrequited love and how she had been so embarrassed that she'd tried to hitchhike home.

By the end, I could tell that Pat was holding back tears, her face tight with the effort as Bobby held her hand. Bobby smiled at me, but I could see that his eyes were glistening. I kept forgetting that before he was my friend, he was Helen's cousin, and they had grown up together.

"And that's what I found out," I said. "I'm sorry if it's upset you."

Pat shook her head rigidly and made eye contact. She had a strange expression on her face—the best way I could describe it was a sad strength. It was as if her grief was just another unbearable burden that she had to drag through life, trudging down a path lined with injustice.

"Oh no, Jenny, it didn't. I'm glad, really, to know what her last day was like. I just hate the idea that her heart was broken."

"I . . . I think Alan blames himself," I said carefully, unsure of what her reaction would be. Pat shook her head.

"Oh, he shouldn't. It sounds like he was a good friend to her. Other boys might have taken advantage of her feelings," Pat said thoughtfully, staring out at the street. The kids had used chalk to make a crooked hopscotch course. I wondered if Pat was seeing Helen as a little girl, jumping from square to square on that very spot.

"Jenny, where did you say he worked? The Trapper?" she asked. I nodded and she continued. "I think I'll go out there this week and talk to him. He must be feeling so alone now. If my daughter cared about him, I'd like to meet him."

"Sounds perfect," I said. It was comforting to think that even in death, Helen had continued to give Alan what she gave him in life: people who would care about him.

We lapsed into a long silence, the warm breeze feathering over the porch and across our skin. I felt a sense of relief, as if I had given Pat and Bobby a tiny bit of closure. I was able to tell Pat about another person whose life Helen had changed. And while it was likely that her last moments were filled with pain and fear, there was some comfort in the fact that Helen had spent the hours before her abduction with Jake and Alan: two people who loved her and would never forget her.

But just like telling Tom about Chloe, sharing the truth about Helen didn't seem to be enough. Nothing I had done had changed the fact that there was a killer out there, that the country was actually full of dangers for First Nations people. I had shed light on Helen's last day, but nothing I'd done changed the fact that she was dead and that more girls in the future would likely fall prey. Sitting on that porch, I felt conflicted about the whole investigation.

Eventually, Bobby checked his watch and realized he had to get home to help with dinner. I watched him cut across the lawn to his house, his feet flapping at the bottom of his legs like the oversized paws of a puppy. I didn't know if Pat was expecting me to leave too, but I had one more thing to talk to her about.

"Uh, this is kind of a weird question . . . ," I began, hesitating over the giant leap in intimacy I was about to take, "but, do you believe in ghosts?"

"Why do you ask?" Pat inquired, her eyes unblinking as she studied me from behind her glasses.

"A while ago . . . I think I saw something. I think I saw my best friend, Chloe, like I was seeing her ghost," I stuttered, sure that Pat would either laugh at me or order me to leave. I didn't mention the dead children; it seemed insensitive when I knew Pat had lost her sister at that school. In a way, the whole thing was callous, asking a grieving mother about ghosts. I hoped she understood that it was only because I trusted her.

"To be honest, Jenny, I don't really know if I believe in ghosts. But if you want, I can tell you what my grandmother told me about Anishinabek beliefs."

"Please do," I said.

We had never learned much about Native beliefs in school, other than the fact that they were connected to nature. That fact was repeated so often that it became stripped of all its significance, implying a winking implication of savagery to a culture based on respect for the natural world.

"Well, my grandmother told me that we enter the world from the east, like the day. So when we die, our spirit moves west like the sun, to rejoin the spirit world and the Creator. But spirits aren't confined to that world. They return to earth in dreams or in visions to convey messages or help those they have left behind, even their descendants who never met them. I've also heard of people building spirit houses on top of graves so that the spirit has a place to stay, in case it doesn't immediately depart for the spirit world.

"My grandmother told me of ceremonies to honor the dead," she continued. "Some people actually call them Ghost Dances. They were held in the fall after the leaves were gone. These dances would last four nights, and they took place during the full moon. People would dance and fast to celebrate the dead and thank them for their help. That, and other ceremonies in the sweat lodge, were supposed to lift grief from the heart and confusion from the mind."

Pat had recited all of this flatly, the way one might read a passage from an anthropology textbook. She ended her explanation with a shrug of her shoulders, as if she were ambivalent about the content.

But it was an interesting lesson. I liked the idea of Chloe's spirit hanging around, visiting me from the spirit world. The Ghost Dance sent chills up my spine as I thought of the full moon that had dangled from the sky that night at Tom's. It was obvious that I hadn't conformed to any of the ceremony's rules.

Natives fasted and danced while I had gotten drunk and gone running through the woods. And yet, seeing Chloe that night had somehow lightened my grief.

"Are you going to do any of those things for Helen?" I asked carefully, not wanting to violate Pat's privacy. Pat bit her lip and shielded her eyes to stare beyond the porch. The sun was low in the sky and the children were packing up their toys and heading home, their chalk drawings abandoned like spills in supermarket aisles.

"No. You know, traditional beliefs are difficult. When I was in school, the sisters constantly taught us that they didn't matter, that Christianity was the way forward. A lot of us lost our faith in the old ways. But many of us never really embraced Christianity, not when the Christian world was so cruel to us. So we were left with nothing to believe, caught between two worlds like ghosts."

I nodded. It was times like this when I realized that Pat's history created a rift between us that I could never really bridge. She was a member of an oppressed minority group who had grown up in a time when it was even more dangerous to be a Native than it was today. I was a white teenage girl who had seen so little of the world. I still had trouble understanding any experience different from mine.

"It must have been terrible, all of those people trying to force you into the white world. Um, I know I'm white . . . ," I began, feeling like an idiot for stating something so obvious; the blond hair and blue eyes were a bit of a giveaway, "and I know I can never really understand what you've experienced, but I'm just wondering . . . is that what you see when you look at me? All the white people who treated you so badly?" I asked the question in a rush of words, unsure if I really wanted to hear the answer.

Pat smiled and shook her head. She patted my arm, her hand soft and warm.

"Jenny, Bobby told me that you met his mother once. Barb had a hard life, and she's never been able to forgive the people who hurt her. But when I look at you, all I see is a girl with a good heart, the kind of girl I would have liked Helen to be friends with. Yes, being white means you may not fully understand what it's like to be Native in Canada. But if understanding isn't totally possible, then caring is the next best thing. And you care."

"I do care," I said softly, bowled over by the poignancy of her words. Pat was quiet, but it seemed like she was always thinking, always mulling things over until she had an answer so insightful that it caught you by surprise.

We sat in silence until it was time for me to head home and start my homework. Pat saw me shift to get up and held out a hand to stop me.

"Wait. Before you go, I have something for you," she said, prying herself out of the narrow chair.

When Pat came back she was holding a folded pile of sky-blue fabric. Mysteriously, the fabric seemed to jingle as she walked, a bright sound emphasizing every footstep.

Pat sat down again and carefully unfolded the fabric. It was a long skirt, horizontally striped with embroidered bands made of every shade and color imaginable. At the base of each band were cone-shaped, silver bells, attached to the dress only at the narrow end.

"I made this jingle dress for Helen a couple of years ago. She danced in a pow-wow with her cousins. She didn't want to do it because she was so shy, but they convinced her. Have you ever seen anything like this?" Pat asked. I shook my head.

"Well, women wear jingle dresses to dance because there's a lot of bouncing steps and look what happens," Pat said, holding the skirt up and shaking it. Every upward movement raised the bells up and then brought them down in a cacophony of metallic melody, like a dozen churches announcing Sunday services. The skirt was suddenly alive with noise and movement and I smiled, imagining a bunch of girls dancing in outfits like this.

"It's amazing. I can't believe you made this," I said. Pat laughed.

"It took some time, but it was worth it. When Helen was out there dancing with her cousins, she forgot all about how self-conscious she was and she just let herself move. It's how I like to remember her—happy and free."

Pat's smile was wide and her eyes were distant as she relived her happy memory. I could almost see it myself: Helen's hair bouncing along with the skirt, her white teeth flashing like the silver of the bells.

"Jenny, I want you to have this. I know it's not really the kind of thing people wear in day-to-day life. I just want you to have it so you'll have something to remember Helen and me by."

She pressed the skirt into my hands and I held it gently, with reverence. I had never been given anything so precious.

"Thank you," I said. "I'll treasure it. But I wouldn't have forgotten you anyway."

Chapter Thirty-Six

June 18, 2006

A
s eleventh grade ended, I was beginning to accept that Chloe was truly gone, and a sense of peace emerged as the realization sunk in. I was even willing to forgive my classmates for how they had bullied Chloe. They had been callous, but I didn't think of them as murderers anymore. They hadn't known how deeply they'd hurt Chloe because to them she was a star, impervious to the everyday indignities of growing up. So many kids heard the stories about Chloe secondhand, and that distance allowed them to be mean.

Some people were capable of directly inflicting pain, but the majority only struck out after they averted their eyes. Their lack of empathy made the kids at my school cruel, but I believed it was only a temporary condition. Choosing to have faith in humanity made it easier for me to envision spending another year in Thunder Creek.

But the one thing that still bothered me was the fact that Devon, Mike and Liam would never know how much they had made Chloe suffer. Devon and Mike had hurt her first, but no boy could have betrayed Chloe more deeply than Liam.

It made me seethe to think of them living out happy and normal lives. I saw them going off to university next year. I knew Devon and Mike were going to party schools, but Liam had completed his perfect four years of high school by getting into McGill University, the kind of school that took great teenagers and made them even better. I saw them all going to college parties, meeting girls at keggers and playing on ultimate Frisbee teams. I saw them finding good jobs in Thunder Creek and marrying the kind of girls who kept their volleyball team jackets from high school because that team was like "family." I saw the guys and their pretty wives building lives together and raising a couple of photogenic children. And someday, those guys would contentedly review their lives, confident that they had deserved all of their happiness because they were good people. Chloe's disappearance would be largely forgotten, other than as an anecdote at a dinner party, or a tragic story about first love that Liam would use to build intimacy with future girlfriends.

It's a sad fact of life that we never know how many hearts we've broken and how many tears were spilled because we existed. But I wanted them to know. I wanted Chloe's memory yoked to their backs, weighing them down with blame. Every time a bad thing happened to them, I wanted them to know that it was no great injustice for life to echo back the misery they had caused.

I never went to the police. I knew my story was weak and that the cops didn't see me as particularly reliable. It also wasn't smart to make hopeless accusations in small cities. Accusations refracted through a million personal connections and could have huge effects on the people around you. Maybe that was right and maybe that was wrong, but it certainly wasn't the most immoral choice that had ever been made in Thunder Creek.

But I hadn't forgotten Tom's offer of retribution. I craved a symbolic act of justice that would ensure they never felt completely blameless again. The night before graduation, Tom and I finally put his plan into action.

I waited until midnight before I left my house, confident that my mother would never know I was gone as long as I was back before she woke up. I snuck down the stairs as quietly as I could, carrying my sandals. I stepped outside, breathing in the muggy air of a June night.

Shadflies coated my car and hummed around the streetlights in infernal clouds. Shadflies were a unique feature of Thunder Creek summers, attracted by the warm, shallow waters of Fisher Lake. For two weeks a year, the whole city was covered in quivering, thin insects with long beaks and transparent wings. They were harmless, but their sheer numbers rendered them disgusting. Shadflies would coat every available surface, so that when the wind blew, the sides of buildings undulated like cornfields. Cars would skid on piles of them, wheels helplessly losing grip on the slick surface. For two weeks, piles of shadflies would form on the beaches like barricades erected against the sea.

And then they would be gone. Shadflies only live a day. In a cruel twist of evolutionary fate, they are born with no mouths and have no way of securing sustenance. Shadflies sit dumbly on their chosen surface and starve to death, their only contribution being to lay the eggs of the next doomed generation. Their story made the lives of humans seem so much more meaningful.

I opened my car door carefully, the shadflies refusing to give up their grip on the surface. I cleaned the bugs off my windshield with spray and glanced in the rearview mirror, confident that the plastic bag from the hardware store was in my trunk. Tom had bought the supplies weeks ago so that no one would remember a guy buying red paint. Our plan would work better if it seemed like an anonymous accusation from the universe.

Driving down the silent streets of Thunder Creek, I felt more nervous than I'd expected. As I parked my car in the Walmart lot where Tom and I were meeting, I tried to convince myself that this would be fun. Chloe would have liked it; I could imagine her watching me and laughing hysterically. It was a comforting thought, but it didn't change the sinking feeling I had in my stomach.

The parking lot was empty, the streetlights forlornly pooling on asphalt still warm from the long-gone summer sun. I lifted my hair off my sweat-sticky neck and tried to ignore my pounding heart. Finally, Tom's truck pulled up, and I watched his lean shadow move toward my car. I could hear the scuff of his shoes over the thrumming crickets in the nearby bushes.

"Hey," Tom said, sliding into my passenger seat. He fiddled with the seat, pushing it as far back as possible to accommodate his long legs.

"Hey," I said, patting his leg.

"You ready?" Tom asked, leaning in for a kiss. I nodded, my lips sticking to his in the humid summer air.

This was it. Our last adventure together. Tomorrow, Tom would graduate, and the day after he would be gone traveling. It was surreal. What had seemed so far off had now arrived: Tom was leaving. It made every moment feel more urgent to me, as if I were trying to feast on every word and touch in the hope that I could remain permanently satiated.

Yes, I had Bobby, Jake, Pat and even my mom, but they all seemed pale and insubstantial substitutes for the throbbing intensity of my time with Tom. Of course, I knew I couldn't ask him to stay. Not because I was too proud, but because I knew he wouldn't do it. Still, this was the second person I cared about this year who had chosen to leave me. This time, at least I knew where Tom was going, but Asia was inconceivably far for a girl who had never left Ontario. Part of me wanted this night to last forever, and part of me wished it was already over so I could be past the part where we said goodbye.

"Which house should we hit first?" Tom asked as I started the car.

"Liam's," I said firmly. "In case something goes wrong, I want to start with him."

"Sounds good," Tom said.

We parked down the street and snuck up to Liam's spacious five-bedroom abode. It was an immaculate home, the lawn lush and meticulously trimmed. Flowers bloomed in the garden and the porch was bright white and smelled of fresh paint. You could imagine the photogenic gatherings that happened in such a house: lemonade on the porch in summer, presents opened under exquisite color-themed Christmas trees, Thanksgiving dinners on mahogany tables where family members actually took the time to say what made them grateful. The house was timeless, and I knew Liam and his siblings would be able to fondly return to it over the decades, college girlfriends in tow, followed by wives, and, eventually, children. Yes, it was a picture-perfect family home, and we were going to vandalize it.

Tom and I shook the spray cans and worked quickly, the paint dripping down the white garage door. We kept glancing furtively over our shoulders, hoping that an insomniac neighbor or random police car wouldn't ruin our plans. My stomach was roiling and I could barely breathe through my panic. When we were done, we hurried back to the car and moved on to our next stop.

We had chosen the night before graduation because we wanted to ruin something special for these boys. Tomorrow, the boys' families would wake up in their cozy, middle-class homes. I could almost hear the pleasant "can you believe how old you've become, we are so proud, on to the next adventure" conversations that typically happened on the big-milestone days. Maybe they'd eat celebratory food, dishes that were famous within the insular world of their family: Mom's special pancakes, Dad's legendary omelets. Then they would get all dressed up, those happy little suburban families, and they'd go outside to get in the car. And that's when they'd see it.

RAPIST—spray-painted in red, dripping letters that completely covered the garage. The family would stand there in confusion, trying to come up with an alternative meaning for the word. They would look around and realize that only their garage was vandalized, that this message had been meant for them. Here they were, enjoying a sunlit morning at home, while every morning jogger, dog walker and Saturday-work commuter saw something they would never forget. It was an accusation, a slur lobbed directly at them. It was a word almost never spoken above a whisper, and yet here it was, splattered across their garage door like eggs on Halloween. And the punishment was more fair than when I had *Psycho* written all over my locker. I had slapped a girl. They ruined one.

Everyone would be frozen to the pavement, their jaws dropping down to graze tie-knots and locket necklaces. Fathers would be scrutinized along with their sons. Mothers would demand explanations, plausible stories about disgruntled co-workers or ex-girlfriends getting revenge. Everyone would swear they didn't know anything, and finally they would conclude that it was a sick joke. Plans would be made to buy cleaning supplies on the way back from the graduation. The family would climb into their car, the father pressing a button to raise the garage door. Everyone would breathe a sigh of relief as they watched the word *RAPIST* fold itself away like a map. The father would spend the entire graduation worrying that someone would steal the expensive road bicycle he bought to stave off aging when he turned forty.

It's likely that everyone would try to pretend nothing happened for the entire drive to the high school. The boys would spend those quiet drives flipping through their memories, trying to figure out who would call them a rapist. Then they would remember Chloe and maybe recover the unsavory details they had ignored in the aftermath. Devon and Mike might remember the slackness of her body, the way her head rolled from side to side as they moved on top of her. Liam might recall her tear-stained face and how she had fled from him on a winter's night. They might try to explain the memories away and justify why they couldn't possibly be considered rapists. They might not be successful, though. They might be left always wondering if they were truly good people.

I knew that Liam would probably connect the spray-painting to me. He knew that Chloe had told me what had happened on that last night. But I wasn't scared of him or the other boys. They were cowards, and I'd faced scarier things than them this year.

At the graduation, I imagined the mothers raising cameras to their faces, pausing to examine their sons through the anonymous gaze of a lens. Surely that wasn't the face of a rapist. It was inconceivable that the sweet little boy who loved books about dinosaurs and wore hockey pajamas to bed could grow up to be a young man capable of such violence. They hadn't raised a rapist. But a voice would linger in their heads, whispering, "What if?" And those mothers would hesitate to have a photo from graduation framed because they didn't want to be reminded of their doubts and the guilt that those doubts provoked.

Maybe those families would momentarily forget during the festivities, but they would go to bed that night wondering what secrets festered in their homes. In the end, that graduation day would always have a shadow over it in their memories; something that was supposed to be wonderful had become complicated.

I should have felt good about all of this. It was only fair. Why should they have a nice graduation when Chloe would never get one? But as we drove away from Devon's house, our final stop, I felt even emptier than I had before. I remembered how right I had felt when I'd sat with Pat, knowing that while I hadn't fixed everything, at least I had provided her with a small measure of closure. Now all I felt was regret. It didn't matter if those boys were bad people; I wasn't sure if our actions were right.

Chloe would have loved it, but I wasn't Chloe. I was Jenny Parker, and I felt nauseous thinking of all those confused mothers and startled younger siblings. I wondered if they would be scared to be in their houses now, holding their breath every time they unlocked the door or went to the bathroom in the night. I had stolen their sense of safety, and I didn't know if it had been mine to take. Revenge made me feel weaker, not stronger, as if it showed how toxic I was on the inside. It hadn't brought Chloe back, and it had made me feel as if I'd lost a piece of myself as well.

Tom saw the tears rolling down my cheeks and lightly grabbed my shoulder.

"Hey, what's wrong?"

"Nothing," I said, the tears spilling over faster. I wiped them away with one hand and tried to think of something, anything, other than what I had just done.

"Why don't you pull over?" Tom asked, pointing at a small parking lot by a public playground. I nodded and pulled into a spot, waiting until I turned the car off before breaking into full-out sobbing.

"Hey, come on," Tom said helplessly. "What's wrong? Look what we did tonight—you should be happy!"

"We didn't do anything! We just spray-painted some shit," I sobbed, resting my forehead against the steering wheel. "This was supposed to make me feel better and it didn't!"

"I don't know what to say," Tom said in frustration. "You seemed all up for it a few hours ago."

"Maybe I just wanted to do something with you!" I cried angrily. "And I thought you knew what would help me, but you don't!" I was still crying, but I also felt mad at myself—for going along with Tom's stupid plan, for convincing myself that a bit of a petty vandalism could fill the hollowness I had felt since Chloe disappeared.

"I'm not a mind reader, Jenny. I haven't even known you that long!" Tom said. The way he was frowning at me made me feel even worse.

"Yeah, you've made that clear! I thought you gave a fuck about me but you're leaving!" I cried out, almost instantly embarrassed. I had tried so hard to play it cool with Tom, but I was really quite bad at it.

Tom's face softened and he pulled me in for a hug, our bodies awkwardly angled by the car seats. I wanted to pull away; instead, I found myself crying on his shoulder, angry and ashamed about how I was acting, about how much I wanted him to stay.

"I do care about you, but I have to have my own life. Jenny . . . I'm not Chloe, and I can't replace her for you."

And there it was. The unspoken reason I had become so dependent on Tom in the last few months. It wasn't that I loved him (although I really did care about him), but that I loved Chloe. I loved Chloe, and I didn't know how to live my life without having someone to love. I thought Tom would save me from being alone, but he couldn't, and it was unfair to expect a teenage boy to solve all my problems. Chloe was gone, and I was here, and nothing and no one could ever change that.

"You're right," I sobbed, feeling my heart break open. The raw emotions I had been trying to contain for months rushed through the cracks. "I just wish you could."

We stayed like that for a long time. Finally, when I had cried myself into a dull calm, I started the car. Tom offered to drive, but I declined. I wanted to reclaim a bit of dignity after my breakdown. Tom had been good to comfort me, but I had to begin taking care of myself. He had been my training wheels as I started a life without Chloe. Now, I needed to learn to go it alone. I wanted to know who I was without another person as a point of reference, how to live a life that wasn't devoted to someone else.

When we got to the Walmart parking lot, I climbed out of my car to say goodbye to him. He pulled me into a hug, and I made sure to notice every detail of how he smelled and the way I fit snugly into his arms. The feeling of that hug made me ache with pleasure. I felt myself waver, shocked that this was the end; he really was leaving.

"Have a good trip," I said, my voice tight and choked. Tom leaned in for a final kiss and then we stepped away. For a moment I felt off-balance and dizzy, but my body steadied under me.

"Thanks, I'll be in touch, I promise," he said. I shrugged.

"Only if you want to. You don't have to worry about me," I said quietly. "I'll be okay."

"You'll be more than okay, Jenny. You'll be great," Tom said firmly. I smiled.

"Yeah, maybe you're right."

Then he got in his truck and drove away. I sensed that Tom was doing the right thing by leaving Thunder Creek. If he didn't go out and discover who he was and what the world was like, then eventually I would outgrow him. Tom needed to follow his dreams and make a life for himself, and I *was* going places. Maybe not this year, but definitely the next.

The fact that we were done with each other wasn't completely sad. In a way, it was beautiful to reach the end of the chapter. I could feel myself closing the book and looking up, wondering, "What next?" And just imagining the possibilities.

Chapter Thirty-Seven

July 15, 2006

I spent the first few weeks of summer reading books and pulling as many double shifts at the diner as I could handle. Working as a waitress—where I was always taking orders, delivering food or tallying bills—distracted me from Tom's absence and all of the things that had happened this year. It already felt like a lifetime since I'd said goodbye to him, the night we'd spray-painted the houses.

The vandalism hadn't been widely discussed in Thunder Creek, but the teenagers all seemed to know. Everyone was debating the identity of the vandal and arguing over whether the boys really were rapists. They were popular, yes, but there were a lot of kids at Thunder Creek High who would be happy to see them fall from grace. Everything just seemed too easy for Liam and the others, and a lot of people secretly resented it.

Meanwhile, I was keeping a low profile and avoiding everyone from school (other than Jake and Bobby). I knew that Liam probably suspected it was me, and if he ever found me at a party, he might lash out. But I didn't go to parties anymore, and I had spent the last six months acting like a loner anyway. Besides, I was sick of the sound of Creeker gossip.

I was enjoying a rare morning off when my mom called me from the diner. I sighed, sure that she was about to ask me to come in because someone had called in sick.

"Hey, Mom," I said, examining a new crop of freckles that

had bloomed on my arms from my time in the sun. I had never totally given up hope that the freckles might someday merge into one another and give me the illusion of a tan.

"Jenny . . . ," my mom said, her voice breaking and shuddering. "Oh, Jenny . . . "

"What? What is it, Mom?" I asked, feeling my anxiety rise. Something was wrong, terribly wrong, and I felt as if, once again, my life was about to change.

"Sweetheart, they found her. They found Chloe," my mom finally said. I could tell that she was crying.

"Alive?" I asked. I knew the answer would be no, but for a single moment, I rediscovered a shred of hope. Maybe my mom was upset because Chloe had been held by some sadistic kidnapper, or maybe they'd found her on skid row, injecting heroin and turning tricks. I'd believed Chloe was dead, but maybe I'd been wrong. I'd never wanted to be wrong so much.

"Oh no, baby. I'm sorry, I shouldn't have said it like that. No, Jenny, they found her body," my mom said in a rush. I leaned against the wall, wrapping my arms around my stomach. I felt as if the wind had been knocked out of me, my lungs left crinkled inside my chest like deflated balloons. I struggled to breathe and felt tears filling my eyes. I thought I'd been ready for this, thought I'd eradicated any doubt I had that Chloe was dead, but a secret wish had remained intact. It was like I'd lost her again, and the thought that it was all over made me cry harder.

"I'm so sorry, Jenny. I can't believe it. She was at our place so much over the years, I feel as if I've lost her as well," my mom said.

"Yeah," I said, not sure what else I could say. I slid down the wall and sat on the floor in the kitchen, cradling the phone.

"Someone's coming in to cover me. I'll be home in an hour, okay?" she said.

I considered telling her that I would rather be alone, but I couldn't. The sheer size of this news made it seem impossible to handle alone. I needed someone to be with me, to make me feel like this wasn't the end of everything good. I didn't want this to be reality; I didn't want this to be my life. I pressed my hand against the linoleum, unwilling to even get up off the hard floor.

"Thanks, Mom. Come home soon," I said, tears running down my face. I hung up the phone and pressed my head against the wall, the reassuring firmness making me feel like I wasn't in danger of floating away.

I'd known this would happen someday. So why did I feel like my heart was breaking?

My mom found me still sitting on the floor in the kitchen. She didn't say anything; she just sat down next to me, groaning a little as her sore back jarred. I put my head on her shoulder and cried, feeling her stroke my hair and make comforting noises. We sat there for ages, my face buried in the scratchy sleeve of her uniform as she held me. I felt like a kid again, needing my mom to chase away the nightmares and monsters that hid under the bed. The world seemed so large and threatening, but I felt safe there, wrapped in my mom's arms in our hot little kitchen.

"I'm sorry, baby," my mom whispered, her voice as soft and familiar as childhood blankets.

"She's gone. She's really gone," I murmured.

"Yes, she is," my mom said. "But you'll never forget her."

I nodded and fell silent again, realizing that words would never fill the hole inside of me. My mom could have said the most profound and comforting sentiment possible and it still wouldn't have been enough. It was better just to be with my mom, existing in the moment without thinking about the next one.

A while later, I got up and went upstairs for a nap. I could hear my mom downstairs, washing dishes and listening to the radio. I lay on my bed, feeling drained from all the crying, my eyelids sore and heavy. I didn't think I would be able to sleep but I did, clutching the mitten I'd hidden under my pillow.

I didn't wake up until around 4 p.m. I could smell garlic from downstairs and knew that my mom would be making my favorite meal, spaghetti with meatballs and garlic bread. But I didn't go right down. Instead, I pulled out my laptop and began searching for news about Chloe. I had to know what happened.

The police hadn't released much news, only that a body had been found by some kids building a tree house in the woods on Blueberry Hill, not far from the ski hill. The body had been found at the base of a very tall ridge, the forest so thick on the cliffs that it was hard to see where rock ended and sky began. The woods were so dense in that area, and so far from any mountain-biking or cross-country skiing trail, that it could have been years before anyone even walked near the ridge. The cause of death had not been released to the public, but the police could now confirm that they had found Chloe Shaughnessy.

I sighed, staring at the picture of the police chief at the press conference he had given in the morning. I felt bad for the kids who had found Chloe; after spending over five months outside, the body would likely have been a horrifying sight. It seemed like it was always children who found the hidden crimes in Thunder Creek. A few years ago, three preteen boys had found the body of a newborn baby abandoned in the forest, left there by a woman who couldn't cope with the idea of having a child. A forest could be the dumping ground for awful secrets, and it was often kids, unafraid to stray off the path and find their own way, who discovered them.

The police may not have released her cause of death, but I knew she had jumped. Her parents probably did too. They were unlikely to think Chloe had gone for a midnight hike in January, one that had resulted in an unfortunate accident. Mr. and Mrs. Shaughnessy were probably sitting in their house right now, trying to understand why Chloe had killed herself. They were probably so confused, afraid that they'd never understand what had happened. But I knew what happened; I had been carrying the secrets around for months. Chloe's parents needed to know the whole truth. I didn't want to do it, but I knew it was necessary. Now that I knew for sure, I had no excuse. I had to act.

I waited two days before I called the Shaughnessys. It might seem like I was trying to screw up the courage to do it, but it was actually really hard to wait. Now that I knew what I had to do, I would have preferred to just get it over with. Still, I wanted to give Chloe's parents a couple of days to process the fact that their daughter was dead before I dropped any more bombshells on them.

Chloe's mom answered, and I asked her if I could come over and talk to her and her husband. She probably assumed that I just wanted to pay my condolences as Chloe's best friend, but in any case, she said yes. I climbed into my car after hanging up the phone and started driving to Blueberry Hill before the gravity of what I was about to do sank in.

I parked my car and knocked on the door. It occurred to me that the last time I had been at this house was February 2, the night I dropped Chloe off. The last time I ever saw her alive. I breathed in deeply, trying to find a trace of her lingering on this porch. Maybe I was crazy but I did feel something. I felt calmer being here. Chloe felt closer.

Chloe's mother answered the door. Linda's face had the swollen, ruddy look of someone who'd been crying for days. Her hair was clean but she was wearing a ratty old University of Toronto sweatshirt and a pair of paint-splattered jeans. I had never seen her looking so casual.

"Hi, Jenny," Linda said, pulling me in for a hug. She leaned on me, and I could feel her weight spread across my shoulders. I started to wonder if this was the right time to talk to Chloe's parents. Were they too fragile right now? But I knew that if I didn't do it now, I would never do it. It was never the right time to tell someone that you knew why their daughter killed herself.

Greg appeared behind Linda, looking a little more pulled together, though I could tell by the bags under his eyes that he was exhausted. Chloe had never been close to her dad, but one look at Greg instantly told me that their distance hadn't reduced his suffering at all. It might have actually made it worse; you weren't just mourning the person you lost but also the possibility that you might have become closer in the future.

"Would you like a drink? We have water, juice and soda," Linda said, pulling away from me. I shook my head.

"All right, then," Linda said, gesturing toward the living room. "Let's go in here."

We sat down in the formal living room, a place I had only ever walked through on the way to the kitchen, the TV room or Chloe's bedroom. The couches were covered in a stiff dove-gray fabric and were firm enough that you never felt like you could relax. I scanned the room, seeing a familiar face staring out at me from every corner. Chloe's school pictures covered the mantel piece and the top of the piano. It was comforting to see her there, as if she were in the room with me for this difficult conversation.

"I wanted to come here and talk to you guys," I began hesitantly. "I know they found Chloe, and I'm sure you're asking what happened. And I don't know for sure, but I thought I would tell you what this last year was like for her . . . "

And then I told them everything. I started with the house party, the bullying and the rumors. I ended with that last night; the date with Liam, the aftermath, Chloe's demand that I drive her home, and my suspicion that the events of the evening had driven her to kill herself. It was really hard to say out loud the things I'd been holding inside for months, to see the shock and sadness on Chloe's parents' faces. By the end, they looked stricken, their faces pale and horrified.

"I always thought Liam was such a nice kid . . . ," Linda murmured. "I told the police that there was no way he'd have anything to do with her disappearance, that he wouldn't hurt a fly . . . " Her voice trailed off.

"I know. If I'd known how that date would turn out, I would have begged her not to go. But I never suspected," I said softly.

"So am I right in thinking you were the one who spray-painted *RAPIST* on those boys' garage doors?" Greg asked. I grimaced.

"Yeah. I know it's dumb, but I just wanted to do something."

"I understand the feeling," Linda said grimly. "Honestly, I could kill those boys for what they did." She looked so angry that I didn't doubt her.

"Is there anything that could be done about them?" I asked. "Like, with the police?"

"I doubt it. But I'll tell them. They might have a chat with the boys, off the record, make it clear they can't treat girls like that," Linda said. She looked as if her heart was breaking at the thought of someone treating her precious child so cruelly. I'd seen the same expression on Pat's face when we talked about Helen.

"Anyways, I came here because I wanted to tell you how sorry I am. I should have told everyone what I knew earlier. I am so sorry. Maybe it would have made a difference to the investigation. Maybe they would have found her," I said, my voice breaking. I was embarrassed to realize that tears were filling my eyes. I didn't have the right to cry in front of Linda and Greg; I was the reason they'd lost their daughter.

"Oh, Jenny, all you could have told them was what you believed happened. You didn't know where she was. It wouldn't have saved her life, and the police might not have even agreed with you," Linda said soothingly.

"There was nothing you could have done," Greg said.

"But I still should have told you," I said, rubbing my face furiously, wishing the tears would stop. "I could have told you what was going on before that night, when you could have done something," I sobbed.

Linda sighed. "And I could have asked. In all honesty, I did wonder if Chloe was okay in that last month. The whole winter, she just seemed so moody. I thought she was still upset over the breakup with Liam, or that maybe she was stressed out about school. I thought all she needed was time, and that I should give her some space. But I was so, so wrong," Linda said, her face crumpling.

"This is what happens," Greg said, wrapping his arm around Linda. "When you lose someone so young, everyone wishes they'd done more."

"But I left her that night. I should have stayed with her," I said quietly. I wasn't sure why Chloe's parents weren't yelling at me, why they couldn't comprehend the million ways I'd failed their daughter.

"She asked you to take her home, and you thought she was safe with us. And you'll always wish you'd done something differently, but Jenny, you weren't her keeper. Chloe made a choice that night. We will always wish she chose differently, but you couldn't stop her," Linda said through her tears. We were all crying; even Greg was covering his face.

"I know, but it's hard to accept that," I said.

"It'll take time," Linda said softly, wiping her eyes with a tissue. "But we want you to know that we don't blame you for anything. You were always a good friend to Chloe."

"Thank you," I whispered. "She was the best friend I could ever hope for."

The room fell silent except for the ticking of the wall clock and our muffled sniffles as we all tried to stop crying. But I felt a strange relief, a lightening that I had been chasing for months. I thought getting revenge would make me feel better, but it had been like eating candy for dinner: it seems like a good idea for a moment, until you end up feeling sick and unsatisfied. Telling the truth, bringing everything out into the open, was different. It had been difficult, but the pressure that had been building inside of me for five months was suddenly gone. I could finally breathe.

Chapter Thirty-Eight

August 30, 2007

It was a year later, and I was leaving Thunder Creek. I had been floating toward this moment all summer, unperturbed because I couldn't quite believe that it was real. I, Jenny Parker, was moving to Toronto.

It had been a beautiful summer, and I had spent every moment that I wasn't waitressing at the beach. Sometimes I went with Bobby or Joanna, a girl who had moved here from Kapuskasing at the beginning of the year. Other days I went alone, bringing a library book and my ancient Discman. Thunder Creek was wonderful in the summer, a sun-drenched town that straddled two lakes. People spent every possible moment outside, savoring the gentle breezes that smelled of warm pine. It made it harder to leave, and I found myself wishing that university started in January. It really wasn't hard to leave Thunder Creek in the winter.

But I was excited about starting school. My mom had been so proud when I got a scholarship to Ryerson University. I was going to study journalism, and Ryerson had one of the best programs in Canada. Helen's death had taught me the value of asking questions, of examining the things that other people ignored.

I knew I would meet a lot of new people in Toronto, but as I'd driven down the familiar streets of Thunder Creek that summer, a familiar person was on my mind. I thought of Tom occasionally, less than I would have expected a year ago. Tom had had a tremendous impact on my life, but when he left, the feelings I had for him began to fade like a healing bruise. I understood now that the intensity of our relationship had a lot to do with timing: I'd met Tom during the most difficult year of my life. That didn't stop me from feeling sad when I remembered how good it felt to be in his arms and the secret things I had told him. I occasionally wondered whether, if I hadn't been so obsessed with Chloe and Helen, Tom and I might have stood a chance. But I couldn't answer that, and neither could he. No guy had shown any interest in taking Tom's place, so I'd spent the year trying to convince myself that I didn't want to date anyone, that I didn't miss the feeling of being wanted, even just momentarily.

He sent me the odd e-mail from Internet cafés in Asia, but I didn't know how to maintain anything meaningful through such intermittent conversation. It was as if, once a month, a man stormed into my room, shouted, "Thailand is awesome! I just came back from a crazy Full Moon Party!" and then left before I could respond. It was a far cry from the way he used to appear next to me in crowded hallways, sending a jolt of electricity down my spine before he even opened his mouth.

We hadn't known each other that long, and while I felt we had shared something important, I had no idea if we would work in any other setting. But I was going to get the chance to find out. Tom's last message said that he was coming back to Canada in November. He was running out of money and needed to work for a while before he could plan any more trips. The message also said that he was planning on living in Toronto, and could he crash in my residence room while he looked for a place to rent? I said yes. I tried to tell myself that we had changed so much in the last year, and that having him stay with me would only bring closure. But I couldn't deny the fact that a mental calendar in my head noted the number of days until I saw him again. I was still young, and had never experienced love independent of loss, but I hoped that someday soon I might.

I still saw Officers Trudeau and Bragg around town every now and then. They usually ignored me, except for once, not long after I'd told Chloe's parents everything. Trudeau had been by herself, out of uniform and in the local mall. Our eyes had met and she'd given me a single nod. She may not have approved of my decisions, but I'd like to think that she understood why I'd been hiding things from her.

I was glad, though, that I'd told Chloe's parents. It had given us all a sense of closure and made me feel strangely connected to them. They no longer lived in Thunder Creek; they'd moved down to Niagara-on-the-Lake not long after Chloe's funeral. Thunder Creek had too many unhappy memories for them, the town still populated with the families of the boys who had raped Chloe. I hoped their new life down south was working out okay. I had a standing invitation to visit them, and intended to do so once I had settled in at school.

The day before, I'd gone to the chairlift. It was the first time I had ever visited it by myself. I went there to think of Chloe, to feel close to her. It was such a peaceful way to spend my last night in Thunder Creek. I had stayed under the stars for hours, thinking about everything that had happened and what might happen next.

All summer, a stack of university things had sat in the corner of my room, growing and colonizing the space around it. These "supplies" were the first thing I saw when I woke up every morning, and the knowledge that tonight I would unpack them in a dorm room in Toronto made my stomach bubble with nervous excitement. I had said goodbye to my mother the night before, but she had still come into my room early in the morning before work and given me one last hug and kiss. I had been half asleep, but the memory of that soft and familiar embrace lingered in my arms.

Now, I was packing my car, grabbing suitcases full of clothes and Walmart shopping bags bursting with twin bedsheets and shower caddies. My car was almost full when I swung my backpack across to the passenger seat, knocking my water bottle out of the cup holder in the process. The bottle rolled under the seat, clattering against the empty pop cans that lurked inside my car. I jogged around the car, cursing its under-sized cup holders, which left only the smallest drinks intact on hard turns.

My mom had been suggesting all summer that I clean and vacuum my car before moving to Toronto. "You don't want to go off to university with a dirty car, do you?" she had asked, as if somehow crumpled chip bags would distract me from study-ing. But I had never gotten around to it, preferring to spend every moment I wasn't working reading at the beach. Now, as I stuck my hand under the car seat, I could feel the grit of a sum-mer's worth of sand and a flock of empty Coke cans.

I frowned as something soft brushed against my fingers. I pulled the mystery item out past the detritus. I was expecting a sandy sock, chucked on the floor one of the many times I had decided to drive home from the beach barefoot. What I found instead made my jaw drop.

It was the missing mitten. I had been searching for it for over a year and here it was, in my own car. I sat down heavily on the passenger seat, tracing the pink and blue stripes that I had knitted years before. This whole time, I had believed that the mitten would tell me where Chloe was, or at least give me a clue about what had happened. Instead, she had likely just dropped it in my car when I drove her home that night. I felt so disappointed that bitter tears began to pool in my eyes. The mitten had been nothing but a mitten, and I might never know exactly what Chloe's last moments were like. Real life wasn't like a mystery novel. Everything didn't get neatly tied up at the end.

Tears were rolling down my face as I clutched the mitten, feeling waves of grief begin to overtake my body. But then, something occurred to me. I had always believed that the missing mitten would show me where Chloe was—and maybe I hadn't been wrong. I found myself laughing even as I continued to cry.

I had thought I was alone during that year, the worst of my life, one half of a pair. But I was wrong. Chloe had always been here, with me. She was with me now.

AUTHOR NOTE

I grew up in Northern Ontario, where this book is set. I loved to read but I always wished that I could see places and people that I could identify with in stories. I wanted to see stories about girls who grew up in working-class towns far from the glamour of New York and California.

After high school, I left my town and had adventures that would have seemed inconceivable as a teenager. I moved to three different countries, I went to law school in London, England, and I traveled the world. At twenty-three, I moved back home from the Netherlands to study for my Canadian law qualifications. I saw my hometown with new eyes and a new conviction that the stories that happened there mattered just as much as the stories that happened elsewhere.

But I also began to notice things about my hometown that troubled me. I learned that there were two former residential schools in my town, schools where First Nations children were forced to go in order to assimilate them and "kill the Indian within the child." These were terribly sad places full of homesick children, abuse and trauma. But no one talked about the schools in my town. There were no plaques or commemorative exhibits. This legacy haunted me.

My parents have spent decades helping First Nations groups set up their own band-operated school systems. Schools that would respect the culture, language and history of each group, institutions of learning that would be the opposite of the residential schools. There are many causes for this vocation but one of the triggers was Helen Betty Osborne. Helen was a nineteen-year-old Cree girl who had left Norway House reserve in Manitoba because there was no high school there and she dreamed of being a teacher. She moved 437 kilometers away to attend high school in The Pas, Manitoba. Tragically, on November 13, 1971, Helen was stabbed fifty-six times with a screwdriver, raped and murdered. It took sixteen years for the four teenage boys responsible to be convicted of her murder even though they were vocal about having done it. A commission later found that the case had been prolonged because of sexism, racism and indifference.

My father was Helen's English teacher. He was twenty-four years old and one of the murderers was also in his class. My parents met a few years later when they both began working at the school at Norway House, which was later renamed in Helen's honor. They have been passionate about First Nations issues, racism and education ever since. I hope that this book, in some small way, contributes to the conversation.

—MacKenzie Common

I would like to thank my agent Gaia Banks, from Sheil Land Associates, for all of her help with this book. She has been a champion of this novel from the very beginning and her insight and suggestions have resulted in an infinitely better story. I feel so lucky to work with her.

I am also grateful to Lynne Missen, my diligent editor at Penguin Random House. She has gone over this book with a fine-tooth comb, making it the best story it could possibly be and astonishing me with her attention to detail and thoughtful suggestions. I know that the book that has been published owes a big debt to her.

To all of my early readers: Chelsea Smith, Kelsy Ervin, Ellie Telfer, Barbara Peddie, Dani Pietro, Caroline Steverson, Abby Cook, Mary Guest, Stevie Shikia, Ella Kucharova, Sara Grainger, Marcelo Serra Martins and Gerald Laronde. If I've forgotten anyone I apologize!

To my sister Lauren, my boyfriend Martin and my dog Frankie, I thank them for their emotional support. I would also like to thank my father, Ron Common. Not only did he give me advice about various points of the story, but I also stole some of his anecdotes for this work. I would never have been aware of the issues in this book if I had been raised by a different father.

Finally, I would like to thank my mom, Lorraine Frost. She was an early reader of this book and combed through it for grammatical mistakes, errors and pacing issues at least eight times. More than that, she has believed in this story from the very beginning just as she has believed in most things I do. I am where I am today because of her.